TC

Antimatter PowerGrid

BY

Victor Appleton II

Published in The United States of America

The graphic used on the cover of this book comes from a website that features some great artworks and many links for such things as "how to contact" the supposed owners, but THEY ALL take you to an advertising page on some other website. I do not like taking what is the work of others without giving credit, and it is perfect for this cover, so I beg their indulgence in my use. If you are the copyright holder please contact me and I will try to set things right. Also, get that website working to protect you!

Chapter 9 contains the first two parts of the poem, *Jabberwocky*, by Lewis Carroll from his 1871 novel, *Through the Looking Glass, and What Alice Found There*. It is in the Public Domain.

ISBN #: 9781710285796

Tom Swift and His
Antimatter PowerGrid

By Victor Appleton II

Tom Swift and his father are among the best in the world when it comes to designing and building safe and powerful nuclear-based power generators. In fact, Damon Swift became the first ever wholly self-funded, private designer and operator of a nuclear power and research center, the Citadel in New Mexico.

Now, Tom is called upon to come up with something so new and radical to create a nearly endless stream of electricity meant to replace several old or even decommissioned nuclear plants in the Pacific Northwest—an area known for its environmentalist activities and demand for safe energy.

He searches for a way to outdo the best of the best, and with his father's help and blessings, sets out to build a better reactor. The problem is, and he discovers this early on, nuclear power may have already hit its upper limits. Ditto public acceptibility.

Is there something he can do that will give the people of Canada, and even Washington, Oregon and parts of Idaho what they need? Will it be clean and, above all, safe?

Or, will a determined group of underground eco-terrorists manage to destroy what he is building before it has the chance to prove its worth?

I am dedicating this book firstly to Damon Swift. His determination and faith in his radical reactor design, and his discovery of the miracle polymer, tomasite, set safety standards no other company has been able to match. It is also dedicated to the people who designed and built the first civilian nuclear power generator in 1948, the X-10 Graphite Reactor, and to the people involved in EBR-1 station in Idaho back in 1956. It is also giving a nod to the Soviet Union and their Obninsk Nuclear Power Plant which, in 1954, became the worlds first power generating station to go on line full time.

When compared even to his father's own Citadel nuclear research facility, Tom's projected power generators would be positively futuristic!   **CHAPTER 10**

TABLE OF CONTENTS

CHAPTER   **PAGE**

AUTHOR'S NOTE

Well, I'm flabbergasted! Thirty novels are now in the rear view mirror for this author. Nobody can be more surprised than I am. I have mentioned this almost *ad nauseum* in other books how I had only started out to write a couple novels... perhaps as many as five. Now look what someone has made me do!

Many of these stories make me proud even when I go back and read them for the fifth time (still, by the way, finding an occasional typo, damn it!) There are a few of the plots or subplots I feel might be a little weak, but they still hold up to scrutiny... and self doubt.

A number of my stories have had an ecological subplot or even theme and that makes them a bit different from any other Tom Swift series. I have tried to not preach (I am chuckling at *that* notion right now) except on a few things I feel very angry or frustrated about. Most of it is based in the inanities of mankind, religions for the sake of profit, and politicians. I was almost the stepbrother to a U.S. Congressman and hold him to be a rare and shining example of how you can succeed over many terms while continuing being a good guy.

Heck. He even does *not* engage in negative advertising when running for reelection. It is mostly, "Here I am... I have done these good things... I would like your support to continue," ads.

Ah, gosh, I've gotten off track, again. So, back to the books. I hit number 29 with a little dread that the next title (*Space Friends Return*) was the last title and basic story in my head. Then, I used the Title Generator created by fellow TS author, Jon Cooper, and came up with ten new ones. I had to pick and choose various words from that list and came up with this and the next books' titles. Not *Tom Swift and His Semi-skimmed Nutrino Refinery*! Or, *Subsonic Potato SpaceCannon*!!! Although...........

I hope I continue to do the coming titles justice.

I am pretty sure you all hope that as well. Erm, *any* of you?

Copies of all of this author's works may be found at:

http://www.lulu.com/spotlight/tedwardfoxatyahoodotcom

Tom Swift and His Antimatter PowerGrid

FOREWORD

I have to tell you this title threw me for a loop when I saw it on the back cover of the previous book. *Antimatter*, the stuff of science fiction, is a known thing. Tom has used it in the past and can even point to a few brief successes, but to think that it might be created, maintained and utilized for long periods of time—without any danger of improperly intermixing with regular matter and...

Well, the word *kaboom* can't quite capture the results. Perhaps "An Earth-shattering **kaboom**!" might do. Thanks, Marvin.

Now, I have practically infinite faith in Tom Swift. His father as well, and his great grandfather for whom the inventor was named. I can even point back a further generation to Barton Swift and his strides in mechanical and chemical inventions back as far as the late 1800s.

Not, of course, Tom's own grandfather, George Swift, but his is another story already covered.

Oh, but to the matter of antimatter. Wait, was that a bad pun I smell? No *matter*.

(Someone please stop me or I <u>will</u> pun again!)

Our Tom is faced with a problem, or half a dozen of them, as he embarks on a project to create the seemingly impossible.

I guess you have noticed that in these books, mine, my father's, and author T. Edward Fox who occupies the current role of "Victor Appleton," do not end in failure. I can be forgiven if I tell you that he might hit snags ranging from the small and insignificant to the almost deadly... but that would also not be a surprise to anyone having read any of the more than 120 novels (the good ones and not the dreck being published in 2019) that our Tom perseveres. His is a combination of quick reactions, incredible intelligence that outdoes his foes, and a dash of luck.

I can promise you that he does not perish in this book as there are several more in the offing where he is the main character and must appear prominently in them all. For now, I beg you to enjoy this tale of a future that is just around that next corner.

Victor Appleton II

CHAPTER 1 /
A POWER DILEMMA FOR TOM

TOM SWIFT, thirty-two-year-old inventor, the son of Damon Swift who had, some eighteen years earlier, created the four-mile-square industrial, airfield and experimental complex known as Swift Enterprises—sitting on a large tract of unused land to the south of the town of Shopton, New York—pondered his recent successes.

There had been many of these triumphs peppered with the occasional lack of one hundred percent success. Not failures, but not the best results he knew might have been possible were it not for the fact he and his father had a few personal and political enemies, and even a couple of unfriendly nations that would love to see them fail.

Or, for a couple of them, hoping that one or both of the Swifts might die. To date both had been occasionally injured, but not critically. At least, by their enemies. Not lately.

One such nation had gone through so many political changes ranging from scientific extremism to militaristic dictatorship to fledgling democracy to totalitarian rule to near total ruin in the fourteen years Tom had been aware of them. Another, also an Eastern European country with roots in ruthless control of its own people and a leadership determined to steal or destroy scientific and technological advancements in other countries, had been through financial and political ruin twice since Tom turned eighteen. And, he had been a major contributing factor to both.

Today, those countries—Brungaria and Kranjovia—had been attempting to make themselves more moderate and to either apologize for previous misbehaviors or at least to assure the rest of the world they had peaceful intents.

For now.

At least *publicly*.

At least Kranjovia...

Tom was sitting, as he found himself doing more and more recently, in the decommissioned Control Tower room set atop the Administration building at Enterprises. The building was a monster at more than fifteen hundred feet in length, one hundred twenty feet wide and three stories tall with this room situated another twenty-four feet above the roof.

Its relatively small size made it appear to be more a wart on the roof than what was once an important hub of air control activity for the company.

Now, it had become his refuge from the world. Triple paned, tinted windows kept ninety-nine percent of the outside noises *outside* and allowed the room to maintain an even temperature even on the sunniest days. In it he kept a small sofa and a "visitor" chair along with a desk and telephone. On the rare occasions he required a computer, he had to bring up his tablet.

During the nearly four weeks since he had succeeded in banishing the reptilian Master creature that had forced their Space Friends to come back to Earth—with the intent on trying to take over the planet—Tom had been in a sad brood.

As part of the Master's attack, she had announced that the small planetoid named Nestria, previously placed in Earth orbit, was to be taken back... even though it was not this Master's race that had put it into orbit between the Earth and the Moon.

Try as he or anyone might to make it otherwise, eight of the colonists/scientists residing on the low-gravity microworld refused to be evacuated. As it raced into the distance all had perished when the thin atmosphere was stripped away.

It had made Tom sick.

It still sickened him.

At the time it had so angered him he had gone to the Swift's rocket and submersibles base, Fearing Island, where a strange manufacturing device the Space Friends had left for him before they disappeared resided. He used it to do something even his father, normally totally against weapons, agreed had to be done. Tom had built a trio of special guns.

Then, Tom, Damon and Bud Barclay confronted the lizard shooting it in the neck, throat and spine area causing it to crumple to the ground. It had been tightly bound and the Space Friends rushed it away back to their home planet. Other than the people on Nestria, there had been no injuries or deaths during the more than five weeks of the angry and unreasonable reptile being on Earth.

Today, for a change, Tom was deep in thought about a new problem dropped into his lap that morning. Actually, it was an old problem *re*-dropped on him.

Years earlier a small Inuit settlement in the coldest part of Yukon, Canada, had all but frozen to death before Tom had installed a very small nuclear power generating station just outside of town. That generator provided all the necessary electricity for the town and residents as well as steam heat—a byproduct of the cooling of the generator—to maintain a healthy environment inside homes and buildings.

It had led him to invent his Power Pod, a small and powerful sphere that generated electricity for use in places where even the smallest nuclear reactor was not appropriate... or welcome.

But, the Northern native people had recently let Enterprises know the power station was starting to fail them. Levels of electricity, and indeed the steam its cooling system provided to heat their town, had dropped in the previous month to only eighty percent of what they had come to expect. And, could Tom come and repair it... or replace it, please?

So, Tom along with his best friend and brother-in-law, Bud Barclay, and a team of other pilots and several technicians had visited the Inuit town where they discovered the extreme cold of the ground in which the reactor had been buried might possibly have worked against it operating for as many years as he'd intended.

That was their cursory finding.

It ought to last another seven or even eight, but the circulating glycol and ethanol in the cooling system just got too cold so the reactor had to work harder to create the same amount of steam, and steam drove the generator with extra being piped into town for distribution to all two hundred fifty-three public and residential buildings. It all had strained the ability of the unit.

Tom sat in the visitor's chair clicking the tip of a pencil against his front teeth as he pondered the situation.

The basic truth was he could easily replace the faltering reactor, but another important truth was he and Enterprises had never been paid for their work or even the existing reactor system. The Canadian government, twice replaced during the intervening time, had stymied attempts to introduce a repayment plan in their Parliament stating they—the current government—had never agreed to the installation.

Statements such as, "They would have died if someone hadn't done anything, and Canada most certainly was not trying," fell on deaf political ears.

And, that meant that several million dollars continued to be out of pocket, so the accountants at Enterprises, and even Damon himself—regretfully—had said "no" to another such gift.

The Canadians had not said *no* to Tom's wish to visit the tribe to check out the situation and to run a series of tests on the power system... so long as he did it for free. That initial trip proved to point out the forthcoming failure of the reactor along with the probability there was little that could be done to do more than put that off by several months. As it was, all indicators said it would shut down as a safety measure in about one hundred days.

Today, Tom was not so much trying to devise a plan to replace the system, or even to repair it, as he was trying to figure a way to build a series of reasonably-priced power generating stations in a country that was definitely anti-nuclear. The Canadian Inuits were not the only people who needed a reliable source of power.

A talk earlier in the day with Jackson Rimmer and Patrick Peck of Enterprises' Legal department had only resulted in an expected statement from the lawyers.

"If you can come up with something that does not use a nuclear reactor anywhere in the loop, they really cannot try to say no. We've reviewed their law and it specifically states only that nuclear fission reaction is out."

"Actually," Patrick corrected his boss, "it says that a nuclear reactor cannot be the primary source of the power generation via a secondary system such as a steam generator. For some reason they were quite specific about that combination."

Tom was thinking about their words. It was one thing keeping the Swifts from exporting their safe and reliable reactors to the North for over a decade. He didn't want to push things too far or take liberties that might sour relations between Canada and Swift Enterprises, or even the United States. But, he was determined to not allow the natives up there to perish!

"So," he began slowly, "if we find something *other* than a nuclear reactor, that would be okay?"

Both lawyers nodded. Neither attorney sought to modify their answer with anything such as, "So it would appear," or, "We'll need to check that."

The three men sat looking at each other and all felt a little smug at coming up with something that might get around political shortsightedness.

If.

If Tom could manage to devise something that could run for a very lengthy period of time that did not require a constant supply of a consumable radioactive fuel, and almost specifically not something garnered from burning petroleum.

Finally, the inventor stood and thanked the two legal minds for their insight.

"The only thing left to do is come up with the practically

impossible replacement of the nuclear reactor that has all the advantages without the possibility—and I know Swift reactors are not going to put out any—of stray radiation before, during or after the thing runs. Look for me to be absent from a lot of things over the coming weeks."

He left the Legal office and headed down the nearby stairs to the second floor and the office he shared with his famous father.

As he approached the outer office, Munford Trent, his father's executive assistant—who also helped with Tom—stood.

"Hey, Trent," Tom greeted the man who was about eight years older by his last name, the one the man preferred over his first name.

"Hello, Tom. Your father has just left for the MotorCar Company and I have a short stack of correspondence for you to go through if you have the time."

Having nothing solid to focus on, Tom reached out and took the nine letters and email printouts. "Sure. Anything to watch for?"

Trent shook his head. "I do not believe so. But, there is a request in there from the government of Yemen. Seems they want some assistance in getting to some very deep oil deposits and think one of your earth blasters would do the trick."

Tom shook his head. That technology was expressly forbidden for export to any of the "Middle Eastern" nations as it utilized a miniature atomic reactor, and those were never going to be allowed to go to those areas.

"Thanks." He entered the office and sat down on the closest of the comfortable conference area chairs. He scanned the first five letters, noting the same thing on each:

Send to Swift Charities

The sixth item was another in a never-ending group of requests for his time at some event the writer believed was:

1) The most important event of this type *ever;*

2) The school that offered the sort of courses the Swifts needed;

3) The gathering that would get the Swift name to, "the right people";

... and a variety—some interesting; some barely clever—of the above.

Having set aside the Yemeni letter, he noted the others to say he had another obligation yet thanked them for their interest.

The letter from Yemen was printed on what appeared to be the official stationary of the country. It bore an embossed, gold leaf covered, seal of the ruling family.

As Trent had mentioned, the bulk of the letter discussed the oil fields in Yemen and how many of them had been explored to the "full extent of the available resources given current petroleum delivery equipment."

He had to read part of it again. And, the impression he had the first read through was only verified.

> Your technology must be made available to the entire world even though your unseeing politicians can not believe it might be put to peaceful use. We urge you to send us a shipping schedule. At that time we will forward appropriate funding. Your understanding and secrecy will be rewarded.

It was rather blatantly suggesting Swift Enterprises just ignore the law and send them the requested twenty units.

Tom walked to the scanner and got an image of the letter, which he prepared to send to the Swift's friend, and a senior Senator in Washington, Peter Quintana. First, however, he called the man's office.

"Hey. It's Tom. Is your pop in?"

"Well, hello stranger," the Senator's assistant—and his daughter —replied. "Long time no talk. And, no... Dad's actually doing some work at the moment. Ought to be back in an hour. Is there anything I can do?"

"I'm pressing SEND on my old-fashioned fax machine and forwarding him a letter we received this morning. A foreign nation is trying to get us to break the law and sell them something we can't. Once he sees it, and after you peel him off the office ceiling, can you ask him to give us a call?"

"Appears to be coming in right now. I'll give it to him once he's back. Unless, that is, he calls in first. Can I check it out so I know if he ought to know ASAP?"

He told her that was perfectly acceptable.

"Thanks!"

Peter called two hours later, and when Tom said, "Hello," the politician answered using a rather nasty term. Tom chuckled knowing exactly at whom that comment had been aimed.

"And, a pleasant 'hi' to you, Peter. I'll assume you received the fax and have some ideas about what might be done to get this off our backs?"

"Oh, yeah. Got millions of them. Billions, in fact. We have an outstanding and total agreement with their government to prohibit such approaches or attempts. That means this is likely to not be truly official. If it is, then they stand to lose roughly four-point-two billion in petroleum purchases, plus they'll get a little something we like to call an embargo."

He told the inventor to just ignore the letter and allow the "proper channels" to handle it and to send him the original. Then, changing the subject, he cautiously asked how Tom was doing. He well knew the affect the Nestria deaths had on the younger man.

"Bashalli has told me that I did everything short of a gas attack and kidnapping of those people up there so I should not be feeling guilty."

"She's absolutely correct, Tom. It was their choice and they had more than ample opportunities to change their minds. From you, the President and others. I hate to cast aspersions on the dead, but there are some people who just can't get it through their heads they are not immortal. Or, that when they travel to foreign countries telling people in a loud voice they can't harm you because you are American is a stupid waste of breath." He paused a moment, then stated, "You are faultless in this, Tom. Absolutely and completely. Do you understand me?"

With not a lot of enthusiasm, Tom responded. "Yeah. Deep inside I know that, but it doesn't take away the hurt."

"Time will do that, my younger friend. Time."

The next morning as Tom and Damon sat having coffee and discussing the situation with the power system in Canada, the younger Swift mentioned his desire to get a longer and better look and make some more thorough on-site measurements of the failing mini-reactor.

"To my thinking, short of having loaded in some less-than-pure power rods when that reactor was constructed, I can't see how any cold up there might be causing the... let's call it the degradation. Can you?"

Damon stated he could not. It all was, after all, a very well known technology and this was the only incident of a failure or an operational issue.

"I'd normally say, 'Go,' but what with the Canadian Parliament deciding that they don't know us from Adam and can't be bothered to either go investigate this for themselves, or even admit that they still owe us more than three million dollars for that system—even in

15

their rather weak currency—that I will not allow us to get into the position of providing outright charity work up there."

"While I agree they need to step up," Tom responded, "I still believe a trip to that little tribal community would be a good gesture on our part. Besides, we can take up some food items they have to do without, and that may not be intended to, but it buys us a lot of good will with them."

He looked over his mug at his father and could see the older inventor's face softening.

"Would you sneak up there through Alaska and then skim over the top of Canada to get to them, or would this be a full announced flight?"

"I've never been much of a sneak," the younger Swift replied with a grin.

"There is that," Damon admitted. "Go talk with Legal and see what they believe. But," and he held up a warning finger, "I still do not want you to go hauling up a replacement reactor. Okay"

Tom nodded, and agreed. He left the office a moment later, walked down the hallway, looked into Chow's kitchen area only to find the chef was not in at the moment, before walking up the stairs near the south end of the Administration building. Stopping at the top, Tom thought how he wanted to word his inquiry and decided to just get it all on the table and let either Jackson Rimmer or his chief associate attorney, Patrick, decide how to proceed. After all, it was not a subject they had not already spoken about.

"Big chief or little chief in... and available?" he asked their receptionist. She smiled brightly at him and nodded. "Both of them are having coffee in Jackson's office. Let me warn them to put the cards away." She giggled and picked up her receiver. After announcing that Tom wished an audience, she listened, said, "Okay," twice and hung up.

"Jackson is trying to fill out a straight flush, he says, and would appreciate thirty seconds. But, *I* think you ought to go right on in."

"Unless I hear yelling from you telling me to stop, I'm going in. Thanks!"

Both men were standing ready to receive him when he knocked lightly and stepped into the office. They shook hands before Jackson indicated they should go to the small conference area to one side and not to his desk.

"What's on your mind today, Tom? Or, do you just like coming to see us?"

"Well... this is not about building anything non-nuclear in Canada, but..." and he launched into a reminder of what work had been done years earlier, the possible condition their reactor system was in, and what he hoped to accomplish in the short term.

"So, just heading up to do some more detailed diagnostics?" Patrick inquired.

"Well, that plus I'd like to take some of our long-storage foods up. They live primarily on fish and some grain they manage to grow during the clear months. The Canadian government ships them powdered milk, powdered eggs and powdered cheese along with some canned veggies. I'd hoped to take them some pasta, dried meats other than fish, and even some of Chow's nutrition bars. I agree with Dad that I don't take up or even agree to bring back a new reactor. It's just that I feel a little guilty about installing what was supposed to last them a couple decades only to have it fail in slightly more than one."

Jackson had been quiet and looked as if he were contemplating something. "Let me have a few minutes of privacy to make a call. Okay?"

Tom and Patrick got up and left Jackson's office, heading for Patrick's.

"Who do you suppose he's calling?" Tom asked.

"I have zero idea, but you do realize Jackson is about the most connected person either you or I know. He likely has the private number of the Prime Minister up there and is going to tell him how things are going to happen."

When the senior attorney buzzed them four minutes later, they rose and headed back to the larger office.

"Okay. Sit and I'll tell you how that went. I have a friend in Canadian legal circles who works closely with their Supreme Court. She tells me that our northern friends are in a bind over this. The current ruling party absolutely hates what they inherited from the other party, including debts to this and about a dozen other U.S. companies. They owe in the tens of billions in total, so our less than four million is hardly a blip on their RADAR. She tells me to have you go on up as long as it isn't going to cost them anything."

"I guess I can spring for fuel costs out of my budget," the inventor told them.

"Bet your dad would cover that. Tom," Patrick offered. "It is, after all, an expense that can be written off. Not that I'm suggesting that is the reason to go up there, but compassion flights are a covered expense."

Jackson nodded. "I agree. Go. Take your measurements or whatever, and come back and ponder what to do in the comfort of your own office."

Tom thanked them and was about to leave when he remembered to tell them about the Yemeni attempt at obtaining a number of the earth blasters.

"Yikes!" Jackson said. "In the words of my roommate at law school, that is *no bueno*! Not even a little bit. Have you thought to call Senator Quintana?"

Tom said he had, and Peter Quintana had been both furious and distressed.

"He's on top of it, but before I send him the original letter, I need to bring up a copy so you guys have it."

They thanked him and let him head back downstairs.

On the way down, Tom stopped to have a thought.

What the heck am I going to do if that power system is actually failing? And, can I do whatever that is in time?

CHAPTER 2 /
TO THE GREAT WHITE NORTH

TOM AND BUD headed to the Inuit town in the Yukon Province in a rather smallish version of one of the Swift Cargo Jets. This one, roughly the size of a regional airliner in the forty to sixty passenger capacity range, was a new Swift aircraft being trialled potentially for delivery firms that required fast and inexpensive access to small airports in more rural areas of the world where propeller aircraft were too slow and jets required too much—often unavailable—runway.

It was capable of carrying about eighteen tons of cargo at speeds in excess of 420 knots over extended distances and could—this was the important bit—land vertically or on very short airfields when necessary using a set of auxiliary repelatrons built into the wings right where they met the fuselage. They would swing down like the landing gear and provide enough lift even when the jet was fully loaded. They were powered by a new form factor of Tom's power pods so that might sit under the lower-than-normal floor rather than taking up valuable cargo space. Actually, it had been designed to work along with a rechargeable battery pack also located under the floor.

"She's flying pretty nicely," Bud commented after taking over from Tom ten minutes earlier. They had, at that time, just passed into the airspace over Montana.

Tom nodded. "Yeah. I'm quite happy with both the handling and the performance. The new power system will get us there and back again without much more than a one-hour pause."

It was planned that the commercial version would be able to utilize the average 20-minute layover while cargo was removed or added at any location, to give the power "tray" a chance to start to recover. This was aided by having a large solar generating panel on top of the fuselage that worked all the time there was sunlight. If the jet could average such a stopover at least every hour of flying, the pod and battery pack was rated to fly the jet for up to eighteen hours per day.

For forward propulsion it carried a tank filled with ordinary water. That was easily accommodated at almost every airport for a quick refill. Inside the jet, a small amount of the power from the tray converted the water into hydrogen and oxygen that were burned to operate two small yet powerful jet turbine engines.

The inventor had begun by wanting to use some of the electricity to run QuieTurbines, but doing so had limited travel to fewer than seven hundred total miles in any twenty-four hour period according to the computer simulation. He knew it needed to cover three to four times that per day.

Canadian Airspace Control gave them permission to cross the border about the time they passed north of Great Falls.

"Thank you, Canada. We are vectoring to Aklavic, Yukon for the evening before we head north to final destination."

Their interim destination was small but had an actual airport while their final destination offered nothing substantial to set down on, other than the nearly permanently frozen ground and quite a lot of it around the small coastal village.

Possessing no real amenities—such as a restaurant or even a motel—Aklavic airport would be where they spent the night inside the jet. Damon insisted they take along foldable cots, snug and warm sleeping bags and a lot of food provided them by Chow Winkler.

"Why not fly directly to that village?" Bud inquired.

"They are having a storm today and dad suggested we hold off one day unless it clears before we get up there. I agree because neither of us totally understands this jet in case we have a little *oops* situation like a bad gust."

Bud considered something before asking, "What do we do about bathroom facilities?"

His companion nodded. "Right. Well, along with the portable bathroom facility we are brining up, the airport in Aklavic has a caretaker's house at one end and visitors can use an outside lavatory there."

"Oh, goody," Bud responded rather joylessly.

The airfield seemed perfectly nice from two thousand feet up. It was only once the wheels got to within about fifty feet Bud and Tom both noticed that what might have once been thought of as a level airstrip had become a rutted and rather uneven surface. Pouring on the power again just before they would have encountered a nearly six-inch-deep rut, the cargo jet headed up for a go-around.

"This time we try out the nifty lifters," the flyer declared getting a nod of agreement from Tom.

"We'll need to use them tomorrow anyway, so might as well get in a little uneven surface practice now."

Without much in the way of weight in the back, Bud was able to tilt the aircraft over about thirty degrees and make a tight right turn coming back to level flight at the same time he slowed them down and came back over the southern end of the strip.

"Good reverse thrusters," he complimented the jet as they slowed to a standstill almost exactly over the small—also woefully rutted—aircraft parking area at the northern end.

Using his innate piloting skills, Bud sideslipped them over and brought them down gently. And, because they were using repelatrons, there was little in the way of anything being kicked into the air.

Bud reached out and flipped the five switches that shut down the drive systems, leaving the radio and lighting circuits still in operation.

"Gonna call home and tell them we got here safe?" he asked.

"Hmm? Oh, yeah. Give me a minute, Bud. I just had a thought I want to flesh out in my mind."

Bud grinned and picked up the headset placing it on his head and keying the microphone. He knew that when Tom wanted a little alone with his brain time, it might be one minute and might be five hours.

"Shopton. Enterprises Control. This is Swift Two Test calling in a successful landing at CYKD, Canada. Over?"

"*Uhh, Swift Two Test, this is Enterprises. We read you and understand fine and dandy landing. Need anybody notified?*"

Bud looked over at Tom who was in such concentration he doubted the inventor was registering anything.

"Roger that. Let my beloved and Tom's lady know we are both fine and will be satelliting calls to them later this evening. And, call Mr. Swift to say we are A-OK. Out."

Slipping off his headset and harness, Bud headed to the back of the cargo hold where their portable "convenience" was strapped down. He was back in his seat before Tom even noticed his absence.

About eight minutes later he got back up and went back to set their cots up, unroll the sleeping bags and take pillows and blankets from a pair of vacuum bags. He also took a look through the variety of self-heating meals Chow had thoughtfully packed for them. Seeing what was there made him laugh.

"Leave it to Chow to take a 'pack for three days for two people' request and pad that out to a week for five!" he muttered as he located what sounded great to him. Lately he had been having cravings for chicken noodle casserole and tuna noodle casserole.

The storage box contained several of both.

He set a chicken one aside and called forward. "Skipper? What do you want for eats?"

He nearly jumped out of his own skin when Tom, standing right behind him now, answered, "Inside voice, Bud. No need to shout when it's just the two of us. And, if Chow packed any of his fried chicken and smashed potatoes with gravy, that'll do just fine."

Getting his breathing back under control, Bud tried to nonchalantly say there were two packs of Tom's request available.

"Sorry about sneaking up on you, flyboy. I finished my thinking for now and just came back to see what you were up to."

"Yeah. Well, as Sandy says, I tend to let my stomach do the thinking after I set down from any flight. So, now or later?"

They decided to eat even if it was only about 2:40 pm local time. They'd skipped lunch in flight and it was going on 5:40 back home.

As they ate Tom asked Bud about how his son, Samuel, was doing.

"The Samster is growing every day and starting to run around the house like he's planning to be a track star! And," he said sobering a little, "Sandy is becoming exactly the sort of mother she has wanted to be. I think she's even fully come to terms with the adoption route we took. She holds him in her arm and he falls asleep most nights after dinner looking very happy indeed. Both of them."

After cleaning up their dinner things, they each made calls to home.

Once the sun had gone down the area got instantly dark. Even the lights from the nearby small community began blinking out an hour later; soon, nothing was to be seen other than the town's one and only streetlight.

They settled into their sleeping bags, turned off their own interior lights and both men fell asleep.

Morning began with something banging on the hatch at the rear of the cargo area. A muffled voice was calling out something so Tom got up, pulled his pants back on and opened the hatch. To his surprise, a middle aged man pulled himself up and into the aircraft turning around to shut the hatch behind him.

When he turned around to face Tom, he yanked off his right glove and held out his hand.

"Brian Muledeer, airport manager. Pleased to meet you. And, uhh, I guess you'd be that famous Tom Swift we heard was coming up?" He looked hopefully at the inventor.

Tom shook his hand. "I am, and I am also a bit confused by you being in my jet right now, sir. May I ask...?"

"Oh, gawd. Where's my manners. You see, I didn't want to let all the warm outside so I generally just come on in. Don't want to startle or alarm you. Should I leave?"

With a shake of his head and trying to finish waking up, Tom told him it was okay, just unexpected.

"I came over to ask you and your crew—and I see only the other gentleman getting up—to come over to the house, which is the airfield office, for coffee and maybe scrambled eggs and a little back bacon. Oh, and of course, more coffee."

"Well, that is very nice of you. Let's let Bud finish getting dressed and we'd love to join you. We, ahh, we have some supplies to deliver later today, but can we give you a little something?"

The man scratched at his multiple days of beard growth before smiling shyly. "Don't suppose you have any tea bags? The wife loves a cup and we're down to just three of them. Won't get to supplies myself for five or six days."

Tom laughed. He was not certain why Chow had packed it, but there was a box of one hundred bags sitting near the top of one of the cases. He grabbed it as Bud came over to shake their host's hand.

"Say, if you don't mind I'll only take a dozen of those so you can deliver the rest to their intended spot."

Two hours later and full from the breakfast they'd been given, Tom and Bud took off using the repelatron lifters before engaging their forward drives at just one thousand feet. They headed to the north and the small town of Inuvik, site of the failing reactor.

The tribal elder, the same man he'd dealt with to get permissions to install the generator station in the first place, came out to where the jet touched down between the installation and the edge of the houses. They exchanged warm handshakes and greetings before heading back to the town's gathering place, a building with a single great room located in the center of the houses.

Tom knew he didn't need to go into great details about the reason of their visit; everyone in town knew their power source was having problems.

"I notice the ground is very green this visit," Bud stated as they took seats.

The older man nodded. "Yeah. Bad year for snowfall, but a very good year for fishing. We have enough dried fish to last us through the next full year if need be. But, you did not come to speak of fish, I suppose." He asked if there was something Tom might do about the irregular power output. "It is mostly in the lack of consistent heat more than electricity," he told them.

Tom said they needed to do some testing and also tracing of the pipes and lines coming from the generator before he might give any conclusion.

Once they returned to the cargo jet, along with six of the town's younger men, Tom helped unload their cargo onto the trailer the men had brought over. It was meant to be pulled by a pair of horses, but they didn't have those. Instead, four of the men slipped on makeshift harnesses and began pulling the trailer toward the houses.

It took them three trips, but within two hours they were finished and everyone sat down to a lunch of a creamy fish chowder.

To the Americans, it smelled and tasted fishy, but not altogether unpleasant. And, as they ate several of the townswomen began unpacking the supplies the American's had brought. There were several "oooh" and "awww" sounds of satisfaction with what they found.

Tom and Bud walked back to the jet and began pulling together their test computer along with a small tent to protect them from the cold. There might not be snow on the ground, but the ambient temperature was still in the low teens. That tent was a variation on the survival structures all Swift spacecraft capable of planetfall carried. One small air tank inflated a series of tubes to lift and form the structure while another typically provided breathable air. In this case, that second tank had been replaced by a small heater powered by one of Tom's solar batteries.

While Bud was getting the inside ready, Tom took a cable over to a raised cement plinth where he knew the plug-in for the data output would be located. He had to chip off a little ice around the edges to free the cover, but soon had his cable plugged in and was heading back to the tent.

"It'll be toasty in about five minutes, skipper," the flyer told him. "Need any help with that?" he asked pointing to the cable Tom had fed through a small zip-able flap and was connecting to an instrument panel in one corner.

"No. Can you get the two chairs unfolded so I don't have to sit on the floor, please?"

Fifteen minutes later the inventor sat back and rubbed his chin in thought.

"What?"

"Well, the readouts say that we have a repeating cycle of dropouts. I'm going to have to check, but I believe that means we have one bad fuel rod inside the reactor. As I recall they rotate in twenty minute operational periods and with twelve of them in there, that means each one gets used every four hours."

Bud brightened and asked, "So, is the intermittent problem about every four hours?"

Tom shook his head. "No. It's every four hours and eleven minutes. That means we have another problem. The gearing and timing for drawing one rod up and the next is lowered is off. And, sure... that rod is going to have to be replaced—which is going to involve bringing up a special handling robot and a tomasite tent so that nobody gets exposed—but the gearing and timing is a poser. I've got to go make a radio call."

He got up with Bud offering to remain in the tent, "Just to watch over things so reindeer don't come in and steal stuff."

Tom's call to the Citadel went through quickly and he was soon speaking to one of the senior technicians, the person most knowledgeable about the small reactor system.

"Don't like hearing that, Tom. Not even a little bit. I can't see how we can service that unit in place. Is there some way you could disconnect it and bring it here for a couple weeks?"

Tom explained about the precarious situation with the town and especially it having no backup source for heat or electricity at present.

They talked about alternatives but could come up with nothing other than to send up something like the *Sky Queen* to take everyone out of the town and to a city where they could live in comfort for the estimated time it might take to troubleshoot the reactor and get it fixed and returned.

Tom told him there were more than five hundred people there and they all could not crowd into the giant triple-decker jet much less be expected to cheerfully abandon their homes even for a short stay elsewhere.

"Yeah. Guess I can see that. So, give me a day to check into what we might do. Would a swap out be okay with everybody?"

"Not really. Dad told me I can't spend much on this because the Canadian government won't reimburse us. The current climate in their Parliament is that *they* didn't authorize anything so they won't pay for anything to do with whatever the other guys did."

"What a bunch of jerks!"

Tom smiled. It was something he'd also thought, but never gave voice to. "Whatever, I'd like to find a way to do this all up here and without halting what they are getting. Give me a call once you and the folks there have talked this over."

It took until the following morning before Tom received a call. It was from Shopton and not New Mexico.

"Tom? It's dad. Listen. I've been on the phone with Ottawa and with DC and the Citadel. Pete Quintana hinted to the Canadians that they ought to get behind this before it becomes a political hot potato and gets to the world press they are abandoning one of their own native tribal locations." Tom heard his father chuckle. "Nothing like a little politician-to-politician hint of scandal to get things moving. So, here's what is happening."

He outlined that the Canadian government was going to issue a contract with simultaneous payment for the full replacement costs of a new reactor system and to finally pay for the first one. The only thing they wanted in return were the assurances guaranteeing this would go no further and certainly not outside of the halls of government in both nations.

"We'll have to sign a non-disclosure statement, of course, and then get the work finished as quickly as possible. As far as the Citadel folks believe, if you can dig them a new location for the reactor and generator, they can pre-pipe it all and do the changeover from the old to the new in about five hours. Can your people up there be without power for that time?"

"I believe so, and especially if we can provide them a temporary source of electricity during that. I suppose I can outfit the *Super Queen* cargo pod with a generator and enough fuel to cover at least that time."

They talked about time to completion and Tom promised to get back once he had spoken to the tribal leaders.

For their part, all they wanted was to not interrupt their lives too much so Tom's solution was readily agreed to.

Three hours later, and with both Shopton and New Mexico having been told to start things moving toward building and programming a new power generator reactor, the cargo jet rose into the sky, spun around to face the southeast, and picked up speed. It disappeared to the town's people within a minute.

They landed just at sundown and both men headed home to their families.

Tom was greeted at this front door by Bashalli who threw her arms around his neck and gave him a soft and fairly long kiss, and by his son and two daughters standing behind her, waiting although not so patiently. Bart was holding little Anne's hand to keep her from charging forward into their mother's legs.

Once Bashalli disentangled herself and stepped back, knowing what was about to happen, Bart released his sister's hand, raced forward launching himself into the air and wrapping his arms around his father's waist.

"You are home!" he stated emphatically just so Tom could be certain of his whereabouts.

"Yes, I am," his father stated giving the boy a hug and then letting him drop to the floor.

Tom knelt down and hugged his two daughters giving them both kisses and telling them he loved them in a whisper.

After they kissed him back both girls ran for the playroom off the kitchen where their nanny Amanda, was waiting to finish the board game she'd been using to occupy them for the past hour.

"I am so happy you are home. I did not sleep at all well last night without you," Bashalli told him as she took his hand to lead him into the kitchen so she could get their diner ready. "I never do," she admitted.

Tom knew the woman in his life cherished falling to sleep beside him and often holding his hand. It made him all the more sad to realize how she must suffer when he was away on lengthy trips into space or under the ocean.

He was glad this new power issue was going to keep his feet on the ground for some time.

At the Barclay/Swift-Barclay residence much the same scene was being played out with the exception of just the one boy and Sandy being a bit more firm with her husband.

"Don't leave me alone to sleep in our bed again for a long time, Buster," she said shaking a fist—but with a grin—in his face.

He kissed her knuckles, twice, and she lost all her resolve.

CHAPTER 3 /
THE EXTENDED INVITATION

LIFE IN Shopton ran at a normal pace for eleven days while Tom and the various experts checked and rechecked the results of his data scan of the power plant.

Nearly everything they discovered pointed to a failure of one particular rod inside the reactor. A further check showed Tom that rod, along with the others in the reactor, had been manufactured in a single week in the New Mexican plant by a small team who had all worked for the Swifts for years. It was one of a run of ninety-six created from the same batch of nuclear materials.

Because he trusted those people, Tom had to believe they'd received some bad uranium ore and that had made its way into the rod. But, he pondered, "Why just the one? Why not four or even ten of them. After all, they all were fed and filled from a single hopper of the super refined materials.

"If that's the case," Bud said around a mouthful of broiled salmon sandwich at lunch, "I'd have to believe something foreign was put into that rod case and just the one. Don't ask me why because I can't think of much else. What's your dad say?"

"He agrees this is suspicious but says he wonders if this might be a one time fluke." He shrugged. "I'm hoping it is just that. Oh, and the timing thing would appear to be a result of the lagging power coming from the pod when that bad rod is down in the core. It likely built up over time and possibly as early on as five years ago. I suppose for any future installations I need to build in some sort of data uplink for remote monitoring."

"Ahhh, but can you find out anything about that rod or the other stuff inside while it is up there?"

Tom shook his head. "No. It will have to be de-fueled at the Citadel, but that won't happen until it is replaced in a few weeks. Luckily, it is very unlikely it will fail before we get a new reactor unit installed and connected."

They discussed the matter a few more moments before Tom had an idea he wanted to follow up on. "Excuse me, Bud. Got to go talk to dad about something that just struck me."

Back in the shared office he sat down at his desk to collect his thoughts a few minutes before asking Damon for a few minutes of his time.

"Certainly, Son. What's up?"

"Well, this Canadian power station thing, and also what I might do next to come up with a new sort of power generating system that requires no or at least infrequent fueling, is safe, reliable, and can be sold and installed in places, like Canada, where they won't even consider one of your reactor power stations. In fact, I can't really believe—given their aversion to nuclear power—they ever allowed us to build that station up in the Yukon." He looked at his father. "They actually gave us permission, didn't they?"

Damon nodded. "My belief is that this was a case of them either turning a blind eye to something they believed would not be discussed publicly, or not wishing to spend any money themselves and just allowing it to happen. The even stranger thing is them agreeing to allow the replacement with the same sort of technology."

They sat looking at one another for over a minute before Tom blinked and said, "I'd love to come up with something that would never have them looking away; I want something they can accept. What do you think?"

Damon took a moment before suggesting Tom sit down and come up with a few ideas for such a system.

"Do that before you even broach the subject to any nation including our own."

Tom thanked his father, got up, and headed down the hall to the large lab.

Nineteen days came and went before he had a pair of solid ideas. One of them he was quite uncertain how to go about and the other one he feared was not a potential for any location that did not receive at least twelve solid hours of sunshine per day.

It would entail the use of a solar collector and concentrator—similar to that used in space to charge the Swift Solar Batteries—but used to super heat a liquid that would run a generator.

Even then, was it actually going to be a better solution than a large solar panel farm? He silently doubted it.

But, what was his other idea? That question came from his father and from Bud as well as his wife, Bashalli.

"The best way to describe what I am considering is to tell you it involves no nuclear reaction either fusion or fission. But, it may include a reaction that is neither one. What that is, I have no idea. I just know it must be a possibility."

"I do not know what that means," she told him.

Tom grinned. "The truth is I don't know either. I just have a hint of an idea I want to look into. Sorry."

She kissed him saying he had nothing to be sorry for. "It will come to you. I know."

Tom held her in his arms and thanked her for her faith in his ability.

"I just hope I don't let myself down on this one."

*   *   *   *   *

He had been sitting at his desk for over three hours that Thursday afternoon when Trent buzzed him.

"Tom? It's the Minister for Energy with the Scottish National Parliament. Line two."

Tom looked at his phone trying to figure out why a senior minister with the governmental body in Scotland, and not the British Parliament, might be calling. With a shrug he poked the button and lifted the handle.

"This is Tom Swift. I understand I have a minister on the line. Is that correct?"

A feminine and very softly accented voice laughed. "I suppose that would be a truth, Mr. Swift. A good day to you. I am Jacquie Livingston, SNP Minister for Energy. Oh, and the first name is spelled a bit differently from others." He wrote it down as she spelled it for him, and he looked at it thinking that it looked like a very nice spelling.

"What might I do for you or answer for you, Minister?" he inquired.

"Well, right to the matter. I don't suppose that you have much knowledge about a location in upper Scotland called Dounreay?"

He had to think. The name sounded like something he ought to know. After a brief pause it came to him.

"Do you mean the nuclear installation up there? As I recall, it is about as far north as you can get and still remain on the mainland."

She laughed. "You are much more knowledgeable than I would have imagined. I'm afraid to admit it but the perception of most Americans over here is you know very little about the rest of the world except for tourist locations and a certain mythical beastie." Her next laugh told him it was not a scold, but more of a little tease.

"Okay, then I will let you know that *most* of the world believes that America and The United States are one in the same thing. All this hemisphere is America in one form or another... North, Central and South. But, I guess we all have small blind spots. So, Minister Livingston, what is it about Dounreay you wish to discuss?"

"Do you know the history of the area by any chance?"

He did, and he told her his understanding was the nuclear facility had been there since the 1950s prototyping reactors for such things as nuclear submarines.

"My belief is the facilities were decommissioned years ago. Is that incorrect?"

She paused and then told him, "Yes... and *not exactly*. Can I assume this is a private conversation and information imparted will not find its way into public release?"

He assured her this was the case.

"Then, I must tell you that when nuclear arms treaties were signed decades ago, all work stopped. All new or publicly known work ceased immediately. *Public* work," she emphasized. "That was in the last years of the nineteen nineties. We were still running some of the facility for years until it could be exhausted of fuel and then stricken from the roles, audited fully, and torn down."

She told him that a few small details had never been released and that part of the facility was still used for testing of everything from nuclear fuel rods and dampening mechanisms to generation of electrical power.

"Now, the thing with the power is, and this is an *important* something, that once the final shutdown occurs, in less than one year, the entire area will have to be powered by generators that burn fossil fuels. Fuels that must be transported in large lorries—uhh, that would be *trucks* to you—over a great number of rather poor roads, or shipped into the port at Scrabster, some thirty kilometers away from Dounreay. Then, trucked. That port is relatively close to a couple of the more populated towns up there, but— Well, there is the but in all this."

The inventor believed he might know what this was leading to but preferred to allow the Minister to speak her piece and tell him.

"The best I can do over this phone line is to suggest I meet you there in a few days, at your convenience, of course. It is then I can tell you what I hope this could lead to. Is that enough to entice you to come, or should I make a formal approach to your company through your own Department of State?"

"If you are simply extending an invitation to me, personally, to come see what you are shutting down, perhaps even getting an opinion or two from me, then I can clear it with my father—who actually runs things here—and come over the day after tomorrow.

Oh, wait... that is Saturday, so I guess Monday. I do need to ask," he said cautiously, "if it is permissible to bring my family. My wife and three children would love to have a chance to see some foreign land."

"Just as long as they don't come over and start asking about the Loch Ness Monster. That is definitely not on the schedule or in even driving range of the base. I will warn you there is not a lot to see other than the natural beauty of the area."

"Not a problem. They do not need to be kept constantly amused."

She told him there was a moderately serviceable airfield at Dounreay that had been used to park cars on for a decade or more, but they could all be moved to accommodate a smallish jet. The field was, however, in rather poor condition.

He described the *Sky Queen* and its vertical landing and takeoff abilities and assured her that if they had at least a couple hundred feet of space, it would be fine and no car shuffling was necessary.

"Then, let this be my personal invitation to you and your family—lovely I am certain—to come over on Monday. I can be there as early as about one in our afternoon."

It was agreed.

When he told Damon of the proposed trip, the older Swift smiled. "I'd heard some small twittering from little birdies about that facility. Something about them having gone dark and underground, but not as it the burrowing maneuvers. Just transferring about eighty percent of the personnel associated with that base and locking the gates to the general world.

"So, what's that about cars all over their runway?" he asked.

Tom chuckled. "As far as I know, those are over supply of cars coming from Sweden and Germany. The Minister said it began as a couple dozen, became a hundred or more and now covers better than two-thirds of the six thousand feet of runway. It's only opened rarely these days but the surface is kept clear of invasive weeds even if there are a lot of cracks."

When he mentioned taking Bashalli and the kids, Damon looked askance at his son.

"Have you taken a good look at a satellite photo of that area? Bleak is the first word coming to mind as well as stark and cold and not necessarily in that order."

Together, using the telejector over the conference table, they did look at a sky view of the surrounding area. Tom thought about what the family might do before he thought of his collapsible SE-11 Toad jet that easily could be fit inside the *Queen's* hangar.

"I can take that and she and the kids can fly around with one of the pilots, probably Zimby."

"If their field is that full of cars, might I suggest folding down a Whirling Duck?"

At home that evening he brought the subject up. Bashalli smiled even though Tom had thought she might balk at taking the two older ones out of school for a day or two.

"Their grade school is closed tomorrow through the following weekend so they can fix some plumbing problem they have that flooded the lunchroom and the gymnasium today," she said. "I was dreading what to do with them since Amanda is back in Nevada visiting her parents this week. I think even Anne is getting old enough to take her on a trip of more than a few minutes. Goodie!"

Bashalli checked several weather sites on about an hourly basis trying to decide what sort of clothing to bring. Even though it was technically late spring there, the typical daily high temperature hovered around 48°F. Jackets and even hats were definitely called for.

Complete with a Whiling Duck and one of the Type Three Atomicars—the four-man size—Tom took the controls of the *Sky Queen* at 9:00 on Sunday morning heading them for Scotland. They would overnight in a small bed and breakfast in Milton of Culloden, a small seaside suburb of Inverness, parking the jet at the nearby airport, before heading for Dounreay the following morning.

Sitting on his mother's lap so she might reach the pedals for him, Bart took a fifteen minute turn at being a pilot once his father stressed he was to only fly straight and level. The boy nodded and took his job seriously until his attention span wore down a bit. Then, he and Bashalli returned to the lounge and allowed Zimby to resume the copilot seat.

"Once he gets to the point he can reach things and stay seated for a couple hours, he should make a good pilot," the man complimented to Tom.

Tom smiled. "Yeah, and let's hope his Aunt Sandy doesn't get to him first or he'll want to become a test pilot."

They touched down at Inverness Airport on the turning circle at the northwest end of the shorter taxiway a few minutes after 4:00 pm local time. Chow, who had come along to make certain they ate well, served a light dinner to them all, including himself, of grilled tuna and cheese sandwiches and some homemade beef and vegetable soup with thin sliced fennel root and lots of mushrooms.

He'd ensured most of them went into Bashalli's bowl as he knew she absolutely loved them.

When he started to clear the dishes she motioned to him to bend over so she might whisper something to him. Instead, she planted a warm kiss on his left cheek. It made the Texas ranch cook blush.

"Thank you, Chow, for the delicious meal!"

"Aww shucks, Ms. Bashalli. I know ya like them mushrooms so I added a few extra fer ya. Wait till ya see what I got planned fer breakfast tomorrow."

They had a quiet two hours before Tom and Bashalli took the kids to the place they would be staying that night. Zimby decided to remain in the jet and soon headed back to the cockpit to make some system checks and to prepare them for the rest of the trip the next morning. He and Chow had a quiet dinner around 9:00 and went to their cabins.

The Swifts got back to the airport before 10:00 am.

Because the trip north would only take fifteen minutes, everyone other than Tom and Zimby remained in the lounge.

Just about on time that day the *Queen* touched down near one end of a runway that appeared to have been almost totally overrun by dusty cars on their right and a rather spartan-appearing base in front of them. They only had to wait twenty minutes before a military transport helicopter touched down closer to the parked automobiles and three people emerged. Two were in Scottish Army uniforms, complete with kilts, and one was a woman in a very thick overcoat.

Tom kissed Bashalli and left the jet to go meet her.

As they came together to shake hands, he saw that a car was approaching from behind the small control room of the airfield.

Niceties concluded, they climbed into the rear of the car with one of the Army men joining the driver up front. The other man saluted then returned to the helicopter.

"What we are about to go into is still classified Top Secret," she told him as they drove around the control building and to a manned, and armed, gate fifty feet away. Seeing his surprise at the closeness of it all she told him, "When they built this base, it was decided there would be no good reason for anyone to come here that did not belong, and therefore cleared, and so interim space was never considered.

She took out her Parliamentary credentials card and handed it to one of the Army guards—these not wearing kilts—who pushed one end into a hand scanner nodding when the light at the end came on green.

"Minister. By authorization of your position, I need to you verify that the civilian with you is cleared for entry."

"He is cleared for full entry," she responded.

"Fine and thank you. Sir, if you will speak your given and family name and nation of residence into this device, please?"

"I am Thomas Swift of the United States of America."

"Also, fine and another thank you to you, sir. You are cleared for entry." He made a motion to another guard who lifted a steel barrier bar and the car moved into the actual installation.

They made an almost immediate left turn and then a right onto the first street that branched off the frontage road. Tom noted the double fifteen-foot fence topped with coils of razor wire that provided protection.

Noting his gaze, she leaned over and said in a low voice, "Fully mined to prevent incursion by most vehicles."

The car soon came to a building that appeared to have at least a dozen sides to it. A sign indicating it was **Dounreay Operations** told him this was likely to be their first stop. It was.

As they drove around to the far side he saw the large, white domed building that would be the location of one of their reactors. He'd heard there were once at least three and asked about the others.

"All in nondescript, rectangular buildings out there," she answered pointing to their west. "That one is the most, well, normal of them all and is the one currently running to provide power to this entire twenty-seven hundred square kilometers of Scotland."

Inside, their military guard excused himself and left them going into a lounge area. Tom and Minister Livingston headed along a short hallway to a conference room about the same size as the shared office back at Enterprises. They took seats in two high-backed leather chairs with a small table between them. Sitting on the table was a carafe of coffee and one of recently boiled water and a selection of loose-leaf teas in tins.

"May I play, as the Brits say, Mother?" she asked.

He nodded asking for coffee.

They passed the next several minutes in conversation before the nearby phone rang.

"Yes?"

She listened and made a humming noise before covering the mouthpiece and asking Tom if he had authorized a flight in a helicopter that had been removed from the rear of his jet.

"Yes. That would be my family and pilot. They would like to tour around the area. I hope that is agreeable and permitted."

Her lips pursed before she answered. "They must agree to not overfly any of this installation and other than when they come back to not fly inside of a one kilometer exclusion area."

"That is already their orders, but I can contact them to remind them."

She shook her head and spoke back into the phone. "They are authorized and will maintain standard clearances. Thank you." She hung up.

"Now, I suppose I need to tell you the reason I wanted this meeting."

The minister began outlining the status of the current running reactor.

"It isn't as bad off as we like to make out, but we are finding that it is running through its final fuel load at a faster rate than ever before. Where the problem is, and this goes to nobody other than your father or the Board of Directors or whatever at your company, is that we are under orders from both the United Nations as well as the European Community governing body to get the installation wiped from the map." She looked into his eyes as if trying to communicate something else.

"Can I assume that means the entire installation gets plowed into the ground?"

With a brief nod she told him, "Yes. Nothing underground, just gone. As in, we have a directive to shut the last remaining reactor off in six months and then defuel in another eighteen months. Not impossible given a few technological breakthroughs, but a rough schedule to hold to."

Now, Tom nodded as he thought about what he wanted to ask.

"So, do you want us to work on those breakthroughs that will allow you to decommission and destruct this site?"

"No. We believe we have that in hand. What we need is something to replace the power generation that is about the only reason we've kept this reactor running for the past four years."

"I see. So, did you want to talk about purchasing a reactor from us?"

Her head shake told him things were likely to be the same in

Scotland as they were in Canada.

She verified this with, "The Scottish National Parliament, the SNP if you will, has declared a moratorium on nuclear-powered electricity generation stations for the next five years. That leaves us in a real quandary we hope you might assist us in."

And, I hope I can come up with something really whiz-bang and reliable in a very short time, he thought. *And, that the Scots agree to let me build whatever that is in their country!*

CHAPTER 4 /
BACK HOME, NOW FEATURING ADDED WORRIES

"BUT, MR, Swift. We strongly believe that a solution to the situation in the Yukon along with adhering to our nation's desires to minimize the deadly effects of a nuclear reactor would resonate in your heart." This was coming from the Vice-Premiere of Canada in a call Damon was taking in Tom's absence.

"Actually, sir, it does not. To put it plainly, our reactors are as foolproof as anything ever devised and built, have a proven track record of never having leaked even a single measurable roentgen of radiation from any of the fifty-seven such reactors now operating in eleven nations, and have a payback period slightly less than half our competition can offer.

"I will be blunt about one thing in particular. We assisted your nation in finding a huge reserve of uranium-rich ore, ore that becomes both nuclear fuel and *nuclear warheads*. Are you stating your government and people are satisfied with others making power or killing people with your processed ore?

"And I also must ask you why keeping your citizens from perishing from the relative cold of a great portion of your nation—not something I ascribe to anything other than your geographic positioning—why *that* does not resonate in your heart as having a priority over unfounded fears?"

There was a silence lasting into the twenty seconds range and Damon believed the other man had hung up. He did not wish to play his, "You already have one of our smaller reactors up near that same Inuit village you have agreed we might replace," *card* as he did not wish to have that questioned by the somewhat ultra-Liberal politicians currently in charge of their government. He also considered, for a split second, reminding the Canadian politician that Tom had made two recent trips to Canada where he had been at the Inuit village ascertaining what might be going on with *no* sign of any concerned Canadians.

Getting that reactor replaced and the continued survival of that village was more important that rubbing the nose of some elected official in the facts.

Finally, the Canadian answered. "Mr. Swift. With due respect to you and your company and, I will add, your record of safety, the people of Canada have entrusted their welfare to this government and we fully intend to see that trust is not compromised. So, with regret, I need to terminate this conversation."

"You never did get to the point of this call, the one you initiated."

"Oh. Oh. Give me a moment to collect my thoughts, please." Music on hold featuring a rendition of *Oh, Canada* played on pan pipes came on.

The inventor rolled his eyes but sat waiting for the full minute it took the politician to come back on.

"Thank your for your patience. The reason for this call in the first place was to inquire if you might extend us a period of one year to make the payment for the power system you installed a decade ago, and *that* money promised by another party, and to arrange for a three-year payment schedule for the replacement for that."

Damon picked up a piece of paper his Legal team had researched and scanned it for a piece of information.

"Well," he began spotting what he wanted, "I see by your latest government budget accounting reports you are sitting on a surplus of greater than nine-point-two billion dollars, computed at Canadian values, not U.S., as of just two weeks ago. Before you ask, that is public knowledge. Because of that I cannot agree to lengthen out the payment terms for the overdue funds.

"As for funding for the new system—something that can be installed as soon as in about three weeks—we are waiting for the official purchase order for that. And, because of the tardiness your government introduced to the payment of the first billings, I also cannot extend anything other than eighty percent down to get the unit brought up and installed and twenty percent within a net-thirty day payment period.

"I hope you can understand our reticence given your, uhh, delays."

The man at the other end sucked in a deep breath. "Mr. Swift, That is unfair..."

"No. It is not. What is unfair is that your government, during all this time you have not paid us," and he put his finger on another line item on his list, "has spent more than seven hundred fifty-three million Canadian dollars on paying for your film and television industry to produce programming and movies that have returned just one hundred ninety-one million in revenues. I would have to say that points to a severe lack of priorities. Wouldn't you?"

The conversation lasted just another minute before the Canadian agreed to get the first power system paid for within the week.

For his part, Damon agreed to get the replacement station

readied for shipment that would occur within twenty days of the receipt of those monies plus a reduced initial payment of just fifty percent of the new unit.

After hanging up, he rose from his desk and headed up to Legal.

Upstairs, he discovered Jackson Rimmer was over at the Construction Company and Patrick Peck had departed for a lunch meeting with a friend in downtown Shopton.

"Guess that'll teach me to just assume they are always here," he told the receptionist with a guilty grin.

"Not to worry, Mr. Swift," she told him. "Mr. Rimmer's meeting just came up fifteen minutes ago and Mr. Peck left a half hour ago, but ought to be back in thirty or forty minutes. Want me to have whoever gets back first come to your office?"

He thought about it. "No. Just give me a call if and when they have about twenty minutes for me to grump and grouse about a nation to our north. Thanks!"

The call came thirty-eight minutes later when Jackson returned.

"Yes, Damon? What can I do for you, and what's this about some nation to the north?"

Damon told him about the basics of the call and offered to play the recording of it.

"No. Just your description sounds like enough for now. Want me to call my friend up there and find out what was behind that?"

The inventor tried to think about it and suggested he come up for a discussion before such a call might be made.

"I stand... or rather sit ready to serve. Come up any time."

"On my way."

By the time Damon arrived, Jackson had decided he needed to hear the full conversation, so that is what both men did over the next ten minutes. At the end, the attorney leaned back and closed his eyes.

"They don't make it easy to like them, do they?"

The inventor shook his head. "No. But I did want you to hear how that went so when they either do or do not send us that money, you will have what you need to either thank them, from a legal standpoint and reminding them of the next payment due, or make the appropriate suggestions to him or them."

"Again, standing, sitting or most other positions..." and he used both hands to indicate himself, "ready to spring into action," Rimmer finished with a smile.

*   *   *   *   *

Since his return to Shopton, Tom had been spending many hours at work and a few at home trying to find some method of power generation that did not include a nuclear reactor. Certainly, his power pods did hold a radioactive isotope-rich gel that reacted with special metallic plates to generate electricity, and they were not classified as "nuclear reactors," but their output was finite, generally requiring a period of recuperation after a sustained release of electricity, and so could not be considered as a full-time replacement.

He toyed with computations showing how many of his largest pods would be needed to replace even the reactor in the Inuit village. In order to provide the same level of power plus enough to replace the steam heating the current system provided, he would need about twenty-seven or twenty-eight of the largest pods and the cost of those would exceed that of the replacement reactor by a factor of 3.4.

Even at that, each one would need to be taken off line at least once per week for over a full day, and they probably needed a semi-annual test and data download—with needed maintenance—to maintain full efficiency.

Other than the pods in many of Tom's space ships, no individual installation had to run 24 x 7 x 365. In offices and residences the pods generally had all night to recover. In space he could unfurl his Solartron sheets and generate added power while allowing the pod(s) to reduce output and rest.

A few more fanciful things came to mind and he made many notes on what he might look into.

One of these was to go out to Fearing Island, the Swifts rocket and submersibles base off the coast of Georgia, and to investigate the possibility the strange manufacturing box left to him by the Space Friends might have something it could build to either test or that might actually function as an alternative to nuclear power.

After all, they had the ability to traverse—physically and with their communications—outside of *normal* space and time. Why not be able to tap some source out there?

Although he and Bud had been gone for two days recently, he asked Bashalli if she had any great reservations about him—and Bud, assuming Sandy did not have a fit—heading for Fearing the next morning.

"My plans are to spend up to four hours with that manufacturing box and then coming home before dinner. Uhh, did you want to come along?"

She smiled at him and shook her head. "No. And I'll have a word with my sister-in-law about not going ballistic over Bud being gone for a whole eight or nine hours." She rolled her eyes. "Sometimes I thing Sandra does not engage her brain before she does her mouth." Now, she grinned, a little guiltily from what Tom could tell, at her speaking about Tom's sister like that.

He reacted by smiling broadly at her and stepping forward to give her a kiss and a hug.

"You know her only too well, Bash!"

She gave him one more small hug before heading for her phone.

"Sandy? Bashi. Listen. Tomorrow Tom needs to go out to Fearing Island with Bud for a few hours. How about we have a nice lunch in town?" She listened for a few seconds. Then, "Yes, I do realize they were gone overnight over less than two full days a couple weeks ago, and will remind you that you and I headed down to New York City and went to a play and had that very nice lobster dinner without them. So, what do you say?"

She put her hand over the receiver and whispered to Tom, "She's softening." She uncovered the phone saying, "Okay," she spoke into the phone. "I'll drop by your office about eleven forty. See you then!"

She made an OK sign with her right thumb and forefinger and then quickly kissed him before heading for the kitchen.

The phone rang a minute later and he picked it up. "Swift residence."

"Hey, skipper. It's Bud. What's this I hear about you sending the ladies out to lunch tomorrow so we can head for the island?"

Tom corrected his brother-in-law about the actual chain of events. The flyer laughed.

"Yeah. Figured it would be something like that. So, what are we up to?"

Tom told him of his hope, even as scant as it might be, about the Space Friends' box. He didn't need to go into much detail as he and Bud had had many conversations about the need for an alternate power generating source. He stopped at one point and asked, "Did you suggest that to me a couple weeks ago?"

"Sort of, but not with a lot of conviction."

"Oh. Then I apologize for not taking it seriously at the time. Once again you might prove to be the wiser of the two of us."

Bud snorted. "Right! Fat chance of that, my friend."

They agreed to meet at the Barn just before 8:00 the following morning.

"I'll have the cafeteria whip something up for us to take along so we don't miss breakfast," Tom offered. As always, Bud readily accepted the idea of some food.

The two men met at the Barn the following morning, but before they could even open the Toad and climb in, Tom received a TeleVoc page from Harlan Ames.

"Answer," he subvocalized.

"Tom? Sorry to bother you if you are in the middle of something, but I need to speak to you as soon as you can come over to the office. Are you," he sounded tentative, "anywhere nearby?"

"Bud and I happen to be at the Barn, so I'll jog over and be there in under five minutes. Any early hint what I should expect?"

There was a pause before his Security man answered. "We've received a creditable report someone is out to do you some harm. We can get to all that as soon as you get here. Bring Bud if you wish. It's likely that if someone tries to get to you when you are flying, he'd be there as well."

"Okay. We're on our way." He closed the connection.

"Come on, flyboy. We're going to put this flight off and go see Harlan."

Without any questions, Bud followed his friend out and around the western corner of the open-sided hangar.

Harlan and his third in command man, Gary Bradley, met them just inside the front doors of their building. Handshakes were exchanged before Tom and Bud were invited into the office Harlan occupied. Tom took a seat close to the door with Bud across from him and the two Security men taking the other chairs in the quad of seats.

"Okay, Harlan," Tom said with a small sigh. "What's all this about a threat? I mean, another threat."

"We have had both a call and an email. Neither traceable... yet, but we're working on that. We don't want to worry you—"

"Because your worry is enough for us all," Gary interrupted with a small grin.

Harlan snorted. "To put it mildly. So, Phil and a couple of our techs are working on those traces while Gary and I wanted to brief you. And, I haven't yet told your father. I'll do that after we've spoken. As to the exact nature of the threat, some standard rhetoric such as, 'The Swifts have destroyed the environment,' and, 'Tom

44

Swift is the greatest threat to mankind.' That load of bull we've all heard before. This time, however, a specific threat of shooting you from the sky is the closer."

Tom's eyes rolled. He'd heard this too many times before. All too often the threat had come after an attack. At least this time he had a measure of forewarning.

"I really can't be tied down to the ground right now. Is there anything we can do to minimize this?"

Harlan and Gary both shook their heads. The senior man was about to add something when the office door flew open and Phil Radnor came inside.

"Big news, guys! With the help from both the FBI and the National Security Division, our equipment was able to trace the origin of the phone call. It was a different number from the one associated with the email, but they are both registered to the same address. And, it is right here in Shopton!"

Stunned, Tom could find no words. Bud, on the other hand, jumped to his feet, declaring, "Let's go get that miserable—" but he faltered seeing the other men shaking their heads. "What?"

Tom spoke for the others. "You, flyboy, need to put that impetuosity aside and think about who is the best for racing off to get the bad guys. And interestingly it isn't either you or me. Besides, ask yourself what Sandy would say if she were here."

"Or," Phil added, "how hard she'd tackle you before you got out the door."

The flyer blushed and sat back down. "Okay. If you put it like that, and threaten me with my wife, I give up."

"As I was starting to say," Phil continued, "the local FBI folks along with Shopton's finest and even a couple incoming cars of Captain Rock's best state troopers are on their way to the address. They ought to be there in..." and he glanced at his watch, "well, right about fifteen seconds ago. I'm going back to the communications room and monitor the progress. I'll be back to you all as soon as I hear anything." He rose followed by Gary.

While waiting for news, Tom, Bud and Harlan talked about Tom's upcoming plans for a new type of electricity generation station.

"I only ask," the Security man told him, "because sure as shooting—and I know that is a poor choice of words right now—this department is going to need to be involved in all security and safety measures wherever you go with this."

Tom admitted he'd been to Scotland and the Dounreay location could very well be a starting point for investigation.

"Even though I would want to build a small-scale generator at first, we do need some location to try things out that will not automatically—"

"And blindly," Bud said.

"Right. We need a country where we won't be up against a massive uphill battle with everyone from the lowest of public servants to the highest member of their government. Local citizens included." He was about to add more when the door opened again, and Phil stepped inside.

"It is over," he stated with a sad smile. That quickly changed as he described all he knew of the operation to get to the person or people responsible for the latest threat. "Uhh, it would appear that, in an effort to get rid of evidence and equipment, the man had explosive charges set up around a lot of his stuff. He..." and he gulped a little before continuing.

Harlan came to his rescue. "Can I guess? He fired those off as the authorities battered down his doors and—of course I'm making a wild guess here—they were stronger than he probably meant for them to be. So, *removed* from society?"

Phil nodded.

Tom turned to Bud. "If you'd gone charging in there you could be in that same condition. And, while I hate there to be loss of anyone's lives, I'd much rather it not be you. Can you imaging how much Sandy would hate me?"

The flyer had turned pale at these thoughts. Not especially the *Sandy* one—he knew her admonitions and even occasional arm punches were delivered from her love for him—but the idea of the violent end of the man threatening Tom's life.

Hanging his head a little, he muttered an apology for still being more of an act first and think later person.

"It's kept both of us alive more than once, flyboy. You keep the instant switch to action mode going and I'll keep placing the metaphorical hand on your forearm to stop you when it's in your best interest."

Bud grinned. "Getting a little flowery prose in there, skipper?"

Tom nodded. "Just thinking back to Junior High English classes and how Mrs. Trunbridge always told us to use more than just a couple, simple words when delivering something you feel strongly about!"

"If the Greater Shopton Literary Society and Coffee Guild can be called to order," Harlan told the two, "then I really need to hear more about where this Scottish installation site might be and find out when—and you will kindly notice I did not say, 'if'—my team can go scope things out?"

Tom did not know. He did know the facility was pretty much off limits to outsiders and that he had only been inside under escort and with one of their senior Parliament Ministers.

"Besides," he said thinking about other things to be overcome, "we may not build right inside their highly fortified barbed wire walls."

"Okay. If not inside that facility, then where?" This came from Phil who had not left the office.

Tom told the others about the flight Bashalli and the kids, along with Zimby Cox, had taken while he was occupied.

She had mentioned the beautiful if a little stark landscape below them along with a small lake, or loch, to the south.

"Both Bash and Zimby tell me there is a lot of forest land nearby that appears to be unused for anything other than trees and wildlife. I'll need to check with the Minister to see if we can bother both of those."

CHAPTER 5 /

"I CANNAE GIVE YA MORE!"

TOM BELIEVED the bulk of his troubles might be solved if he could spend some time out in New Mexico at the Citadel. If anyone could shed light on power generation, it might be Dr. Timothy Slade and his folks in Nuclear Research.

He did consider that they might be so finely tuned into the nuclear side of things they might find it difficult to shift gears, so to speak, but a phone call convinced him they were, "...always looking at alternatives, Tom. Just not finding any viable ones at present."

But first, he and Bud flew the Toad south and east to Fearing Island where they landed at about 11:20 in the morning.

After checking in with the base commander, Tom found he needed to spend forty minutes with one of the rocket crews to help with a small issue of a payload release refusing to test positive when installed on a two-stage Swift Sampson rocket, yet working perfectly when removed and set up on a test bench. While he did, Bud walked over to the control tower to see a couple friends.

After watching the process of bench testing and then installed failure, the inventor stood pondering what might be the cause.

"Have you checked the connectors?"

They had. Three times.

"Okay, how about the gyroscopic inputs? If I had to guess I'd say the payload doesn't believe it is the upright orientation."

That stopped the two technicians from nodding again. They looked at each other and a small level of embarrassment passed between them.

"Oops, Tom. That's about the only thing we didn't check. Hang on..." and they lowered the rocket from its launch rail one more time. In minutes the fairing on one side was detached and Pete—of the pair known to many as Pete and Re-Pete—reached inside with a practiced hand and withdrew a thick circuit board from the very lowest part of the payload bay.

The three men headed to a computer where a pigtail was plugged into the board with Tom calling up a test sequence.

The green bar was interrupted by a small band of red near the middle.

"Yep!" Pete stated as he tapped the screen. "That's the gyro output and it's not outputting. Orient that board ninety degrees, will you, Tom?" The inventor obliged and the test was rerun with the same results.

"Gee. Not just failing to tell us if the board or the rocket is upright, it's downright refusing to send out anything!"

Tom smiled, held up a "wait one" finger and walked over to a parts trailer where he pulled out a replacement board. This one, once attached, tested out correctly in both orientations so Pete and Pete installed it.

Nine minutes later the rocket was upright and everything checked out normal. The launch had to be held for another two hours and fifty-seven minutes so the small satellite they were launching, even into what was technically a low-Earth orbit, could be "inserted" into that orbit at the correct point in the planet's rotation. Otherwise, as they all knew, it would fail to overfly the fifteen geographic points it was meant to during daylight hours.

They thanked Tom for his insight.

"Foo! You'd have come up with the same answer if I weren't here in a few more minutes!" he told them.

Eleven minutes later he rejoined Bud at the large hangar next to the Administration building. This was where the manufacturing box —left on the moon of Mars known as Phobos by the Space Friends when they departed the system a few years earlier—sat covered with a light woven Durastress tarp.

Once it was uncovered, Tom placed his right palm on an area he knew to be the activation pad, the one that would verify to the machine his identity and would authorize access. He knew he was the only person that could make it respond and even turn on.

It did.

A disguised screen appeared where he'd touched showing him the standard hand-signing of the aliens telling him hello. After having used it on more than a few occasions, he understood it could, and would, go though a complete introduction sequence of about twenty minutes unless he overrode that with a press of his palm again, only this time in the middle of the screen.

The image changed immediately. He recognized the alien hands now telling him, "Hello, Tom Swift. Please make a selection or upload a design."

He scrolled through the display of about one hundred devices it was already programmed to build. It was only once he arrived in the early 90s he began seeing what appeared to be anything having to do with generation of power.

From behind him came Bud's voice. "Anything already in there, skipper?"

"It's not looking great, Bud, but there might be something here at the third from the last device." He stepped to one side. "What does that look like to you?"

Bud, who watched a lot more science fiction television and movies than Tom responded. "Looks like a special bead condenser from an Interocitor."

Tom turned. "A *what*?"

The flyer grinned. "Interocitor," he repeated as if it were an every day word. "It was something an alien race provided to the main character in the book and movie *This Island Earth* back in the nineteen fifties. It was a key component to communication. And that," he pointed back to the screen, "looks a bit like the extremely high voltage bead condenser at the heart of the device."

Tom looked like he was digesting this new information.

When asked what this Interocitor could do, all Bud could recall was that it was used as a communications device, a controller for an airplane and also a weapon to destroy things including itself once used.

Tom's face looked bothered by that last piece of news.

"I'd hate to build something only to have it self-destruct. Of course," he said brightening, "until I see what that thing can do I'll never know. Let's make one."

Tom tapped the image on the screen then followed the unspoken prompts to make a single unit. It came out of a hidden door that slid up three minutes later.

This was the quickest anything had come from the machine so it had Tom wondering if the blue piece had any practical use.

"You don't suppose," he said in a low voice to his friend, "that this piece of whatever it is might have something to do with power? Generation, modification, control or something I mean." He pointed to the metallic-looking contact pads on each end.

Bud gave an exaggerated shrug.

Only to see if he'd missed anything, or find some indication this new small device required another component also available from the box, Tom searched back through the entire menu. He had a sudden shiver run down his spine as he came to the energy weapon screen, the one he had used to create three hand-held devices used by himself, his father and Bud to defeat the Master brought by the Space Friends when they recently revisited Earth.

The flyer also recognized the image but thought better than to mention it. He knew that both Swifts had hated the idea of using an offensive weapon but had been forced into that by the actions, demands and anger of the reptilian being.

Tom located a compact device that appeared custom made to accept the first small sphere-with-end-knobs piece he'd had made so he also had one of these built. This time the box required over nineteen minutes. He believed it must be much more complex than the first piece.

He also wondered why, if they did fit together, they were not on the menu next to one another.

Not certain why, he made another pair of the blue beads, possibly as backups.

Within the hour he and Bud radioed the control tower asking for permission to take off, departing the island four minutes after that.

His trip to the Southwest the following morning was with Bud and Red Jones in his Toad jet. While Bud and he would remain behind, Red needed to fly to Flagstaff, Arizona, with a parcel of spare parts for another of the Swift aircraft models being used by a small charter airline company. He would return the following afternoon.

"See you two tomorrow," the older pilot said as he closed the canopy and prepared to taxi back to the single runway.

Tom and Bud headed for the main building cluster of the nuclear facility. They checked in with the secretary for the manager and were assigned a pair of rooms in the Visitor's wing of the dormitory building.

After that, Tom headed for the office of Dr. Slade while Bud headed out to the airfield and the hangar where one of the Swift's cargo jets was landing. He intended to assist in the unloading as he felt he had nothing to contribute to Tom's discussions.

"Well, hello there, Tom. Of course, I know why you are here, but I feel a little small talk is always a nice way to get comfortable. So, anything new in your life? A new kid on the way?" He smiled at the inventor.

Tom, for his part, also smiled but shook his head. "Not a lot new that doesn't involve work and no new kids on the way. Three is about all we plan to have. It's just this power system problem weighing on my mind right now."

The Doctor pointed to a couple chairs to one side of his office. "I would suppose that a bit of sitting and some serious conversation is called for, then. Let's take a seat."

Tom sat and leaned forward as he sought to find the way to begin what he wished to discuss.

"I suppose I need to ask how familiar you are with the situation up in Canada. By that I don't so much mean the power station as I do the people and what they have gone through."

Dr. Slade nodded. "I believe so. An isolated native tribe village that found themselves without power a decade or so ago. I do recall the special fast build of that system once you and Barclay headed up and installed a tank of diesel fuel for their old generator as a temporary measure." He looked over the top of his reading glasses at the inventor. "I am also painfully aware that we have a bad rod, or at *least* one, in that reactor. And, I have to tell you, we've been both racking our brains as well as our build records to try to figure out why that has started to fail."

Tom sighed. "Then, I suppose we need to start talking about how to complete the build and fully test another one for them in as little time as necessary. I believe the current installation will last under one year and the Canadian government is starting to pay for the first one, but we can't be absolutely certain they will follow through on the second one. Especially—and I am not certain why this has not come up so far—given the problems with the much shorter than expected life of the first system."

"I believe," the Doctor stated, "we also must come up with some systematic way to check this reactor fueling and then all others we make from this point on. Some way to determine the absolute purity of the pellets we pack into each rod."

His guest nodded. "Right. The thing is, since we've never had this problem before, I am not sure just how effective it is going to be to do much more than what we currently do."

The conversation turned to the build of the new reactor and how it would be incorporated into the current circulation system. Dr. Slade asked if Tom believed the rest of the system would be sufficient to last through the expected life of the new reactor.

"We are going to perform a pressure test of the system and also inject a dye into the liquid to watch how quickly it circulates and comes back to the reactor. If it is within five percent of what it was all those years ago—and dad and I have no reason to suspect it will not be—then our opinion is it will last another two decades."

They rose to go look at the current state of the build. Because nothing would be fueled until it was ready to deliver, everything was in a secure room but without the need to have people in any protective gear. In the middle of the thirty by thirty-five foot room sat a trio of reactors of the same size.

"Two of those are destined for Spain," Dr. Slade explained, "but the priority one to the right is the one for up north. Come," he invited Tom to step over with him.

Both men watched in fascination as two of the technicians used an intricate hoist system to raise and then lower into the open-topped core area the first of the nuclear material rod holders. In less than three minutes it had been trued using a laser system and bolted solidly inside.

Tom knew it would remain in that position, all within about five microns of perfect, for the life of the reactor.

As they watched over the next ten minutes two slightly smaller holders were installed on either side of the first holder. These would be used for the dampening cobalt rods that would help control the reaction within the core.

"They should have that finished before the end of tomorrow, tested the following day and then filled with the internal coolant and sealed on Monday."

"Great! So, how long for the proper operational testing?"

Dr. Slade laughed. "You are certainly in a hurry. It will take a week for the NRC inspector to give us the certificate necessary to fuel, another two days for that plus a week of initial small-scale running and tests. Then, let us say three weeks from yesterday, the fuel rods will be withdrawn, the protective shroud installed and it will be ready to go up. I'm assuming you want to be part of the delivery." He looked at Tom curiously.

"Absolutely!"

By the time Red returned, both Tom and Bud were more than ready to get home to their families and regular jobs. Talks with Dr. Slade and his team had failed to yield any ideas for an alternate method of generating electricity.

Evidently, Tom's mention of an "Interocitor" and the movie *This Island Earth* that evening after visiting Fearing had intrigued Bashalli. She'd found it on an online video streaming service and had it ready for them to watch that evening after dinner.

Amanda, the nanny, suggested the two girls ought to perhaps not watch it due to one of the 'monster' characters toward the end.

"I think Bart will be okay. He can distinguish between fantasy and the movies and real life, but I'm afraid Mary and Anne might have a few nightmares."

After the movie finished, and while Amanda came to get Bart cleaned up and in bed, the two Swifts sat discussing the movie.

"Well. I, for one, am glad Amanda did not think that was suitable for the girls," Bashalli stated. "But, I liked it!"

Tom grinned at his wife. "Me too. And, now I know what Bud was talking about with both the Interocitor and the condenser bead. He's right. The thing the box out on Fearing gave me looks a lot like that. Now, all I need to do is try to use it to see what it actually does."

Being possessed of a life-long love of intriguing movies, Tom picked up the remote and set their TV to record the movie so he could watch it again some day.

The next morning Bart was trying to describe the movie to his sisters when Tom came into the kitchen.

"I hope you aren't describing the Mutant to your sisters," Tom warned his oldest.

"Nope! Not gonna tell them about *that*," Bart declared with a small gleam in his eye. "It's too good for *girls*!"

"And," his mother warned, "you are never going to... isn't that right, Barton Swift?"

The boy's eyes went wide. He knew when his mother or father used his full first name it was a very serious thing. He also knew if they used all three of his names, he was in trouble.

"Never. I swear," he said crossing his right index finger over his heart.

Bud joined his best friend in the large lab on the second floor of the Administration building at nine-thirty that morning. Tom was just sitting in front of the large worktable against the right wall looking at the small, slightly red bead. It was mounted in a small, padded vice and attached to a couple of small leads that ran into a multi-tester.

The flyer was about to pull over a stool when something reached his brain.

"Red?" he said in a loud voice. "It came from the box all blue. What gives?"

Tom looked over to his brother-in-law for a split second. "Not sure. As soon as I hooked it up to see if anything was coming out of it, it did *that*," he stated pointing at the bead.

"And?"

"There is a sort of energy I can detect, and even measure, but it doesn't seem to be electricity," Tom admitted. His gaze was back on the bead.

"Now what?" Bud asked with a tone of great curiosity.

Tom sighed and reached over to turn off the tester. He disconnected the left lead before answering, "Now, we put this inside the test chamber and see what happens if I put electricity into it."

His companion nodded and helped move the test equipment and its small roll-around table into the tomasite chamber.

Tom did the honors of hooking things up before the two men stepped out and closed the door.

Once they were both seated on the safe side of the clear wall that covered most of the left side of the lab, Tom asked Bud if he was ready.

A nod told him what the answer to that question might be.

He reached out and turned the tester's outside controls to the **ON** position. Seconds later he adjusted the settings so it was not testing what the bead was putting out, it was about to put some electrical power into it. He sat thinking about how much to give it and came up with the decision to begin with half a volt at exceptionally low amperage, likely to be half that of a small AAA battery.

"Here goes," he announces almost under his breath.

The bead inside was being watched by a camera and displayed on a high-resolution monitor just above the panel. It started out its normal blue color and remained so until the inventor had raised the power to twenty volts and 5,000 milliamps. At that time it turned orange.

"Getting some reaction now," Bud commented.

"Yes. We are. Not sure what that means but it's something to note." He wrote a short note on a pad sitting to his right. Then he returned his looking to the monitor as he reached out to set the equipment to slowly raise the voltage—keeping the amperage steady... for now—at the rate of a volt per twenty seconds.

Nothing different could be seen until he reached his preset maximum of two hundred volts. DC. He had decided to not attempt alternating current for the time being.

He knew his equipment could provide about five times higher output—but only to a certain point—and decided to give that a try. If he burned out the small bead he knew how to create more.

"Along with adding more power in, I want to hook up a

tangential switching circuit to see what we get back out."

Bud looked askance at Tom. "Uhh, how?"

The inventor explained that he could use a special circuit that would perform many switches per second with the output alternately turned off thirty times while the input activated the other thirty cycles each and every second.

"That way, flyboy, I see what comes out for what goes in. My hope is that the power does not just disappear inside that thing. I'm expecting it to put at least the same level back out."

Over the following two hours and right up until it was close to going home time, Tom slowly fed in increasing amounts of power. The two men looked on in increasing amazement as the power coming back out exceeded the inputs.

Halfway through the test the two exchanged places. Tom wanted to more closely monitor the output.

"Keep going up," he requested fifty-six minutes later.

Mimicking the character of Montgomery Scott from the old science fiction television series, *Star Trek*, Bud grinned, exclaiming, "Sorry Captain Tom, but I cannae give ya no more!"

Tom turned to face his friend, momentarily puzzled before it came to him what was being said.

"Ahhh... so you're at top input now?"

"Yep!"

"And I'm getting about three times that back out. Hmmm? While I'd like to explore the upper limits, I guess I have to be satisfied with what we have. However," he said with a hint of mischief, "tomorrow is, as someone once said, another day."

Bud grinned. "You do have to admit it is pretty impressive already. Right?"

Tom grinned back and nodded. And, the inventor was already planning on what equipment he could have delivered to the lab to see just what the Space Friends' little electronic bead might be able to do.

CHAPTER 6 /

A DEFINITIVE DEAD END

IF TOM believed that everything would be solved by the Space Friends' manufacturing box, he was about to discover that line of thought was not leading him straight to success.

On the other hand, it was not going to lead to total failure for the inventor.

To begin with, he started by using one of his smaller power pods hooked to a circuit feeding an ever-increasing charge into first one of the power beads and then a trio of them. Measurements of the output showed that it exceeded the input levels by a factor of five, but it was raw voltage only at low amperage.

That was not enough to suit him, but it was a start.

The more power he fed in, the more came out, but only to a point. The limit seemed to be anything above four hundred volts and six hundred watts at a maximum draw of twenty amps.

As he and Damon discussed this, the older inventor asked a good question.

"Remember when you first started playing around with processing videos on your computer and discovered what I believe you said was once called 'the rubber band effect'?"

Tom smiled at the memory. In an old book he'd taken out from the Shopton Library, the authors discussed how there was a balance point between image dimensions, frame rate and amount of data necessary to support that. Increase one—for instance the image dimensions—and for each slightly larger image you either needed to add more data, sacrifice image quality if you kept the same data rate, or do something with the number of frames you could display.

"Sure. If you only stretch one part of the band it wants to pull in the others. So..." Now, he stopped and considered how this applied to his power experiments. "Okay," he finally said. "If I want more of one, say voltage, I need to find a way to increase the others, or at least one of the other factors, or give in on one of them."

It made sense. If he wanted higher voltage using his current setup, he would either need to feed in more watts of power or be satisfied with lower amperage.

At least, given the evident capabilities of the alien power bead.

"Tom? Changing the subject for a moment, I know you wanted to be involved in the changeover, but the Citadel team took the replacement reactor up two days ago and made the swap in just two hours. Disappointed?"

"Not really. I'm just glad that is taken care of!"

Ten minutes later he headed back to the lab to try other ways of using the beads. As it stood, they were not the universal panacea Bud's reference to the ones from the movie hinted at.

Tom spent the remainder of the day and the two that followed trying to eke out a little more power from his system. He managed to get small results from a dozen more volts and about ninety more watts, but the amperage could not be brought any higher. Finally at the end of Thursday afternoon, he slid his chair back from the computer where he'd been taking notes and put his face in his hands.

His eyes stung—something that had happened to him a few times over the years due to what Doc called Uveitis, or more commonly known as an eye infection. But, today it didn't feel like that. His eyes just felt exceptionally dry.

The more he thought about it, the more he realized his throat was dry and his lungs felt as if he'd been in a desert.

For a birthday gift when he turned seventeen, his aunt had given the boy an indoor weather station that included a barometer, a thermometer that read in both Fahrenheit and Celsius, but it was the sensor that indicated the relative humidity he was most interested in. He checked his instrument.

To his amazement it was reading just 4%.

"That is *way* too dry. I wonder what's going on?" he croaked.

Standing, he realized just how bad he felt, so he walked to the door, opened it and nearly swooned when the normal 39% humidity hit him. It felt a little like a damp cloth being slapped onto his face.

Now confused, he headed into the hall, closed and locked the door, intending to try to find out what was going on the following day. But first, he headed for the Dispensary. He'd had enough experience with extra dry conditions to know his body likely needed both water as well as some electrolytes. Doc would have just the thing.

After explaining his situation, Doc walked from the small exam cubicle and down the hall. When he returned he had an orange one-quart sports drink bottle in one hand and a green one in the other.

"It's gonna make you have to find a bathroom, but I want both of these down and into your stomach in the next half hour. It's either this or an IV. Okay?"

Taking the orange one, Tom nodded. The truth was he was very thirsty. He managed to drink that bottle in just thirty seconds and taking only four breaths.

"What a nice and behaving young man you are being," the medico told him. "So, sit there for five, then take the other one and please head home. Have a nice dinner, using a little extra salt because your body really needs that right now, and then drink as much plain water as you can before bed. No coffee, tea or sodas. Sorry to tell you but I believe there will be at least two trips to the little boys' room before you get up tomorrow. If you need a note for Bashalli, I'll jot one down for you."

With a tired grin and a nod, Tom promised he would pass along his plight and ask for her understanding.

"Just tell her it isn't so much a *plight* as it is a... hmmmm? Circumstance? Yes, that one."

He was no more in the front door when she almost jumped into his arms, but stopped on seeing how pale he looked. "What is going on, Tom?" she asked with deep concern.

He told her about working on an experiment in the lab and suddenly finding that he was getting dehydrated. "Doc says you have to make me drink a lot tonight and then put up with my heading for the bathroom a couple times. If you insist I'll take the sofa down here so you don't lose any sleep."

"Thomas Swift. If you think I could sleep comfortably with you exiled down in this living room, think again! Just try to tiptoe and be sure to shut the door before turning on any light."

She started to turn away, but turned back. "Oh, and I love you." Now, she headed for the kitchen while the three children took their turns hugging their father and receiving forehead kisses.

The next day he stood outside the lab door, took a couple of deep breaths and went inside closing he door quickly. His weather station said the humidity was back to 39%, so he took a breath. It seemed to be fine.

As an experiment, Tom brought the station over to his desk, set it up leaning against the wall, and decided to repeat what he'd been doing the day before.

Setting the power experiment to run automatically, but over a shorter period of time, he watched the gauges. They barely twitched during the first half hour, and it was only as the power neared the top of his previous attempts that he watch in fascination as the temperature gauge rose by two degrees in a few brief seconds and the relative humidity started to go down by about a percent every thirty seconds.

He turned things off. In minutes the humidity started to go back up as the air circulation from the rest of the building filled the room. He wondered what might have happened if he'd shut down the outside circulation and had just been using the air within the room. He now believed he might have gotten into a more desperate situation had that been the case.

Without any humidity, he might have actually done some small damage to his lungs before he thought to leave the room. If he'd been able to leave.

This was, he knew, not a good thing and had ultimately not led to much success on the power front.

Well, he thought, *at least I may have discovered some sort of industrial dehumidifier!*

After disconnecting his equipment and storing a few of the pieces he used over and over, he made a few final notes before heading out of the building to go tell Doc he was doing fine and had figured out what happened.

"I thought that electricity was our friend," the physician told him. "At least that is what an old radio ad told people. I'mg lad you drank enough and found out what caused the troubles so you can avoid it in the future."

After leaving the Dispensary, Tom headed for the parking area of a few of the electric runabouts used by employees on the Enterprises' premises. He climbed into one that had a green, or **AVAILABLE**, light on the dash, checked it out using his TeleVoc and headed for Hangar 6 where Bud kept his office.

The flyer was sitting on the front edge of his desk perusing a test printing of the manual update to the Toad.

Now available in three engine configurations, it was the best practice to print separate manuals for each type. This meant no chance of looking up incorrect information.

"Hey, flyboy!" Tom called out as he rounded the corner and headed for the office door.

Bud looked up, smiled and made a "come in" gesture with his head.

"What's up, skipper? Great news about impressive experiments?"

Tom's look told him this was not to be the case.

"Oh. Sorry. Uhh, is there something I can do to help?"

Letting out a rather heavy sigh, the inventor took a seat a few feet inside the door. "Nothing I can think of, Bud." He told his friend about the power bead failure to improve much on what they already had seen and how something in that circuitry had either drawn out moisture from the air, or somehow dried the actual air with no sign of where that water might have gone.

"So, we'll not be seeing a Swift Interocitor then, I suppose," Bud said a little sadly.

"Nope. Now I am left with just about nothing to show for my troubles and not a lot of ideas for how to replace a nuclear reactor with something capable of making enough power to do more than keep a few hundred watt lights burning."

"You *will* find that, Tom. You know I never have any doubts about what you can do. Give it a little time."

Tom shrugged. Their talk turned to the Inuit village in Canada and how well they had reported the new reactor and generator system was working. The tribal elder had sent a message telling Tom that the level of steam heat was incredible.

"I think we forgot just how hot things had been at one time," the man had messaged to Tom three days after the reactors had been swapped. "When I think about it positively, we will have no more nights when anyone questions if they might beg for a little extra. We even run the heat in the meeting room and in the tribal offices all day and all night."

"Once we got that message," Tom told Bud, "I offered to create a sort of thermostat program to control the overall system. After that gets uploaded to their system, and at night when they don't use a lot of electricity, the rods only go into the reactor about forty percent. Less heat, less power and overall things should run five years longer. By that time I hope I can tackle this generator thing and find a way to run power out to all villages like theirs."

Tom wanted to spend a lot more time on his energy project, but he was called to Washington, DC, to meet with Senator Quintana and the Vice President. The subject: how to replace the now-missing planetoid, Nestria?

As Peter Quintana explained on the phone, the reason it was to just be Tom and not in conjunction with his father was that Tom had the most experience with the small planetoid and also had designed the technology that had made it habitable.

Namely, his atmosphere machines.

Slim Davis accompanied him saying he would spend the day with his sister in Georgetown. He offered to come along so that the inventor could spend the time considering what he would be telling the two politicians.

As frequently happened, when trying for a landing at the Potomac River Airport, formerly Reagan International and before that, Washington National, the controllers made a call to all approaching aircraft notifying them of the forthcoming flight through airspace of the President's Marine One helicopter. That meant everyone had to go into holding patterns miles away, or to declare an emergency and vector to Dulles International.

With plenty of fuel, Tom told Slim to go ahead and do "the circuit" until they received clearance.

That came only eighteen minutes later, and at a time when they actually were heading back inbound.

As they approached over the area known as Fort Hunt National Park, Slim received permission to descend from the current four thousand feet to one thousand and to prepare for final instructions. Those came when they crossed over Freeway 495 and Alexandria.

Tom put his tablet computer aside about then and watched as they aligned on to Runway 1 coming over the outer markers sitting in the water to the south of the airport.

Not that he would have expected anything different, Tom smiled when Slim set the Toad down just after they crossed the threshold stripes. They slowed and were directed to turn to the left at the third crossway, about forty percent down the runway. As it was a slow time of the day—all morning commute flights had come and gone an hour earlier—they received permission to pull into the first circular terminal and take the spot closest to the south side and nearest the main building.

A short walk across tarmac and in through a security doorway got them into the last straight part of the terminal building before the main arc and the outside doors.

A black limo was waiting for them with U.S. Government plates and a driver who was speaking to a young police officer. As he spotted Tom and Slim, he pointed over the officer's shoulder and then waved.

The young man, who had his ticket book out, turned and looked. He dropped that hand to his side and walked away, a defeated man who really had wanted to write up a citation for the limo refusing to "move along!"

"Mr. Swift? I'm Leon, the man who generally drives your father around this town. And, you are?" he directed the question to Slim.

After introductions were made, Leon suggested he could take Slim into Georgetown and drop him off.

"Not really on the way, but we are a little early. The Senator and VP had to call to say they are running a half hour late. So, unless you already have transportation, hop in."

They raced off a minute later. Slim was let out at a restaurant on Wisconsin Street where he would meet up with his relative promising to make his way back to the airport in a few hours. After that, the limo headed for a building where Tom, Damon and the previous Vice President—a man who had definitely *not* been friendly to either the Swifts or to any technology company—had once met, and the Swifts had walked out when the demands and insults had become too much to take.

Tom thanked Leon and asked how to get him or someone else back to pick him up after the meeting.

"The secretary will give me a call when it looks like things are wrapping up, and I'll be right out here."

Following a prolonged check-in process where he received a very old style security badge, something that had been in use for more than a decade and had been proven to be ineffective, Tom was shown up one level and into a conference room where the two other men were just getting settled.

"Well," Peter said reaching out to shake hands, "right on time, or at least on time after our delay. Thanks for coming, Tom."

Tom shook the Vice President's hand and exchanged a few pleasantries.

They all sat and the V.P. took over starting the meeting.

"Let me begin by stating that this government and indeed the world owes you and the entire Swift organization a huge debt of gratitude for the way you handled that alien... well, I suspect that 'invasion' is far too strong a term for what happened. But, the fact is that handle it all, you certainly did. And, other than the loss of those scientists, nobody else was hurt, unless you recall those soldiers who tried to invade the wrong side of your local lake. They had two broken legs, a half-dozen wrenched ankles and one smashed thumb when a young soldier slammed the breech of his rifle closed without taking the digit out of the way." He rolled his eyes and shrugged.

They spoke about a few of the lesser known facts on how the alien Master was subdued with Peter nodding appreciatively and the V.P. quite astounded in hearing of the eventual showdown.

Within moment talk turned to Nestria.

With Peter now rolling his eyes just out of line of sight with the V.P., the number two man in the country asked a straightforward question.

"Can we replace that little chunk of rock and when?"

A sudden itch in Tom's left ear took his attention for a few seconds giving him a little time to formulate an answer.

"Well sir, and Senator, that chunk, Nestria, was a specially shaped piece of either a planet or even an asteroid from another solar system. It was moved by means we still have zero understanding of, by beings—not the dinosaur being that came here recently—to be used by the other aliens we know as our Space Friends. On its own, it would have so little mass and gravity that we could have never built our atmosphere unless the whole space was covered by a dome."

He told them about the gravity stone and how that could not be duplicated. He did not mention the defunct one he had left on Mars more than a year earlier. He did not believe it would further the discussion.

Peter spoke up. "Replacing that small moon is not a possibility, sir. Earth, and even the Swifts, do not have that engineering capability."

"Oh." The senior politician seemed disappointed. "I see." He now looked at Tom. "What about one of our own asteroids? Like the one you pulled into orbit to build that giant space station of yours?"

"It was about one tenth the size of Nestria, sir. The likelihood of bringing in more of them—which might unbalance the asteroid belt —and trying to stick them together is exceedingly slim. Nearly no chance."

"Damn! I was afraid it would be like that. So," and he turned to Peter, "what can we do? There was evidently some very important research going on up there. How do we recapture that?"

Peter Quintana looked at Tom and his eyes told the story. Tom nodded ever so slightly.

"Sir," the Senator began, "the absolute truth is the scientific research going on up on Nestria mostly entailed the study of... Nestria. People were studying it to see if it has, or had, similarities to what is inside our solar system. It was a peaceful and out of the way place for study. Well, other than the whole kerfuffle at first when at least one foreign body believed it would make a nice base from which to rule the planet!"

He slowly shook his head. There really was not a lot more to say on the matter.

66

But, if nothing else, the Vice President had proved time and again to be a man who took a bulldog's approach to things. In other words, once he sank his teeth into something, he hung on.

"Fine. Granted. But, what about all that lost science? How can we recreate those conditions so we learn something from the terrible tragedy that happened?"

Tom asked for a moment to access his tablet. He had to have the military guard outside the room obtain a password for him to use the network in the very secure building, but eleven minutes later he had the answer he wanted to find.

"Okay. I thought this would be the case, and it turns out to be true. Just about every bit of research gleaned from Nestria during the more than thirteen years it was in orbit was sent down to a large server farm in, of all places, Washington. It is part of the National Archives system. I had to remind myself, but everyone up there agreed it would just take too much to store things locally. So, and knowing how quickly it orbited Earth, and with its rotation period not conducive to always being in position as it passed above the United States, just about once every twenty-nine hours whatever they had was sent down and filed away.

"In other words, gentlemen, what they knew up until the day before—" and Tom faltered as the memory of what he'd witnessed hit him like a hammer. Finally he was able to finish his statement.

"Everything to within about seventeen hours of the taking of Nestria from its orbit sits right here in this city. All that needs to be done is to have the Archive people assist in retrieving it for whomever needs it."

When Peter accompanied Tom downstairs and they arrived outside, he chuckled. "I told the V.P we had it all, but he just doesn't believe politicians can either know things or tell the truth. Thanks for coming down, Tom. You have done a tremendous thing by giving him that info. Possibly saved this country untold billions in unnecessary research, development and deployment of exactly what we do not need."

CHAPTER 7

THE GREATER SHOPTON NUCLEAR PLANT AND LIGHT RAIL SYSTEM

AS OF the previous year, Shopton, New York in particular, and the greater Essex County in general, had joined the nuclear power club with the addition of a generating plant built into the hills to the southwest of Swift Enterprises and the Swift MotorCar Company.

It had been quite the uphill battle until the Vice President of the United States had gotten behind the program. His reasoning was simple; he had been on final approach to Enterprises for an important meeting with Tom and Damon one stormy day when all power for the landing lights at Enterprises went out. His pilots were military aviators and immediately reacted by performing a missed approach and go-around.

Power was restored and they landed just five minutes later, but it had been enough to get him angry at the lack of a reliable local power source and not just the shared trunk lines coming from a hydroelectric dam a couple hundred miles away.

So, he had gone back to Washington and pushed through an emergency power act allowing any of the more remote communities to set up their own—clean power only, please—generating facilities.

Because the Swifts owned and operated the safest nuclear facility in the nation, the Citadel, Shopton had approached them to provide such a facility to benefit everyone, and especially the Swift companies who would be repaid for the generating nuclear reactor over a period of eight years and would be allowed to use as much electrical power as they required for free.

Shopton was a growing town with more than thirty thousand people living within and just outside the city limits, nearly four thousand of them working at the three Swift sites. With that nine-fold growth in the past seventeen years had come a couple new challenges. The first had been power. That was now taken care of so the City Council sought advice from many people and businesses about what they might next tackle.

Overwhelmingly came the opinion there were now just too darned many cars (and a few buses) on the streets and there was now at least a fender bender accident every day or two.

"Can't we get some sort of shared transportation services?"

That had come from Jake Aturian at the Construction Company

during a closed session of the Council with the town's "business leaders." These included Damon, Jake, Charlie Van deGroot—manager of the MotorCar Company—and the owners of three other companies, each with at least fifty employees.

All eyes turned to Damon.

He looked back at them before smiling and standing up.

"Now that we have our power plant, and everyone is benefiting from that, we are discovering we have a surplus of electricity so I would say anything we do ought to take advantage of that. I honestly do not believe we need to try to bring in hundreds or a thousand or more new families to use what is available, but might be able to use the power in a streetcar or trolley system that can benefit most of our citizens and businesses."

That got two side discussions going which he and the Mayor, with a nod between them, allowed to go on for a minute before the gavel came banging down.

"And, what might that entail, and also what does it get us, Mr. Swift?"

Damon spent twenty minutes outlining his ideas for a constantly-running system with one main north-to-south track beginning at the Shopton Regional Airport running around the top of Lake Carlopa and then south through the heart of the downtown, past the Construction Company, looping around Enterprises outer wall and eventually to the MotorCar Company before continuing the loop and returning along a parallel track back north.

"There could be a perpendicular line from the park downtown running to the west out to the newest residential area past the old Reason Hill mansion. And, where I see at least four trolleys running the fifteen mile main line this spur can be a single one of about three miles going back and forth."

He told them how calculations showed anyone could get from almost anywhere along either line to someplace on the other inside of nineteen minutes and from one end to the other in twenty-two.

In town travel would take no greater than nine minutes.

"Right now it takes me twenty-two to get from my house out to my company which is close to the airport," Peter Stilson, owner and CEO of StilsonArts, a company making high-quality titanium golf clubs with fifty-seven employees. "Depending on where the line runs through Shopton, I'd say easily more that eighty percent of my people would jump aboard a trolley rather than drive each and every day."

So began the discussions and planning for a system that would require fewer than nine months to complete—but only once all studies, permits and reams of paperwork were complete—and would benefit at last sixty percent of the population, something that was twenty-three percent higher than nearly any other mass transportation system in any town or city with under one hundred thousand people in North America.

As they generally do, discussions turned to the costs of creating such a rail system. Nobody could agree on what those costs would actually be—Damon attempted to interject that nothing could be known until the City Council agreed to order a cost and project estimate be developed... but not a single attendee seemed to listen—and the meeting broke up twenty minutes later with nothing much accomplished.

The next morning a call from the Mayor's office was waiting for the inventor as he entered the outer office.

"You have a call from City Hall. He says it is imperative you take it... and it is the Mayor, by the way."

Damon rolled his eyes. The man had scurried out of the meeting as if he were attempting to avoid either a confrontation, or at least further discussion. After entering the office and setting his tablet computer on the desk, Damon sat and reached for the phone.

"Yes, Mr. Mayor?" he asked into the receiver.

"Oh, Damon, Thank God! We didn't get the chance to talk after yesterday's meeting and I just have to get you on side with this all. Is now a good time to ask that you come to my office?"

Damon glanced at his schedule for the day on his monitor. It was fairly empty until 11:00 and then full the rest of the day.

"Not really. I am about to go into the first of back to back to back conferences. Now, I am not certain what you wish to discuss, but I did hang around yesterday in case anyone needed to speak. You left quickly so I assumed you either had nothing for me or another meeting to get to. Ummm..." and he took the receiver from his ear and sat there for a half minute before continuing, "could we make it the day after tomorrow?" Damon was beginning to regret even bringing up the subject of a commuter system.

It was the politician's turn to say nothing for a moment. When he did, he was stammering. He stated that the meeting had to be that day or the entire project was off.

"I'm sure you can see the importance of getting my approvals on this."

After ensuring the call was being recorded, Damon told him, "Sounds like a little threat, sir. You wouldn't be threatening me or the success of this town. The town, might I remind you, that elected you primarily because the former mayor refused to allow his name to be placed on the ballot for a third term. So, and having said my piece, I must run. Call when you can schedule a meeting that does not expect any business owner in this town to drop what they are doing just to meet your convenience."

With that, he hung up.

He buzzed Trent.

"The Mayor is going to be calling back very soon. Please tell him I am now heading to a meeting and it is the first of a full day's set of such meeting, and that I will be unable—as far as you understand— to return any calls until tomorrow, mid morning."

"Happily, Mr. Swift. I take it you will still be inside your office?"

Damon assured his secretary that he would be there until his late morning meeting at the MotorCar Company. "Other calls can come through, but nothing that originates at City Hall. Not today. Thanks!"

But, a minute later he did head out of his office notifying Trent he was going up to see Jackson Rimmer.

When he was ushered into the lawyer's office, Damon began by explaining the meeting the day before.

"Can I assume that the next thing you will tell me is that you hung up on the Mayor ten minutes ago?"

Amazed the man in City Hall had reached his chief legal council in record time, Damon nodded. He stated he had told his caller about a meeting schedule that would not let him just drop things and race to the center of town at that other man's whim.

"And, you should never feel you are in that position. So, what I got from a panic call from the City Attorney is that his boss is in a snit over what he sees as a rudeness on your part. I told Alexander that it is more likely that windbag in the office one floor above him is making up a story and that if either of them want to take it further, we will show up at the next City Council meeting with the recording of the conversation." He looked at his boss with a question, to which Damon nodded.

"Of course I recorded it. Standard procedure for all calls to my office."

"Knew I didn't have to ask."

When the inventor inquired what the reaction to Jackson's suggestion of a great public release of the conversation, Alexander Miller, someone who had been an attorney for about six years and a public servant for just five months had sputtered and said that was *not necessary* at all!

"I told him to clear that with the Mayor and get back to me before ten this morning. We'll see."

Before he had the chance to stand and leave the office, his TeleVoc pinged Damon to say Trent was attempting to get him. Knowing of Trent's aversion to using the actual pins, and that Tom had finally built the man a small desktop box to use with several prerecorded messages, the inventor knew the secretary only used the box in what might be termed extreme conditions.

Jackson handed Damon his phone receiver and pressed the numbers to connect him.

"Yes, Trent?"

"I am so sorry, Mr. Swift, but the Mayor's office is in what would appear to be a melt-down situation. He is begging to get a message to you. He told me his phone has not stopped ringing since the news channels here got hold of the story of the forthcoming *light rail trolley system*. He evidently came in this morning before calling you to say all fifty of the phone voicemail messages were from citizens insisting they find out exactly when they could start taking the trolleys."

"Not that he was getting angry calls about how dare he consider such a thing?"

"Not that he indicated. I said I would try to get some message to you as quickly as possible. I am sorry. He did sound sincere."

Damon thought a moment about whether he wanted to get into another situation where politicians said one thing only to hit him, or Tom, broadside over something else. "Okay. Call his office and tell him I can arrange for ten minutes in about twenty minutes from now. I cannot come down—and please stress that as I know you will —but will call him back. Thank you, Trent."

When he did call it was to find a man who was nearly in tears he was so panicked.

"Oh. Damon. You can't imagine how grateful I am you could call." He effused over his valuing of the Swifts and how he personally held Damon to be the pinnacle of being a great American before he got to the point.

"That trolley system you came up with has hit a real nerve. And, in a great way as I stated in my release yesterday late afternoon. But also, not such a great way. Each and every call, and I do mean *every* call, I have had since about 6:10 last night, have been calls of 'When can I use the light rail?' And, 'You absolutely have to make this finished and ready for this coming October when my family is coming to visit!' I have only had my assistant log them and then erase them. I can't say anything in response because I have no idea. Was talk at the meeting just a pipe dream, or can this happen... and how soon?"

Inwardly, Damon let out a very heavy sigh. Into the phone he said, "Mr. Mayor. To begin with yesterday's discussion, which you ducked out on about a second after it was finished, was extremely preliminary. You really should not have made that a public release. I only suggested a rail system as one way to use surplus electricity. I did not propose a specific design. Such systems, even the relatively short ones such as ours could *someday* be, take years. A decade or more in fact. Think about the obstacles from the perspective of the city, the county, state and even Federal regulations. In point of fact, the actual build is short compared to all that other stuff."

There was an almost horrified silence at the other end of the call.

Finally, Damon continued. "Okay. So, if this needs to be spelled out right now, the ball is in your court. You and the City Council must pass a resolution to start the process. Then, you and the Council need to follow all the well-established rules and procedures for obtaining studies, arranging right-of-way for not just the tracks, but the stations, road crossings that require automatic barriers, and power."

"But, I thought you'd take care of the power."

Oh dear, he thought. "Mr. Mayor, while Enterprises can and will help with the construction and installation of the track, and we can help the rail system tap into the area's new power grid we've helped get running, we will not be providing those services, nor the electricity, for free."

Damon did agree to come for a meeting the following afternoon when the entire City Council would be in a special session. He did stress, before hanging up, that once all the proper steps had been completed, he and Tom and the entire organization would work to make the possible light rail system a reality as quickly as possible.

Tom had been working six days a week on his attempts to come up with a unique power generating solution. The most improbable, and yet likely to provide the most power for the least amount of materials, was to construct a generator that "built" its own fuel.

Of course, this could not be petroleum-based, nor could it be a polluting source of energy used to make higher levels of energy. His mind kept coming back to ways to create an absolutely clean method of nuclear energy—fusion.

Gone would be the heavy radiation in both the fuel and in the energy created.

Gone, theoretically, would be the objections from nations—or even states and cities—to using a "reactor" to make power. What would remain was the need to generate such a tremendous level of heat to start the process, but once the reaction had been started, it could be sustained using a much lower level of heat and energy.

And, that should leave enough extra energy—plus the dissipating heat—to run the type of steam-based generators that currently made power in everything from submarines and large marine vessels, to giant power plants.

The problem was going to be making that level of heat and then keep making more heat to make things continue to run.

But... Tom had a notion forming in his mind that he already knew how to achieve the necessary star-hot heat, and how to control it!

It was something he'd used several times—successfully—in the past to drive a spaceship into and through a micro wormhole in space and to travel to a nearby solar system. It was in that distant system Tom had discovered two of the most amazing things he had ever seen: a black hole that not only ran in the assumed direction drawing all materials around it into its interior, it also periodically reversed directions and spewed that same material back out. The second thing he found was an anomaly that appeared to allow for travel through time.

That one had ultimately been brought back to Earth and to Enterprises where experiments on it over more than two months had shown that in that environment it could only send items backward in time and only by a few seconds short of twenty-four hours.

The truly unfortunate aspect was that whatever traveled back in time ultimately disintegrated once it came back to its "normal" time.

This is something Tom found out the hard way when he was forced to use the anomaly to send himself back in time to save the lives of his wife and their unborn first child. In the end, Tom had to watch as his other self broke apart in an obviously painful death.

But, that was, as some say, another story.

What had made the opening of the wormhole—something so tiny that a typical sewing thread would barely be able to be shoved inside the opening—had been to release a small charge of antimatter directly in front of the opening and then to hit that with positive matter.

The results were that the hole was hit so hard with the released energy it opened for an instant allowing Tom's *Galaxy Traveler* needle-shaped ship to shoot inside.

Now, as he sat in his lab thinking about that he realized the almost unthinkable energy released in that negative and positive matter collision could be the solution to kick-starting his fusion reaction.

Later that afternoon he was discussing this with Bud and was trying to describe how the reaction would, once begun, continue with only the occasional input of additional antimatter.

"And, as I recall—painfully—we have the ability to make that antimatter ourselves and do not need to rely on any of the other outside nuclear labs for it."

"Exactly right, Bud. When Fermilabs decided to discontinue their experiments we picked up their equipment. After we used it for the time anomaly it went into storage down on Fearing Island, but about once every six or seven months a few of the scientists from the Citadel go out there for a week, perform any maintenance and do a small run to make certain it all continues to be available to us."

This was something Bud well knew as he often was the pilot flying the five to seven people from New Mexico out to the island off the Atlantic Coast and back a few days later.

What he had never been curious enough to ask was what happened to the antimatter they made. He did that now.

Tom smiled at his best friend. "Because of the huge amount of power necessary to keep an electromagnetic containment of that pinhead-sized bit, we can't just store it out there. I'll bet you've wondered why they drag out a couple large suitcases each visit. Those," he said as the flyer nodded, "are their field lab to test the power, stability and purity of the antimatter."

Bud's forehead scrunched in deep thought. "So, does that sort of eat up the antimatter?"

"No. But they also bring out a small self-contained ball into which that dot of destructive matter is placed and that goes into a small sounding rocket you likely will have seen each time you've taken them to the island. Up it goes aimed to the sun. Those rockets are just powerful enough to launch the ball into a path that sees it hitting the sun about eight months later. There, it disappears into nothingness."

"And, it stays contained all that time?"

"It does because the inside of the tomasite sphere is a layer of neodymium magnetic material that keeps the dot centered and safe.

Dad and I figured it can to that for more that fifty years if a ball should go way off course. If it ever did, that same magnetic layer would let us track it so we could go up with the *Challenger* or something like that and get the Attractatron on it before slinging it into the right course."

They talked a little more about how Tom envisioned using the antimatter, but the inventor noticed his friend's eyes glazing over as he started to talk about nuclear theory, decay of isotopes and the differences between fission and fusion.

"That's enough for today's lesson, Mr. Barclay. I suggest you read chapters fifteen through twenty, inclusive, before the next class." He grinned at his friend and Bud grinned back.

"Thanks, Prof. While I have to believe everything you say is true, and being a man who married into this family makes me pretty open to believing some pretty wild and crazy things, it still takes a bit of work for some of it to soak in. Even then, I don't have the educational background to absorb some of it."

He looked at Tom, a small level of either sadness or even regret showing.

"There are times when I think I should have taken a few other classes in school. Physics actually fascinates me these days, but I believed that football was more important. Now look at me. I don't play football; heck, I don't even watch much football on TV these days. But I sure the heck live in a world where physics is important to understand."

To himself the flyer was pondering if he might not take a few evening courses offered at Shopton's Essex County College to try to pick up his levels of knowledge on things like that and even chemistry.

CHAPTER 8 /
IT'S ALL UNDER CONTROL

AS TOM was struggling to come up with a way in which to take his latest idea and see it turned into something that actually could generate more power than it took to create, Damon continued to work with the Canadian government on obtaining the necessary permissions to build an experimental power generating station in their nation, and probably—to benefit the most distantly-positioned people—in central to northern British Columbia.

Any work on his part toward the light rail system for Shopton had been put on hold when the City Council found out they simply could not snap their fingers and acquire all the needed right-of-way through most of the area, but specifically the downtown of Shopton. So, with that off his list for at least a few months, he resolved to get things back into a moving condition with the nation to the North.

"Well, I had thought this was all talked out, Mr. Swift," the Vice Minister for Energy Affairs for the Western part of Canada told his caller. "I mean, we are not going to budge on the non-nuclear reactor demands, so what more is there to say?"

Damon smiled to himself. "Possibly a lot more than you realize, Minister. For instance, this morning your Parliament passed a resolution to open more productive talks with outside agencies, such as Swift Enterprises, to solve the power issues your Minister had stonewalled for more than three years. I have to believe he has been informed of this already and had not passed that message on to you."

He wanted to add, *It isn't my place, but you really should ask yourself why he hasn't told you...* but he held his tongue.

"Making up lies and falsehoods is not something I would believe a man in your position might do," the politician stated boldly.

Now, Damon did not hold back and did respond with his recent thought.

"I'd suggest before either of us allow this conversation to degrade away from being polite or progressive toward a solution we both know you have been tasked to come up with that you go speak to the Minister. I cannot hold for you to do that but can arrange to be available for a call—either you to me or me to you—this afternoon at 3:00 pm."

The other man grumbled and suggested that Damon might be

delusional, but he would ask a simple question about anything interesting happening that day. He did not agree to any further call.

It was with only a tiny bit of surprise when Trent announced a return call just eleven minutes later. On the line was the Vice Minister and he was in a considerably more contrite mood.

"Uhh, Mr. Swift. I find that I was in the wrong about what I assumed during our conversation today. And, it turns out you are better informed than I. That is a situation I am about to tender my resignation over as the Minister told me point blank it is not my duty or right to question what he tells anyone or when he does that. And, when I told him that had placed me and the Ministry in a position of embarrassment, he outright accused me of pandering to Americans." The man sounded miserable so Damon decided to not say anything.

"I mean, the man can't get it through his head that we are all Americans. North Americans at that! I must apologize for my previous attitude and ask that whomever replaces me in this position be given the chance to work with you."

Damon chuckled, which must have mystified the man in Canada, but he said, "I'd rather you didn't quit right now, and especially now that you and I are on the same page. If at all possible, I'd love to receive permission for my son, Tom, and a small team of surveyors to head over to B.C. to look over a couple sites they have identified where we might be able to accomplish our goal, which should be your goal as well, with minimal impact on both the people out there and the environment."

He described, with GPS coordinates, the sites.

The first of the three Damon mentioned had to be denied. "That is a special tribal reserve even a unanimous act of Parliament cannot overturn. It is an ancient area where three of the tribes had a war for over a hundred years, and that was in the time of the first Pilgrims landing on your East Coast. Sorry, but they are actively defensive about even discussing positive uses for that tract. What is next?"

The other two areas were, in the Vice Minister's opinion, acceptable, but his reservation on the second one was along the lines of access to the area.

"There are no roads that are more than muddy ruts in winter and hard-caked ruts the rest of the year."

Damon assured him the intent was to fly into each area with a vertical-landing-capable aircraft that would do no damage on the ground other than the possibility of its tires sinking slightly in damp earth.

It was agreed in principle and the man in Canada offered to send down a signature page for the Enterprises people to fill in with specifics. After that it would be only a day to approve.

"And that is because, as long as I do hold this position, I am the approval chain. Thank you and good day to you, Mr. Swift."

As he stood in the shadow of the *Sky Queen's* left wing, Tom noticed a dark, green SUV approaching, bouncing on the rougher off-road ground as if in a hurry. It had a very serious-looking light rack on the top—not currently turned on—and when it turned slightly to the left he saw the RCMP emblem on the front door.

A woman, shorter than him by ten inches but very muscular-looking, stepped out and leaned back in to speak to the driver. He must have told her something she liked because she nodded, smiled and closed the door before coming over to Tom.

"Hello, Mr. Swift," she said walking straight toward him. "I am Commandant Dimmock of the RCMP. But, you probably noticed that from the truck." She hooked a thumb over her shoulder. "Anyway, I am the senior Mountie in the Provence and as such needed to come speak with you about security."

Tom pointed to Phil Radnor who was standing about fifty feet away. "We brought some of our own but it is nice to have the official local enforcement folks to back us up. Or, is it to take over?"

"Part lead and part support. We try to do what is right, not what is politically correct. This isn't the city. Does my name ring any bells with you by chance?"

She looked at Tom, her eyes narrowing as she attempted to decide if she ought to say anything more.

"Umm, maybe not my place, Tom, but I know your mother. Or, I worked with her once upon a time..." She trailed off now dreading she might need to explain Anne's former association with the Agency.

"Oh," he said brightly. "One of Momsie's, ummm, FBI medical mystery people? Wait! I *do* know who you are. I've read the stories. You're—now, don't tell me—you have to be *Cheryl* Dimmock!" He had glanced at her name badge with just her last name on it, all the while trying not to stare. He looked very pleased with himself.

She also was pleased. "Yeah. I first knew her as Barbara Boone, but soon found out about mythical names. Mine used to be Lindsey Archer. Didn't hate it as much as your mom hated hers. I got the chance to work with her again while I was still in the States with the FBI. I don't miss the Agency, but I do miss people like Anne. She's one in a million; I hope you know that."

Tom smiled at her, nodding. "Yep. I sure do. So, I see you're back in the RCMP and with a lot more fancy stuff on your shoulders and chest." Now, Tom reddened at the thought she might think he'd been looking... well, not at her eyes.

Patting the ribbons above her left shirt pocked, she grinned. "I certainly do. And, don't be embarrassed by looking down. You have to be one of the few men who have looked at my face *first* in years. Most stare slightly lower than the ribbons." She smiled at him. "I thank you for that, Tom."

The truth was, Cheryl Dimmock had an extremely well developed bust. She had tried disguising it starting at the age of about fourteen, and had given up once she reached forty. For reasons only known to her fellow Canadian Mounties, she'd acquired the nickname, "Moose."

Tom decided to *not* mention he knew about that.

Anne Swift had once told Tom it likely had to do with that very large animal generally possessing a prominent chest.

"Cheryl did a great job of camouflage, but having experienced... well, having a slightly smaller yet similar build—and you know Sandy had to go through this as well—I hear she just got tired of the slouched shoulders, the loose garments and even the special panels she told me she had to sew into her uniform."

Tom looked at the now senior officer. "I am quite happy to finally meet you, and I have to say Momsie actually did you justice in saying you were, and are, a very beautiful woman. She is very proud of how you have advanced through the ranks over the years. She'll be tickled to know I met you. Any message?"

"Oh, we can talk messages later. The reason I have come out here is to tell you a special team of Mounties are being detailed to shadow you. We may be a nation known for being kind of soft and nice, but we have a 'radical element...'" and she made finger quotes, "that have stated any U.S. company trying to do anything up here is going to get attacked."

Tom's shoulders sank. "I can't tell you how tired I am of having people I'm just trying to help suddenly hate me or attack me or my people." He sighed heavily. "Are they a credible threat?"

"Sorry, Tom, but I wouldn't be here if they were just blowing steam. These are the sort of thugs who used to hammer steel spikes in trees due to be felled by loggers. They have been known to set off explosives at construction sites to knock over the first couple floors of buildings.They even did that kind of malicious destruction two years ago in a small town of Red Dear in Alberta. It was going to be a hospital."

They looked at each other, both shaking their heads sadly.

"Do they have any concept that we are just looking into some possible sites for a totally safe and very beneficial power generating facility? We aren't going to break any more ground than to do a few core samples to ensure we don't try to put anything up over an old uranium mine?"

"Unfortunately, these sorts do not listen to anything other than their narrow-minded and often invisible leadership. On the possibly positive side, if they show their faces we may have to opportunity to ferret out those leaders and put them in jail. We'll see. In the mean time we are going to take care of you and your people."

They discussed how she and her Mounties would be providing both visible and less-than-visible protection for whatever Tom decided he was going to be doing in Canada.

The younger man from the truck came over and whispered something into his commander's ear. She nodded and turned back to Tom.

"Oh, that's Sergeant Preston, my assistant. And, please don't rib him over the name."

"I'm not actually sure I understand that," Tom admitted.

"Well, back in the nineteen sixties there was a television show about a Mountie with that name. Made us look either too smart and good to be real, or sometimes made the general Canadian population look like criminal idiots."

"Was that back when you all wore those red and black wool uniforms and the furry hats?" he asked with a grin.

She returned the grin. "Ceremonial and heavy and itchy and you wouldn't catch me in mine other than last year when I got these extra bars."

They chatted another minute before Tom had a thought.

"You do know Mom is going to rush up here to see you the moment I tell her we touched base. She is also going to ask me all sorts of, well, personal questions about you. Is it okay if I tell her you are still a very beautiful woman, or is that a bit chauvinistic of me?"

She smiled warmly. "You can tell her everything including that I have stopped keeping them covered." She smiled again and let her gaze drop downward. This had the result in making Tom's face turn bright red.

"Uhh, I'll only mention that if she brings the subject up."

They spoke about her time with the FBI and how she would be forever thankful for Anne and to Quimby Narz for them sponsoring her through her acceptance and training. She reminded Tom she had two more opportunities to work with Anne Swift over the ensuing years.

"Both times it was in your home town. I truly would have loved to come meet you, your sister, and your father, but that was when she was still in Total Confidential Mode." She looked at her watch that had just thumped her wrist. "I have to go, but please tell Anne she is welcome to come up any time she wishes. Very good to meet you after all these years," she declared pumping his hand a couple times before turning to jog back to the SUV she'd arrived in.

Before she got in, she called over to him, "It's all under control, Tom. Don't worry; the RCMP is on this!"

Phil wandered over just then. "Weren't you going to introduce me to that very lovely woman? Friend?"

Tom reddened once again and Phil noticed it, preferring to not ask about that. "She was in uniform and I'm going out on a limb here, but as she came in a RCMP vehicle, she might just be something more than a local constable."

Tom explained Cheryl's position and the RCMP's interest and the suggestion there might be trouble coming their way.

That got Phil's attention. He asked many questions the inventor could and also many he could not answer.

And, once he called Harlan to report it, the Security chief's attention was also well engaged. "Did Tom get her number and full rank and location?"

"Harlan? Will you calm down, please," his second-in-command requested. "She knows Anne Swift. They worked together a couple times when Anne was still undercover with the FBI Lab. I believe you even met her once or twice. Cheryl Dimmock? She's the Commandant for the whole of British Columbia and from all reports not out to jump our time on this."

He heard his boss take a deep breath and let it out slowly.

"Oh. Right. Uhh, Sergeant back then... *way back* then. All right. I'll get in touch with her main office in B.C. and see if she can call me back. We'll coordinate things, unless she told you she's taking charge. I hope she didn't say something like that!"

"Not to me, Harl. And, Tom is standing here overhearing both sides of this call and shaking his head. Hang on."

Tom took the cell phone. "Harlan. She wants to RCMP to be under full investigation and even what she calls *invisible* mode and let you and Phil and the others take the visible part of protecting us. I get the impression she really does not want to step on anyone's toes so be nice when you speak to her."

"Right. And, I will. Can I speak to Phil now?"

The inventor handed the phone back and wandered back to what he was doing before the recent arrival.

His Security men discussed how to best use the Canadians coming to the conclusion that locals generally knew who they were dealing with better than outsiders. But, they also felt Enterprises' Security was better suited for taking care of Tom and his team.

"I'll give the Commandant an hour to get back to civilization and give her a call," Harlan promised.

The truth was Harlan knew Cheryl and liked the woman. He'd even taken her out to dinner at the end of the third of her FBI lab experiences in Shopton. It had been at Anne's suggestion, one he gladly followed through on.

Their conversation regarding the anticipated threat in BC went well and by the end he had only suggested that her people be briefed to expect at some point he might insist on taking over if the threat became real and directed specifically at Swift employees.

"Okay, Harlan, but only if your people give my Mounties the feeling they are moderately in charge of things. These young guys and gals have a bit of an inferiority issue with folks from the U.S. You can't imagine how hard it was for me to come back and be accepted with something less than deep suspicion after nineteen years down there."

Harlan chuckled and told her the arrangement was between senior security people, and he wasn't even going to tell his bosses.

"Same goes for me, Harlan. Good to catch up with you. Bye!"

Two days later the same team who'd checked out the first site headed over from a day off in Vancouver to look over the other site on their short list. This one was a little more difficult terrain but it did have the advantage of a nearby highway for those cases where ground transport would be an advantage.

Not that the road into the proposed site was in any great shape, but at least it was something and had the advantage of a good landing place within just a couple miles.

One of the older Swift Whirling Duck helicopters, that could have its rotors folded back and was just sized properly to fit inside the hangar of the *Sky Queen*, was packed away and ready to go once they landed. As soon as the lifters shut off, the three technicians began the process of opening the hangar door, extending the ramp and rolling the craft to the ground.

A press of one button inside the six-man cockpit served to start the electrical system moving the rotors out and around into position.

Three minutes later it was finished and the system shut down while showing green lights on an outside panel, one per rotor blade.

"Everything's out and locked, skipper," the lead tech announced when the inventor came out the side hatch and walked to the rear.

"Great. Let's get in the air and do a site survey from about a thousand feet," the inventor suggested.

It was from that height they all spotted the Mountie truck at the base of the hill Tom wanted to investigate. Standing just outside and waving her arms was Commandant Dimmock and her driver, the man Tom assumed would be Sergeant Preston.

Two hours later Tom called for the coring equipment to come make a total of eleven borings, all marked with stakes he'd personally driven into the ground.

Damon asked Tom to take a seat. He paced a little giving the younger Swift the impression he had something very serious on his mind. Finally he came back and sat.

"I know it is early days and all, but if this power project of yours is going to get off the ground, and make some money for this company..." he looked into Tom's eyes and both knew this was a demand and not a suggestion, "then you are going to need to come up with a direction to head. It's okay to have a place in mind for, well, whatever you intend to build, but that must change to a definite thing quickly. Do you have a good direction?"

Tom nodded. "Oh, I do, Dad. I really do!"

He told his father about his thoughts of kickstarting a fusion reaction using antimatter. It intrigued the older scientist and inventor so much he almost slipped of his chair he sat so far forward.

Slowly, so he could choose his words carefully, he asked, "Are we speaking about initiating a true fusion reaction?" Tom nodded, his face nearly a blank. "I see. So, do you really believe it can be sustained and used for your generating station?" This time Tom not only nodded, he grinned. "How?"

It was a simple question so Tom gave a simply answer.

"About once every couple of hours we boost things with another tiny shot of antimatter. A fairly simple system can generate that much in that timeframe. Now, before the question comes up, we do have the technology to contain that plus the materials to hold in the forces that will build up. After that, it's just a fancy steam engine turning a wheel that makes electricity!"

CHAPTER 9 /

THE DREADED "A" WORD

"ANTIMATTER" Tom declared to the assembled people in the room. "I know it is sort of a misunderstood, and dreaded word because of all the misinformation spread by bad—or perhaps a better term might be misinformed—science fiction, but the truth is we have used it rather successfully on multiple occasions. We even have the ability to make it. We *have* made it."

He looked for signs of recognitions in the faces of the forty or so people gathered in front of him. One face, Bud's, was bright and sunny. He had been with the inventor all the different times they had used small charges of antimatter to drive open micro-sized wormhole entrances so they could travel into a nearby solar system.

The first time had been to see if they could actually get one open and how wide. It had nearly ended in disaster, but not from the antimatter.

At another time it had been to send an unmanned probe back to watch a particular phenomena in that system... a black hole of some size was sitting inside the system, running forwards—half the time— and *backwards* the rest of it.

Tom and Bud had next gone there in search of something incredible the probe detected. It had been the sight of them and not from the first visit, but from a future one.

That led to the discovery of another phenomena, a "singularity" capable of generating a time shift. It had been brought back to Earth, used in a series of experiments, and finally had led to Tom's death and the salvation of his wife, Bashalli, and the unborn first child.

That was, however, another story. As far as the flyer was concerned, as long as he personally didn't have to use antimatter to travel through the galaxy, he would trust his friend to use it correctly.

"Can we generate more energy than we consume in creating the antimatter?" came from one of the chief physicists at the company, Dr. Andrea Palmer.

Tom nodded. "Yes we can. The creation of enough antimatter to get our ship, *Galaxy Traveler*, into the wormhole required the expenditure of about one hundred fifty megawatts. According to instrument readings, the resultant... *interaction* with the positive matter resulted in nearly one hundred times that amount of released energy."

He looked at her to see if she had a follow-up. She did not.

"I intend to build a small power generator using the trio of giant power pods we mounted back then to the cargo deck of *Goliath* along with the collider equipment we got from Fermilabs when they stopped using it. They can be transported and set up in a day and begin creating the antimatter in the cyclotron that goes with them within two additional days."

He wasn't completely certain how he intended to use the resulting energy release to create electricity, but he had computed the amount of antimatter necessary to give the energy release he knew was required was in the neighborhood of one-tenth of a gram.

That could be created in a matter of two hours.

And, once it started it could keep a target material burning for hours. It was from that other materials Tom knew he would generate his power. He told them it would most likely not be a direct generation.

"It may even be a more traditional form of electrical generation, but one fired by the power of a matter/antimatter interaction!"

Creating the antimatter would use the generated power from Tom's power pods equaling about fifty megawatts and could, if the reaction was manipulated property, result in more than a half-million megawatts of energy.

"And," he concluded, "assuming we capture that and use it to generate electricity and continue to create more antimatter, that means a single installation that might ultimately be about the size of a large grain silo—which would use a fairly small cyclotron at the base surrounding the power pods necessary and the interaction chamber and generator equipment up on top of that—that we would build to be self-cooling much in the same fashion some computers use their own generated heat to draw in cool air at the bottom and exit the hotter air out the top."

He brought up a color image he'd created in his CAD program the day before. There was an audible "oooohhh" from the assembled people as they saw the relative size versus an image of Tom's old *Star Spear* rocket he'd inserted next to it. The generator stood nearly two times as tall and seemed to be ten or more times the width.

Just because he had the ability, the inventor had given the generator an overall bluish color with a few bands of darker or lighter blue, and the slightly flared base an even darker bluish-green. They could see the thin colored bands at five heights Tom told them would be the aircraft hazard light rings.

"They might be steady or flash or even pulse to catch someone's attention. I intend to have them inset slightly so they are best when viewed from straight out or from above. I'd sort of like to keep them from shining too brightly onto the ground."

Arv raised a hand. "Skipper? Wouldn't that give workers on site some light to walk around during the evenings and at night?"

Tom smiled and nodded. "It *would*, but the intent is to have only the first generator station manned twenty-four by seven. Once we prove the concept and safety, I hope these can be run with minimal personnel, and those would be in a nearby outbuilding." He paused. "Actually, there is darned little anyone might do outside unless there is an intrusion or a pilot who does not know enough to avoid a large, lighted structure." He shrugged.

While Tom's meeting was going on, Damon was downtown meeting with the Mayor, City Council and several business leaders from the area. The subject, now back on the Mayoral front burner: how to make a light rail or trolley system a reality faster than any city ever had.

It was a two-sided discussion with the politicians firmly of the belief that just because it hadn't been done before, that was no reason to believe Shopton's very own system could not be up and running in a very short period of time, and all the business people attempting to be the voices of reason. They all understood the many, many hoops that had to be first located and then jumped through to do practically anything.

Laura Crater of the Downtown Business Association had the floor but could see she was barely being listed to.

"Please heed this. A trolley system—and I do not believe we can justify a light rail system because of the shorter length of the two runs—does not spring into existence just because of a wish. Likewise, it does not become realty from threats, entreaties or begging. We," and she indicated the business people in the room, "have all asked more than once to see or hear your plans for obtaining the necessary land for the tracks and right of way." She looked at the Council. They were not looking at her so nobody answered the unspoken question.

When she sat down and said nothing more, it took the five members of the Council more than a full minute to realize nothing was being spoken.

It was Councilwoman Esteves who said anything about it. "Umm, what was that?"

Ms. Crater just stared. She said nothing, so the Councilwoman Esteves looked back down at a piece of paper she'd been studying.

Another minute passed before Damon stood.

"May I address you?" he inquired. When the Mayor absently made a hand motion, one the inventor believed was a sort of "go ahead," prompt, he cleared his throat and began.

"Okay. Given that... 'twas brillig in the slithy toves did gyre and gimble in the wabe: All mimsy were the borogoves, And the mome raths outgrabe." He looked to see if anyone other than his fellow civic leaders had caught on. None of the panel at the front of the room had although the youngest member of the Council had one twitching ear.

Damon decided to continue. "Beware the Jabberwock, my son! The jaws that bite, the claws that catch! Beware the Jubjub bird, and shun the frumious Bandersnatch!"

He sat down after thanking the Council for allowing him to make his statement.

It was then the Recorder, sitting at her shorthand machine to the right of the bench, burst into laughter and applause.

She was joined by the other business people with the Council finally looking up, confused to a person, and with scowls on their faces.

With a bang of his gavel, the Mayor announced, "That will be enough of an outburst. Good God, you are professionals. Act like them!"

Damon re-stood. "What do you think of my statement? Or, like with most of what we have been telling you, did you utterly fail to listen?"

With another scowl, the Mayor answered, "Been hanging on every word, Swift! What was your point?"

Damon motioned to the Recorder; she picked up her machine and took it to the center of the bench. The Mayor was about to tell her to take it back to her station when a few of the inventor's words made it thought into his brain. He stared. He stared some more.

He also alternately scowled and looked shocked. Finally, he looked a little contrite.

"Okay," He sighed. "It would appear we have not caught each and every word coming from the floor. So, everybody up here will put down whatever they are looking at and pay attention to Mr. Swift. And, officially, I apologize for the outburst a moment ago."

Damon looked as Ms. Carter. "You feel up to covering the five minutes of your talk again?"

"Sure." She took his place at the microphone and told the Council again about her reservations, ending with her question regarding what their intent was to secure the right-of-way property. "It will need to be a minimum, according to Federal law, of track width, spacing between north and south tracks so the passing trains did not collide, plus eight feet, fenced, on either side of the outside of the tracks. Unless you decide to place it along a route that people will think is too out-of-the-way, the only thing to do is to close down the waterfront road and place it there. You will not be allowed to dig up our beautiful park or take away beaches, the docks or even the Yacht Club property."

The Council sat, silently, contemplating all that. Nobody had an answer and they all looked miserable because of being hit with a dose of reality. Finally, the Mayor spoke.

"Mr. Swift? *Is* there some way you and your company could build this as an elevated system coming through town? That way only the minimal support... things... uprights? would need to take up any room."

"Well, have you considered access to the platforms above? Places for elevators and stairs. The area of overhang for the stations that have been discussed? And, the answer is of course we can do that, but it would be at a cost premium over a ground-based approach by a factor of about two-and-a-half times."

Ms. Carter added, "And, you will still have to gain right-of-way for anything that will touch the ground. And, come up with a foolproof evacuation process—possibly individual plans for each station—to get people to the ground in case of a problem or even a power outage."

The only woman on the Council tapped her microphone. "It sounds to me as if you business persons do not want a light trolley in Shopton. If that is so, why are we here?"

All the people on the floor looked at the Mayor. His face was a very deep red.

The discussion back at Enterprises had turned from the physical outer appearance to some of the inner workings. This included safety concerns.

"Tom," the representative from Facilities asked, "We have implicit faith in you and your dad, but I think you have to admit this is far outside anything we've ever tried. Even the antimatter we have used came from another company. Right?"

"At first," he admitted, "it did come from somebody else, Fermilabs in Batavia, Illinois. They were the only company willing and able to create the necessary antimatter for us on our schedule. It turned out they needed to keep their people busy so we won. Then when we needed more, and they were in the process of dismantling their equipment, we bought that, hired their top people for a one-year contract, and made our own. Now, I will grant you that we did that out in space and not here on the ground. We did it as safely as they had, for far less, and have retained that equipment and ability. I feel, as does my father, that technology can be replicated time and again and stay as safe. The containment is easy to set up and requires only a little electricity, something that can be handled, even in emergency situations, using the smallest of our power pods."

"How's that possible?" one of the other attendees asked.

"It is mostly magnetic containment with a small electromagnet charge to keep things on an even keel."

"Okay. I agree it is possible to do safely, then. How about from a facilities point? What will we need to do to support this?"

"Because the design I presented is really preliminary—heavy emphasis on the syllable *pre*—about all I can tell you is this will be a Swift facility with all that entails. Personnel comfort, personal space, entertainment and all that. But, this first one is in a location we have not selected or been accepted for... is unknown. There may need to be more entertainment options, a gym, and cafeteria."

He reminded them this was not to be a facility with hundreds or even dozens of people. "Maybe eight to twelve for the first few months and then we scale down if possible."

Harlan raised a hand with a knowing look on his face. He said a single word. "Security?"

Tom considered this a full thirty seconds before responding. "I have had the concept of setting things up in some location with existing security. Perhaps a military base? The truth is, I am not sure exactly where we will look. Of course, we are already checking out a couple places in Canada for a permanent location. The thing is, even the Canadians will not allow us to do our testing up there."

The meeting went on another half hour before Tom called an end to it.

"We all, and that mostly means me, have a lot of things to do. I need to get a good handle on a finished design, come up with the exact antimatter chamber design and a lot of other things. But, many of you can get a start on your areas of expertise. So, Facilities can get with the building construction team to plan out the basics of an installation similar to the Citadel. Reinforced concrete pad to build on, housing for personnel and the like.

He outlined eleven other things to the attendees who all took lots of notes and even had a few brief side conferences to set up times they could hold their own meetings.

As the others filed out, Harlan held back.

"So, I get the idea you are not too thrilled with a lack of Security preparedness, Harlan. Am I close?"

"Tom. Cards on the table, you are in danger up in Canada. The Commandant of the Mounties, Miss Dimmock, and I have had a few conversations and she tells me there is a lot of Internet chatter between a few of the more radical of the ecoterrorist organizations and their fanatic— I mean their followers. None of it points to a warm welcome for you or anyone from the U.S. coming up."

Tom frowned. "Is it just this power project?"

"No." It was a blunt answer, but it did not soften as Harlan continued. "These groups are so blind to anything beneficial if it does not come completely and solely from Canada, and even then they have mistaken home grown projects for what they seem to so hate. You did hear about that Albertan hospital they blew up?"

Tom nodded. "Yeah. Commandant Dimmock told me about that the first time we met." He paused before changing directions. "Why are they so resentful about progress?'

Harlan snorted. "They are equal opportunity haters. If it comes from south of their border, or to the east or west, and I suppose from over the North Pole, they automatically believe it to be something they need to destroy."

Tom brought up these groups previously having harmed and even killed Canadian citizens such as lumberjacks and even a few Mounties in their zealous pursuit of what they saw as "the enemy."

All Harlan did was to sigh.

After the City Council meeting was called to an end, Damon and the other businesspersons headed to a nearby coffee shop and bakery, which also happened to be the business of his daughter-in-law's brother, Moshan.

It was a bit after the lunch crowd and before the end of workday crowd, so they had the largest table to themselves. In fact, they had the entire shop. Moshan greeted Damon with a big hug and many kind words.

"I can never thank you and your wife enough for the way in which you raised Thomas. It is because of you two he makes my little sister the happiest woman in all of Shopton. Name what you wish and I shall bring it out to you!"

Damon smiled and patted his son-in-law on the shoulder. "I do thank you, Moshan, and must say that your sister is about the most wonderful daughter-in-law we could have hoped for." He motioned to the others in his group. "We are here for a small meeting. I am not certain about the others, but I could use one of your Mocha drinks. Maybe I'd best skip the whipped cream, though."

The others all just wanted cups of coffee although Ms. Esteves asked for a whopping six packets of artificial sweetener in hers.

Even Moshan, generally able to maintain a straight face no matter what people ordered, wrinkled his nose and muttered, "Ick!" But, he brought their drinks to them along with a plate on which he'd cut several of his pastries into bite-sized pieces.

By silent agreement Damon became their meeting leader. He smiled, a little reluctantly, and got things going.

"We all know the impossibility of the Mayor and Council's idea of an immediate trolley solution." The others nodded with two rolling their eyes. "Okay. I probably have the largest pool of people to ask to perform some basic research and can put together a packet of all applicable laws and perhaps even a broad estimate at the costs."

"Given more than a single route scenario?" This came from Ms. Esteves.

Damon nodded. "I suppose I can work up two scenarios, both will be, I must tell you, ground-based and not railroads in the sky as he suggested."

He requested that at least two of the others get in contact and work on coming up with a map of possible station locations along with details of all businesses—or neighborhoods—within perhaps a six block area of each.

"It is my belief that we would have a difficult time selling anything with stations spaced by more that eight blocks to the general populace. They are fairly used to parking within a few blocks of their destination, so walking no more than four blocks is likely to be about the maximum for many. That goes especially for our older citizens and the disabled."

Together they came up with a date and time for a second meeting and even a proposed schedule for giving their findings to the Mayor. When they departed, most "forgot" to offer to pay for their drinks. With a small chuckle to himself, Damon reached for his wallet.

Small price to pay for hopefully getting some of this off my shoulders, he told himself.

CHAPTER 10 /

THE SPOT

"SO, WHERE is this marvel of modern power generation going to be located, Tom?" This question came from Hank but the looks on everyone's faces told the inventor it was an important question in their minds as well. "I know you've looked at Canada, but I've heard they are balking so far. So?"

Tom had called another meeting four days after the last large group gathering to see where everyone was in their parts of the planning process.

"Do you all want the easy answer or the more involved one? And, I will say there is likely to be a different location for the small test unit as opposed to our first—hopefully only the first of *many*—full-scale installations. Legal is still working with DC and the Canadians to get us rights to a western Canadian installation."

"Go easy on us with details, skipper," requested Arv. He glanced around before adding, "At least one of us is trying to come up to speed, mentally."

"Well, then the immediate answer is I just do not know. Not exactly, at least. Hank is correct about Canada. They, and I mean their government, are vehemently against nuclear power right now. They are also the only technologically advanced nation to be in a real pickle when it comes to providing power to their people, but especially their Native American populations who tend to live in small communities in out of the way areas. The trouble is, according to dad, they can't see this is a practical and political jam they could get out of fairly easily.

"It will obviously need to be in a location where we have ample ground water for the coolant jacket I am certain the generators will need—"

"Hang on, Tom," interrupted Jake Aturian. "Generators as in plural?"

The inventor nodded. "I believe it will be necessary to have a pair of them operating in shifts for final installations. Now, whether that is running alternate days or even alternate hours, I just don't know, yet. But, to keep the power flowing even when a generator is being refueled we may need them in duos." He glanced around the table; nobody had the look of concern, or of a forthcoming question, so he continued.

"If we find we can run them continuously, we can effectively double the electricity output on a part time, or even a full time, basis."

"So," Bud asked, his left hand raised, "do these get planted at the edge of some huge city or out in the boondocks?"

"It might help if the location was not in such direct sight of civilization. Then again, I don't think absolute desolation and the most remote sites will be advantageous. I have been thinking of a place that is naturally cool and perhaps naturally obscured from sight."

"Meaning?"

"Possibly meaning a place where it is often foggy." He looked around and could now see great curiosity. "It could be a place that is also covered by clouds a great deal of the time. Like on some mountains here in the United States and a few other—and I must stress—*friendly* nations that are in need of assistance with their growth and power needs."

"Uhh, Tom? Why foggy?"

"I can think of a couple reasons. First, an element of disguise. What people cannot see, like from the air, they may ignore. Second, there can be some cooling effect to be had from damper, and cooler air."

Hank looked at the others. "I love it when he has the answers!"

"One thing we might need to take a look at is will these work in hotter, drier locations? Could they be used in equatorial placements as well as cooler ones. Will those need a measurably higher level of cooling water?"

Jimmy Dawson raised a hand. He was one of the engineers from the Nuclear Materials Management team at Enterprises.

"Yes?"

"I know of one place that'd be practically perfect," he offered. "My grandparents live on a farm in a part of Scotland that isn't on much of any map or even the Ordinance Survey charts over there. It's not beyond civilization, but it's pretty close to the end."

Tom's look told the man to continue. In the inventor's mind he was smiling as he believed he knew exactly where Jimmy was going with this. He did not speak up preferring to allow his people to formulate complete thoughts and to not be interrupted.

"Okay. I'd guess everyone knows about Edinburgh and Glasgow and probably Inverness. That's close to Loch Ness, by the way. Oh, and Aberdeen. Well, farther to the north there are a lot of hills, or *mountains* as the locals call them. But you have to get all the way to the top of Scotland to find any settlement of much consequence like Armandale, Halkirk or Thurso. To the southwest of Armandale and along the coast is a spot with an actual airport, Lower Dounreay, and fifteen or so miles south of that is where my grannie and gramp live. Sort of a valley near another loch, Loch Shurrery."

Tom spent a minute calling up a satellite view of the area. Of course he knew about the vicinity to the base and airport at Dounreay, but he did not want to cut off any discussion that might be productive.

"There!" Jimmy exclaimed jumping up and tapping the part of the 3D image. The spot he indicated looked a little ragged around the edges, like it had been part of another image and was pasted onto this one, but it was almost clear enough to see there were hills close by. "It's not much of a spot, but their house and another couple who live near them is on that hill. And, I have to tell you that image has been manipulated because there just isn't that level of brown at any time of the year and certainly it is never that clear. Maybe just hazy and not foggy. I wonder who changed that?"

The hilly area he meant was to the west and mostly to the south of the loch, which was closer to eighteen miles south of the nuclear installation. Both Bashalli and Zimby had remarked about the hilly and green nature of that part of the countryside. There was evidently a road through the area that allowed the few residents to get to places where they could shop.

Hank raised a hand. "Uhh, hate to be a killjoy, but that Lower Dounreay on the coast is the former site of a nuclear reactor facility, and it was decommed back in the mid-nineteen nineties. The Internet says it had an 'incident' and still registers a little bit of contamination. Oh," he said seeing something else on his tablet computer. "They originally commissioned it back in the mid-fifties so it lasted nearly forty years."

Tom mentioned to the group about his trip to Dounreay and the meeting with the Scottish Minister.

"Glad to hear you believe it might be a good spot, Jimmy," he complimented the young man. "I'd say it is worth looking into."

As he lay out the results of his Scotland trip and meeting, and that minister's request regarding doing something about the quickly approaching day when everything had to be truly shut down—with the loss of electrical power—his audience sat forward waiting to hear more.

"How many reactors did they have, or do they still run any today?" Hank asked. "From what I've read, they started with a pair of them way back at the beginning with more when they went dark."

Tom nodded. He was uncertain if he were cleared to let anyone know of the still functioning status of the base. "Their first was a fast breeder reactor and the next one was used to test nuclear submarine reactor technologies. From what she told me they did shut the first two down and evacuated nearly all that base in nineteen ninety four but came back soon after that and did a clean up. They evidently ran a few more years before they shut everything down. I'd say that area had and lost a good power source and might be willing to have that back."

"On the other hand," Jake offered, "having once had a little problem perhaps the people of the area are well and truly happy it has all gone cold."

Tom agreed that might be the case, but he came to a decision. He had to inform them there were still two of the newer reactors running to generate electricity and for small-scale experiments. It was, he stressed to the group, very top secret information.

"It is those final two that have to be removed fairly soon," he said. "And, we have been unofficially asked to study and suggest and, perhaps, build a *non*-nuclear reactor solution. I'm happy Jimmy brought up the area to the south because I doubt we'll be able to build anything on the Dounreay site, but as close as possible would be nice. Now, it might be a case of convincing the locals. We'll see."

He turned the meeting now to the design of his radically new system. He'd worked the previous three days on a layout for inside the generators then asked Bashalli do her artistic magic to give them a more complete and realistic outer "look." If anything, she'd made them look more futuristic than before and certainly might have been painted from actually seeing the dual towers.

Tom switched the display from a satellite view to a series of moderately detailed internal architectural drawings and started by showing the basic layout of the insides of each generator. At the base of each structure would be a circular breeder to make the actual antimatter. That would be transferred up and into the generator through a magnetic containment tunnel where the introduction of minute amounts of normal matter would be controlled and turned, in some manner he had not yet come up with, into energy.

"A cooling jacket will run around from just below the actual power area up to a few feet above with the entire thing taking advantage of naturally radiating heat to draw cool air up and around the jacket."

It was only once he showed them Bashalli's concept the team sat forward and made appreciative noises.

When compared even to his father's own Citadel nuclear research facility, Tom's projected power generators would be positively futuristic! They would be several shades of a tannish-gray and could blend into many types of surroundings.

Gone would be the hourglass-shaped or tulip-shaped cooling towers. Gone would be the squared buildings with their shielded reactors.

He explained these would be self-contained units.

Her graphic idea appeared to be domed silos sitting side-by-side, ringed by three bands of lights. Tom explained she believed those could be turned on and off in succession giving an outside indication of which generator was being used and also the level of electrical power output.

"We'll see on that one," he told them. "It might not be good to advertise how much they are putting into the system. And, for this test unit I hope to sell the Scottish government on, it might not look at all like these images. Perhaps something a bit more like a concrete building."

"Mausoleum?" Bud quipped.

Tom shook his head. "We'll have no association with *that* sort of structure, Bud!"

There was precious little information, even on areas of the Internet you could typically find just about anything, regarding the Scottish base at Dounreay. For a variety of reasons, it had "fallen through the cracks," even so far as rumor or guesswork.

Available satellite images were of low enough resolution they were all but useless for the inventor for a detailed site survey, so Tom decided to head up to the old Outpost in Space and to avail himself of their Megascope and SuperSight imaging capabilities.

The original twelve-spoke wheel had been doubled toward the end of its usefulness to the Swifts, with the building and opening of the *Space Queen* super station, it had been partially sold and partially leased to others. Even though only two spokes technically remained under Swift control, Damon had negotiated for three places for his employees that could be permanently open and ready to be occupied.

Resupply rockets, filled with air, water, food and even people, left from Cape Canaveral each week on Swift rockets.

Now, Tom wanted to take two of those places inside the wheel for about twenty-four hours.

To make it easier on the current occupants, he and Bud would not remain inside during their off and night hours; they would return to the *Challenger* they'd pilot up and park just a hundred feet from one end of the station.

Chow, who used to regularly head up to the station for both a visit and to bring some of his home cooked foods to the appreciative men and women of the Outpost, asked the inventor if he could come up.

"I'll stay mostly in the *Challenger*," he offered, "an' just head over fer the occasional visit ta some o' the folks I still know up there."

"Come on along, then. I'll have a supplemental tank of oxygen strapped to the outer deck in case they get a bit snotty about our consuming theirs!"

When they arrived the next day at noon, the central hub was abuzz with residents and the few paying guests all having their lunches dished up. They barely looked over at the trio when they stepped inside and up from the lower level.

In fact, nobody came over to Tom at all.

With a shrug, he asked if the chef wanted to remain out in the open area, but Chow had sniffed the aromas of the food, wrinkled his nose in a way that told Tom and Bud he did not find it to be pleasant, and said he'd follow along with them.

Chow and Bud did know about nine of the residents who worked in the solar battery command spoke still owned by Enterprises. That is where they headed as Tom walked two spokes to the left and into the Observation Department.

Everyone in that area knew Tom and many of the other Swift people, so they greeted him warmly. When the manager inquired why he was up there, Tom looked curiously at him.

"Didn't the Commander pass the word to you? I called up yesterday and told him we were coming to make a couple hours of Earth observations."

The other man shook his head. "Sorry, Tom. We heard nothing. What is it you want a look at?"

When Tom told him, he was informed that the upper part of Scotland was just a little too far over the horizon, even from their 22,300 mile altitude.

Thinking he should have known that, Tom was a little peeved the station Commander had told him to come up and they'd get some good shots for him.

Tom reached out and shook the man's hand. "Then, we'll be going and not take up any more of your air. Bye!'

He turned and left, stopping only long enough to tell his companions their trip, at least to this station, had been in vain."

"We'll head up and over there and use our own SuperSight to see what we might find," he said and the trio headed back to the airlock, leaving the station just twenty-three minutes after they arrived.

Tom used a couple of the recently-installed nitrogen reaction rockets to move them to the side of the station and to rotate them. Then, a push on the planet below and one against the Moon had them heading to their next destination.

On their way a quarter of the distance around the world, Tom tried to decide whether to tell his father about the lack of internal communication. Knowing it would bother the older man, he put it to the back of his mind; he would decide later.

Chow asked why they were not heading for the *Super Queen.*

"Easy, Chow. Because Tom needs a stationary place from which to look down," Bud explained. "The giant station still orbits, albeit slowly, so we'd only have an hour or two at a time to be close enough for a good look."

The chef looked at Tom for verification Bud was not pulling his leg.

Tom nodded. "He's right."

When they arrived over the northern part of Scotland, Tom set the controls to keep them stationary where they were before moving over to the SuperSight station. Now they had reduced their altitude from the Outpost's height to just 900 miles, he felt the Megascope was not going to give him the best results.

As Chow headed into the tiny galley to fix them a snack, Bud sidled over standing behind Tom's seat.

"What, if you don't mind me asking, are you looking for, skipper?"

Tom explained he wanted a nearly foot-by-foot survey of what was currently on the ground inside the security fence, what seemed to be missing all these weeks after his first visit, and what looked like it was being readied for destruction.

They remained above the installation for five hours, but Tom only spent the first half hour in the seat. He activated a program designed for specific scanning of defined areas. After identifying the corners of the base and setting a fifty-foot additional border area, he got up and came over to where Bud was munching on a sandwich.

"It's a hot ham and cheese," the flyer explained around a

mouthful. He tried to smile but lost a small piece of the bread as he did. It was not subject to the personal artificial gravity they were so it floated in front of his face a moment before he leaned forward and bit down on it.

Chow looked on happily. "Got another couple-a them plus roasted chicken breast with some o' them Indian tandoori spices." He looked hopefully at his young boss.

"What're you having, Chow? I'll take what is left. Either one sounds great!"

It required a little convincing to get the chef to take *his* choice first, but Tom ended up with one of the chicken sandwiches which he ate quickly. It tasted wonderful to him and reminded him a little of some of the moderately spicy dishes Bashalli made on occasion.

By the time they were getting ready to head back to Fearing, it was nearing dinner time. The chef had brought along a bulgur wheat, grape tomatoes and a tender, fragrant beef casserole he dished out to them. Tom had a little squeeze of hot sauce on his while Bud went without.

Chow followed Tom's example with the sauce and was scooping and eating his portion with some gusto.

They landed and headed for the Toad in which they'd flown down. Tom had a computer thumb drive full of all the images and the complete survey he intended to go though the next day.

When he got to his lab in the morning, Tom sat down and loaded in the video from the SuperSight. Watching the scan that started at the front gate, he could see nothing at the front entrance was different other than a large carrier truck, filled with some sort of dirt or former building materials, was heading out. As the scan started to move on, the truck turned to its right where he believed it would head for the nearby highway on the far side of the airport.

Of the five buildings he absolutely had noted from his initial tour, the two closest to the gate were gone. He could not recall if the Minister ever told him their function, so he could not guess their importance in the scheme of taking the base out.

What did catch his eye was more than an hour into the video. The building he knew had contained the very first, breeder-type reactor was missing. Even the components of the building were gone. With some likelihood that structure had ended up with minor radioactivity on the inside walls, at the very least, he believed there was some dumping site, somewhere, and everything had been well buried there.

Four other buildings were now missing.

Two buildings were actively being torn down as his video showed with a resolution making things look as if the camera were less than five hundred feet away at the very most. He could make out the operator cages on the tractors that would, he knew, be totally enclosed to protect the men inside.

Tom fast forwarded through the rest of the video watching everything—even though it was at eight-times normal speed—and making a series of notes about what he could no longer see versus what the Minister had described to him.

Two things he knew were still there, and likely to still be in operation, were the final two reactor buildings.

But, what he believed he detected were a series of forms, probably for concrete, that surrounded both buildings.

He wondered if the intent was to entomb them rather than tear them out.

And, he wondered if that might indicate the intent of the Scots of close off and then try to forget the base ever existed.

Tom sat back hoping he was wrong. He really could use that land.

CHAPTER 11 /

LOCATION, LOCATION, LOCATION

TOM CONTACTED the Scottish Energy Minister via official channels. It took three days to get a call back, and she was somewhat rushed for time. That is, until Tom said what he believed to be the magic word.

"Dounreay."

"Please give the five minutes to clear my schedule," she requested placing the call on hold. Tom had to chuckle at the Scottish government's choice for music on hold. It was a bagpipe band playing Clare de Lune.

Not a good match of instruments and style, he told himself while he waited.

When she did come back it was with a hint of nervousness to her voice. "Uhh, Mr. Swift? Tom. Is this something that might be best suited to talk about face to face? I mean, given..."

"Possibly, Minister, and forgive me for the unannounced call, but I have a question regarding the facility grounds. Do they disappear or might we lease some portion for a new power generator experimental station?" He knew that would pique her interests.

It did.

"Oh, goodness! Well, that will, of course, depend on any number of things. Is there the possibility we could meet again? Same as before?"

It was the inventor's turn to place her on hold. *Hope she likes old disco music played on a pipe organ*, he thought as he looked at his schedule. Then, to ensure there would be nothing to surprise anyone, he opened the door and asked Trent about his availability at the end of the week.

"Well, as this is Thursday and the end of the week is tomorrow, I have nothing that is not already on your schedule. You *have* looked at that already, haven't you?"

Tom's smile was his answer. "In that case you are actually clear through Tuesday of the forthcoming week. Where are you going?"

"Scotland."

With a nod Trent turned back to his computer and made the notation.

"Minister? I hope the music didn't either lull you to sleep or annoy you enough to hang up." She assured him her mind was so full of what the forthcoming meeting might entail she hadn't actually listened.

"Okay. Then how about tomorrow?"

"I have a very vital vote in Parliament tomorrow at eleven, not, by the way, regarding this matter; it is just something for which I feel strongly and must be there. Could we either make it for later in the day—and you can stay the night so we might continue the following day if necessary—or just begin things on Saturday morning around ten?"

They agreed to start on Friday at 2:00 and to reserve the next day as well. Tom offered to have her stay the evening on the *Sky Queen* and to have dinner prepared by Chow. Her small protest that her security team—all two of them—needed to be housed nearby was quickly overcome by the knowledge there would be sufficient cabins onboard for them as well.

"And, the jet is very secure. Plus, we could take off at a moment's notice if necessary!"

Minister Livingston had to place Tom on hold a moment while she made a side call to check with her Ministerial Protection manager. When she came back her voice told him all was going to be fine.

"Personally, I hold you in rather high esteem, Tom. Our protective team holds your Harlan Ames in even higher esteem. Is it true he was once the Vice President's personal Secret Service agent?"

"Yes. He was shot protecting that man and when they wanted to take him off more strenuous duty, we hired him. We have all been happy since then."

Bashalli told him as they had dinner that evening she hoped he was not expecting the entire family to come along this time.

"The children do have a full day of school tomorrow and I have another meeting with some of those Eastern European people on their 'Come and vacation in a land where your personal safety cannot be guaranteed,' advertising campaign."

"Is it really that bad?" Amanda asked from the breakfast bar where she and the kids were eating their ravioli.

Bashalli nodded. "Unfortunately, it is. They just had two French tourists kidnapped and held for a day. No harm came to them except it has put a bad taste in all our mouths. Tomorrow, we may be telling them to take back the money we have not yet spent and go elsewhere."

Tom swallowed his latest bite before commenting, "I can't begin to think how bad it might become if someone watching or reading one of your agency's ads were to come to harm. Lawsuits, for one thing."

It was agreed she would tell her manager she no longer felt it proper to work on that campaign and would tell the woman they should back out of the agreement.

In the meantime, she hoped Tom's trip was going to be a success. She even was mostly philosophical about his needing to be gone for two days and not coming back the same day.

She remained very close to Tom that night, even taking up more than a little of his half of the bed. He woke a few times and had to smile to himself on finding she was still touching him and even caressing his arm in her sleep.

When he rose it was to find her still asleep. He was about to jostle her when he noticed the clock, on her side of the bed, said it was only 5:32 am. She didn't have to get up until 6:30, so he slid as quietly as he could out of the bed and went to the bathroom to take a shower.

Twenty minutes later he came out to find her on her side, head propped up on her hand, smiling at him.

"Now that you no longer smell of a good night's sleep, come and hug me, please," she requested.

He was happy to oblige.

An hour later, once he arrived at Enterprises, he headed to the office to gather up the few things he wanted to take along, including a portable telejector unit in case he did not have access to the unit in the *Sky Queen*, and the data cube in which was an animation of both the outside of the proposed system as well as a moderately detailed set of views of the inner workings he believed would be part of everything.

Of course Bud was ready and had done all the preflight work and checks on the *Sky Queen* while Hank and Gary Bradley, their assigned Security man, played a little two-handed solitaire in the lounge. Chow arrived about the time Tom did and they climbed up the two flights of stairs with the chef turning to the right to take his two bags of supplies back to the kitchen while Tom headed forward.

Nothing of any note happened on the flight and they arrived at the Dounreay landing site an hour before the Minister was schedule to be there.

As the giant jet settled onto the open space they'd used before, Bud whistled. "That's one mostly barren old base out there," he stated pointing to the now largely bare spaces around inside the high fence.

"Looks like they have been either proactive or forced to get things torn out," Tom said. "But, they must still have a good reason to keep their guard station at the gate."

With things soon shut down and only the basic electrical power from their power pod keeping lights and the heating running, the young men headed back to the lounge area.

Hank was just throwing his latest hand of card onto the table.

Glancing up at Tom, he smiled. "I should have stayed with solitaire. I let this ranch swindler talk me into playing some three-handed poker." He nodded over to Chow who was sitting there with a smile on his face and most of the poker chips they carried sitting in front of him.

"How much you in for?" Bud asked.

"It has to be well over fifty cents now! My mother warned me of the evils and heartache of gambling."

With little to do to prepare for the coming arrival, they all sat and had a quick snack of some pre-made sandwiches Chow had put together just before takeoff.

Nearly ten minutes early they saw the helicopter of the Minister and her team touch down to the right side of the *Queen*.

Tom headed down the stairs and to the right side hatch. A trio of people climbed from the helo and came walking toward him. The Minister smiled and waved while the other two looked constantly around them, and especially at the parked automobiles where anybody might be hiding. The military men only seemed to relax once everybody was inside and the hatch had been shut and locked.

Pleasantries were exchanged and Tom took them up to the third deck and to the cabins they would occupy. One of the men had two small cases and the other one a single. The first man slid one into the cabin assigned to the Minister and took the other to his small room.

"I'll see you forward in the lounge area once you get settled."

The three Scots were there in about two minutes.

"Not a lot to unpack right now," she told everyone before Tom introduced everybody. Even the two soldiers relaxed enough to shake hands and tell the others they were Dougal Gordon and Frankie MacIntosh.

While Hank asked about whether Dougal was a member of the Gordon Highlanders clan and Frankie of the MacIntosh clan, Tom and the Minister headed forward to the small conference room closer to the cockpit.

From her shoulder bag, she took a ten-page document and placed it on the table. Sitting, she pushed it over to Tom.

"That is the agreement from the Scottish Parliament to allow Swift Enterprises to lease and build on a one hectare plot of land inside the fence. In case you do not know that measurement, it is equal to about five thousand fifty three square meters, or—and I had to have help with this conversion—a little greater than one-point-eight American football fields." She looked at him. "I hope that is enough space because that is all the ground we believe is totally devoid of any possible contamination from our... well, *former* life."

He asked if he might take it back for review by Jackson Rimmer and the Enterprises' Legal team.

"Well, you can do that, but it is really a permission slip for you requiring nothing by way of signatures from your company. You do what you wish, though. And, with my delivery of that, let's talk about your plans."

Tom asked if they might go look at the actual hectare site before he got into the details of what he wanted to build there. She agreed and they along with Bud and Hank, plus her guard, headed to the hangar of the jet where Tom had brought a Model 1 atomicar... the first and largest of that vehicle made.

The guards at the gate checked her Ministry identification, asked each of her guests the same questions they had done with Tom months earlier, and waved them through with one admonition.

"Please do not travel within fifty meters of any of the former *major* building sites." He told them those areas were ringed with a series of red flags.

Being their first time within the fences, both Bud and Hank marveled at the look of the base.

"I can only guess how this might have looked before things started getting demolished," the engineer told them. "I have seen the aerial views so I know this was never futuristic city sort of amazing, but now it looks like a nearly abandoned old industrial area in a rundown U.S. city."

As Tom drove them around, always keeping the mandated distance from former buildings, which made the route somewhat odd and circuitous, they arrived at an area, nearly a square, about three hundred by three fifty in size and staked out with metal posts in the corners.

"It's awfully close to the ocean, isn't it?" Bud asked his friend.

"We can make do, Bud. Not much closer, but this should be fine." Turning to Minister Livingston, Tom asked, "Do we have to build dead center in that, or can we bump up against the inland side?"

She told them the building or buildings could be any place inside that rectangle, and that the farther from the ocean might be the best.

Everyone got out and walked to the closest side. Like the entire parcel it was hard packed dirt all around. Unlike other locations on the grounds—some of which were now only large piles of rubble—it had never featured a large building, but had once been the site of two utility buildings holding and repairing base vehicles.

Once they all walked around the perimeter and she and Tom strode across the center, she asked if they wanted to go into the base operations building or back to the jet.

"Where would you feel more comfortable?" Tom inquired. "I brought my presentation materials and portable equipment with us but we can absolutely use the more permanent setup in the *Queen*."

She suggested they stop in the base's Admin building while she retrieved the site's survey files. They included stability and coring reports going back twenty or more years.

When the got back to the jet, Chow had an afternoon snack waiting for everyone.

"If'n ya pardon my familiarity, ma'am, and I don't know what all pro-tee-cols I oughta go by, but if you an' yer friends'll take a sit, I'll bring out slices o' pizza an some special fruit bars I made early this mornin'. Pizza's are veggie and an all-meat. Yer choice."

She laughed lightly and placed a hand on his right forearm.

"That will be marvelous, and inside this jet, your home turf I believe is the saying, I'm either Jacquie," and she decided it wasn't worth spelling, "or at the very most, Miss Livingston. And, pizza sounds delicious! May I have a slice of each?"

Shortly after they had eaten and Chow cleaned up the plates, she, Tom, and Hank headed forward. As soon as Tom turned on the telejector and the first images appeared in thin air right over the table, she sat, slack-jawed, in amazement.

The presentation took about fifteen minutes and Tom was surprised she had no questions during it. Only after he turned the projector off did she start.

He had shown her both a nondescript possible outer building as well as Bashalli's futuristic looks. She asked if they could get by with the more plain building.

"The less people believe they have to see that could be impressive, the better I think."

"We believe that as well. I should have prefaced that by telling you the fancy look is one of the ones we are investigating for all final and full-size installations." That answer and information satisfied her.

During the course of the following five hours, before they called an end for the day, she had questions about nearly all aspects of the generator, and that had included a half hour during which Tom had to explain, and even call up a video of, the absolutely safe use of antimatter. He chose to show it being stored in a magnet flask and placed into the *Galaxy Traveller*, but did not show her the explosive force it created allowing that ship to enter the wormhole.

Later, Hank asked about that "missing" video. Tom said he did not want any impression in her mind that something he knew to be usable in a safe manner could create that level of potentially destructive energy.

After dinner, another of Chow's excellent meals, everyone retired to the lounge seats where Tom brought out the standard, "This is Swift Enterprises" video tour cube and showed it to his interested audience.

Along with footage going back to the original build of the giant facility, it showed many of the modern day operations including flight services along with a aircraft by aircraft display of everything the Swift's had made going back to the very first *Pigeon*.

One thing he noted might need to be changed in the narrative was to differentiate between scenes taken at the Construction Company versus Enterprises footage. Nevertheless, it was impressive to the Scots.

When it concluded, the Minister said she needed to file a report of the day and then answer correspondence, so she excused herself.

Because they needed to be ready for any time she woke up, the two Army men also left the lounge within ten minutes.

Discussions after breakfast included her asking about the volatility of antimatter. She had done some research the previous evening and it worried her.

Tom nodded. "Can you tell me the source of what you read?"

When she provided the name of a man from Sweden who was

known for his radical scientific statements and total lack of a supporting educational background, Tom smiled and asked for a moment.

He pulled out his tablet computer and entered the man's name in the search engine. A moment later he'd located the article he wanted and handed the tablet to her.

The first four paragraphs she read had her eyes opened and her head shaking.

> The man identifying himself as Swedish authority Dr. Johann Jorgensen was, in fact, Hans Jorgensen, a fifth generation Norwegian swine farmer by trade and a dropout from organized education by the age of eleven. Of the twenty or so technical papers he managed to have published before being called out by the scientific community as a phony, he provided no proof for any statements given or observation he is purported to have made.
>
> He ascribed this attack on his integrity as being "another case of personal attacks on his great reputation that were politically motivated and coming from an advanced manifestation of professional jealousy and an attempt by those who just do not know what they question" to discredit him and to drive him into poverty.
>
> He claimed to be the only voice of reason in a "technologically-obfuscating world of politicians disguised as scientists out to take people's freedoms and money." His behaviors came into question frequently during his final two months.
>
> Mr. Jorgensen was shot and killed by Swedish Army sharpshooters during a standoff when he took the Swedish Science Minister hostage threatening to kill the woman by slashing her throat. Jorgensen was screaming about how everybody was "killing true science." He died from at least five bullets hitting in his torso and head.

The tablet almost dropped from her hand as she lowered it. She was actually shaking.

Tom gently took it from her hands and set it aside.

"Jorgensen was a blot on the scientific community for less than five years and yet he did more damage to public perceptions of simple facts and well-established procedures that his affect is being felt twenty years after his death," he explained.

"Why are his lies allowed to remain on the Internet?" she asked incredulously.

With a shrug, Tom told her there were still freedoms allowed to even the most ridiculous of claims. "Just look at the horrible lies some people hand out. I think they feel safe in anonymity and do not think about any consequences of what they say. It is sad, but it is a fact we have to live with."

They discussed what antimatter was, what it was not, and how it interacted with normal matter.

"It is true that matter and antimatter cannot be in the same location, or allowed to touch, just willy nilly." He checked her face to see if she understood the reference. She did. "In fact, and forgive me for not showing you this last night, but I believed it might give a wrong impression."

He pulled up the video of the first time antimatter had been used to open a wormhole. Before the actual video he explained what they were about to see, and specifically why antimatter had been used. He told her that the visible results were mainly from the effects of performing the experiment in a total vacuum.

She was a little startled by the violence of the exceedingly brief explosion, but not so much that her logic was overcome with fear. She asked if it might be shown again, and in slow motion; Tom did just that.

"You explained that your fuel was not going to be nuclear in nature. Is antimatter a nuclear fuel or does it provide a typical nuclear reaction?"

With a shake of his head, he explained that it was just a method of heating and setting fire to the actual fuel, "which we will make on site using electricity and seawater.

"And, you are certain this is a safe environment for your, well, facility?"

"Madam Minister... Jacquie, this location is practically perfect for what we wish to prove. It has the advantage of being remote enough and in a location already used for much more dangerous things. For decades. With no accidents we've been able to find in all that time. We do not intend to damage that reputation. So, the answer is yes, I believe it is exceptionally safe."

Her final question before telling him she was satisfied was, "Would you allow your family to visit or stay nearby?"

"Absolutely!"

CHAPTER 12 /
A MORE SUPPORTIVE MIDDLE GROUND

ACCORDING TO Damon, things were actually moving forward with the government of Canada.

This was both a delight to the younger Swift and a curiosity. In the past, when a government or a political functionary said, "No," to nearly anything they could not see as an immediate advantage to themselves, that meant days, weeks, months and even an eternity to try to overcome.

"I have a feeling we are seeing some backdoor pressures being placed, or at least suggested, by Washington." That was Damon's take. "The political embarrassment their leading party might have been subjected to over the Inuit village—and coming from what I later discovered on the heels of their Prime Minister making a very public speech about how their party is so fully into helping and saving and nourishing the native tribal population up there—did the trick."

"In other words, they backed themselves into a corner?"

His father chuckled. "It would appear they went out and bought the lumber and nails, drew up the plans and built that corner before stepping solidly into it, turning around and hoping nobody could see them!"

Tom grinned recalling a neighbor's cat who would stand next to an open door with its head sticking into the dark place behind, body fully exposed, and believe it was invisible.

"So," he asked, "may I go ahead with more than just plans for the test system for Scotland?"

"If you will allow me a day to check with people like Peter Quintana and let him do the sort of magic and inquiries he is so darned good at, then I say you have a better environment of support for a non-nuclear solution than you did at this time yesterday."

That was all the encouragement Tom needed. He headed for the big lab down the hall and got to finalizing what he saw as the actual process of turning a matter and antimatter reaction into something useable that would sustain itself over a reasonable period of time. *Anything,* he thought, *would be better than a few recent experiments in Germany and France where the fusion reaction he sought had been measured in milliseconds at best.*

If his theory would bear out, then the exceedingly brief explosion would cause temperatures inside the reaction chamber to come close to that of the sun. And, it was the sun's heat that took the available fuel and burned it in a never-ceasing fusion reaction. After that it should be as easy as harnessing that heat to run a steam generator system. Unless, that is, he could discover or devise a manner in which to capture that raw energy release and turn that directly into electricity.

That was something he considered to be a possibility so minute and close to zero he wasn't going to devote a lot of time or energy into it.

Hank and Arv showed up just before noon.

"We heard from a little birdie by the name of Damon that you have good news. That's all he would tell us. So?" the model maker inquired looking hopeful for enlightenment.

Tom told them the Canadian government was opening the door for a more supportive approach to what he and Enterprises wanted to create and offer.

"Actual middle ground from their politicians?" Hank looked as if this were a completely foreign concept.

"Yes. I could say it is about time, but I honestly don't believe I'd be any further along on this even if they had been begging us from the very beginning."

Tom showed them his slightly modified plans and talked about the fusion reaction. Hank had a good understanding of the theory behind it, but Arv was a special effects model maker by training and trade.

"So, if I get this, colliding the two types of matter—"

"States," Tom corrected. "States of matter and I'm sorry..."

Arv shook his head. "No. I need to get this right. So the slamming together of two *states* of matter causes a reaction that gives of such a tremendous amount of heat that the introduced fuel source, the isotope of hydrogen, spontaneously combusts and that keeps burning with such an intensity that it sets the next droplets, or micro-bit of the fuel also on fire and so on and so on?"

Now, the inventor was nodding. "That is the theory. Nobody has been able to sustain the reaction so we only have the briefest of instances where such fusion has been possible."

"Did I once read some early experiments were trying to use simple carbon as the fuel?"

"Yes, Hank. Carbon, calcium, sulfur and even helium-4. To date just the expenditure of energy getting things up to a high enough temperature have been nearly astronomical. And, searches for the illusive cold fusion have turned out to be mostly mistaken beliefs in what has really occurred, or outright lies."

He added that he could locate no instance where the reaction had started by the use of antimatter.

"That might give us a leg up in doing this."

Hank and Arv nodded at what seemed to be the logic in that statement.

"What can Arvid or I do to help at this stage?"

Tom, who felt he was just getting a handle on how to contain the reaction took a moment to think about that request.

Finally, he said, "If the two of you could take my drawings and build a, well, perhaps one-twentieth scale model of the entire generator building for me? It will help not only for my own uses, but hopefully others can be shown it and get a better idea other than from theory and a few line drawings."

The two other men readily agreed to do that. With the names of all Tom's files pertaining to the generator, including Bashalli's initial outer views, they departed, heading first for Arv's workshop where they would do a little extra work in the CAD environment. Once that was finished—or at least for some elements that could be built self-contained—one or more of their 3D printers would be employed to turn out parts and even whole assemblies.

Tom had a good feeling about how things might progress from this point. If his team members were at the point they could turn out various items, even moving parts for normally static models of the generator components that set the stage for actual construction when the right time came.

A small knock on the lab door was followed by Damon stepping into the room.

"I was out chatting with Trent when Hank and Arv walked past. They mentioned something about making a semi-working model of your antimatter generator. Is that true?"

Tom grinned as he turned around to face his father.

"Well, perhaps not so much the semi-working part, but I believe they will do what they generally do, and when I ask for just a static shape, they will give me a miniature steam and turbine generator loop that includes moving parts. Might even be able to make a small level of electricity if they think to add an outside pump to flow water or something around."

His father sat down. "There are times," he said with a bit of a sigh, "when I have to believe we have people who are too good for us. I can't count the number of times those two, together or individually, have been sent away with a request to make a rather simple box with wheels, and they come back—days early, for that matter—with a fully designed, sleek vehicle that has a drive system that either proves what you or I would eventually want to test, or the word that it just could not be done in that form factor!

"How did we get so lucky?"

Tom put a serious look on his face. "Well, if you can remember back that far, a certain man with a vision for a giant industrial facility began hiring an ever-increasing group of men and women to work there, and he did a darned good... no, a *great* job in who he hired!"

Damon realized Tom meant him and he blushed slightly. "Yes... well... anyway, before I saw those two I was checking with Trent on your schedule. Your mother wants a gathering of the tribe this very evening and I wanted to make certain you hadn't scheduled yourself to be on the Moon or something." Now, the older inventor smiled.

"Oh? Am I scheduled to be off the planet?"

Damon shook his head. "No. In fact, neither you nor I have anything after four this afternoon, so I suggest that you plan to leave right after that, pick up your wife, children, and Amanda, and get over to Casa Swift before five. With this nice bout of weather we are having, I am being pressed into grill duties and I need an able-bodied young man to assist. And, no, that is not going to be Bud. I love the man like the son-in-law he is, but something about your sister's negative influence in the cooking arena had rubbed off on him, and he has lost the ability to time the proper cooking of meat."

Tom had to agree. Where once Bud had been a great help in backyard cookery, over the past five or more years he seemed to have forgotten fundamentals. With the more recent coming of his son, Sammy, his attention to mundane things like poking a finger into a rib eye steak to check for doneness had been put, with the unintended pun, on the back burner.

"It'll be nice to cook with you again, Dad."

"Looking forward to it, Son."

When the three parts of the family met at the Swift home, Ann had all the meat on a platter with a flavorful spice rub on each piece, large pieces of vegetables that generally went well on the grill, and a pasta shrimp salad in the refrigerator.

Bashalli asked if she might do anything to help.

"No, dear. I think Sandy needs the experience while I make a salad dressing and some lemonade. You go out with the men and make certain they are not horsing around. Send Bud in for the meat. Oh, and could you take the veggie platter with you, please?"

Understanding his limitations, Bud stood and watched as the steaks, pork chops and half chickens were grilled to perfection. Even Bart came over to see how it all happened.

Tom's oldest had become quite a little foodie since he turned about three. He loved all meats, fish and seafood, had an affinity for spicy hot and flavorful spiced dishes, and really not much of a sweet tooth.

He also became a little exasperated with his younger sisters over their fondness for sugary things and what he saw as a failure on their part to understand that vegetables were delicious!

During the meal—the four children at a lower table off to the side being entertained by Bart telling the others about several books he'd recently read—the adults talked about Bashalli's agency and their eventual refusal to go through with the European country's ad campaign, and then all eyes turned to Tom when she said his tale as much more interesting.

"There isn't a lot to tell you that I haven't already, but Dad had some great news about Canada and their, well, almost *willingness* to talk about this as if they would be okay with having us work up there. And, we are a couple signatures from having a location in Scotland to build a smaller test unit and then a couple locations in Canada where I hope to set up a full-scale dual generator placement."

Amanda, who liked hearing about her boss' projects, had only heard small pieces about the antimatter generator. She apologized for her ignorance regarding what all might be on the inside such a generator, and even said she would be willing to hear about it offline, but Tom told her it was fine. He would tell her more right now.

On hearing the word, "antimatter," she let out the tiniest of gasps, but shook her head and muttered to herself, "He knows what he's doing Amanda!" Then, looking into his eyes she asked, "Is it a lot safer than people who write sci-fi could lead us to believe?"

"Truth? Well then," he said as she nodded, "uncontrolled it can be exceptionally harmful. Those writers have one basic piece of info right. Matter and antimatter do not play well together when they come in contact." He pinched his thumb and index finger together and they pulled them quickly apart. "But, keep them apart, even by a very tiny margin, and you get nothing. What you don't want, and what my system will ensure, is that you never get a lot of them touching."

He told her, with Bart listening intently as if he were filing all this away for future use, his generator would work with particles of antimatter that were smaller than what might fit on the point of a pin.

"Not the head?" she asked.

"Nope. We are talking perhaps a thousand atoms, and even in that number you could barely see them under a powerful microscope. Except, you could not use that microscope unless it was outfitted with a containment system that doesn't let anything touch!"

"So," she started but seemed unsure where to go with her question. He gave her a moment. She looked back up and asked, "Just how small will this, uhh, thing be? I mean, the whole generator thing."

When he told them all of the probable size of even a small test version, all except for little Anne stared at him in disbelief. Even her older sister, Mary had to question her father's statement.

"Can it be bigger than grampa's car? Really?"

Tom smiled at her and nodded. "Yes. Your grampa Swift's car is a pretty big thing, but remember that giant spaceship I took you into last summer? That's my *Challenger*, and it is so big I will take my test generator up right on the outside deck."

Her little eyes widened in wonder. Damon's car was the biggest thing she recalled being in so it was her best point of reference. Even the large spaceship didn't figure into such mental equations; it had simply been too much to take in at the time.

The arrived home a little before nine.

"Okay, kids. Let's go get cleaned and in jammies," Amanda suggested. Mary and Anne liked getting a warm bath, even though Mary had recently asked to not have to take one at the same time as her sister.

Bart, being a boy, didn't see the use in a nightly bath. He knew he'd just get dirty the following day, so why bother? But, he secretly did like his comfortable pajamas that looked like a little business suit just like his grandfathers both wore.

With just Tom and Bashalli sitting of the sofa, she leaned over and kissed him softly.

"That is for being such a great father that you find a way to teach the children something practically every day. I love you!"

"And, I love you, too, Bash. Do you have any secret doubts

orfears I need to get straight?"

She thought, then stated, "No. There have been times when I have asked something that has made you decide to change something, but this time it really sounds like you have everything thought out and under control. I only want one promise, please."

"Name it and if possible I'll do it."

After taking a deep breath, she said, "When you go to test your generator, please do it away from people, and I mean that includes you. If you can do it a mile under the ocean with you back here in Shopton, wonderful. Anywhere so you will always be safe."

"How about I take it up into space and then move a long way off?" he offered. What he did not mention was that his own *Galaxy Traveller* had used slightly more antimatter and at a point only a few yards in front of where he and Bud were sitting... and on at least five occasions.

"Okay. Just as long as you stay safe," she repeated.

The next Tuesday morning brought an invitation for Tom, and Damon, to appear at a two-day Parliamentary "investigation" in Ottawa. There was no amplifying information to the statement, "You are encouraged to attend a special meeting of key Ministerial personnel..."

Both Swifts headed up to Legal to a quickly arranged meeting for a discussion about this latest.

Jackson read through the single page that had been delivered by an overnight carrier that morning. He read it twice as he sought to find any hidden meaning, or even a hint of threat in the wording.

He found nothing.

That did not, he told them, mean this was a friendly meeting or that they might not be raked over a few coals.

"In fact, and as it is an accepted practice, I will accompany you along with quite a number of facts and figures, some of which a few of these Ministers might not know, or may wish to have kept private." He said nothing more, but Tom felt he was silently suggesting he would not be above using some of that information as leverage.

The meetings would be Thursday and Friday with a start time the first day of 1:00 pm.

So they might talk on the trip up, Bud came along as pilot and Slim Davis as co-pilot of the *Sky Queen*.

"It'll be much more impressive for them to see the giant jet than for us to arrive in what is basically a business jet," the lawyer explained.

A rather long and large Cadillac limousine was waiting for them when they arrived holding a pair of somewhat worried-looking politicians.

"We didn't expect you would be coming with a huge retinue," one of them, the Minister for Energy told Damon.

The older inventor turned and glanced over his shoulder at the jet.

"May I ask what gives you the idea we have that full of people? We brought it because it contains our living quarters. Nowhere in your letter did it mention we would be accommodated in a hotel... or otherwise. So, we brought the hotel rooms with us."

That statement seemed to mollify the man and so he swept his right arm toward the limo. "Let us be on our way, then."

Jackson mentioned under his breath while they waited for things to start, "Looks as if our homegrown politicians aren't the only ones who find it difficult to abide by their own announced schedules."

It was now 1:27 and only half the seats at the table before them held anybody. It also seemed that for every man or woman sitting at the table, each had a minimum of two assistants or associates sitting or standing behind them.

Two minutes later a woman who the Enterprises people believe to be the Master at Arms banged a ceremonial staff into the floor and announced in a voice sufficient to fill a space three times that of this meeting room, "This official meeting of Parliament and the Ministers and assistants is hereby called to order. The Honorable Marcus Gibson, presiding!"

A side door opened and a man in what Tom thought of as full court or military regalia entered, followed by five others. First, he took the center seat with the others sitting to his left and right. Seconds later and without pomp, the individuals who would be behind them all sort of slinked in and the door was shut.

"Please allow me to do the initial talking," Jackson whispered to the men on either side.

With a bang of what looked like a simple piece of dark wood—not exactly a gavel—onto the desk, the chairman raised his face and smiled.

"Let us begin. You gentlemen in the front can see our name and title plates up here, but it would be nice to have some formal introductions. So, allow me to begin."

He introduced himself and stated that during the meeting he should be addressed as "Mr. Chairperson." He had scowled at that and muttered something about why it was so impossible to be called a "Chair*man.*"

The others at the eleven seated positions introduced themselves and each simply suggested "Minister" or "Minister of (whatever there function might be)."

Finally, the Chairperson looked at Damon. The inventor stood and introduced himself, along with his title and position as owner of the Swift holdings, nodded to Tom and made similar statements, and then to Jackson Rimmer.

"Mr. Rimmer is our Corporate Attorney and is an expert on International relations. I am afraid your invitation was rather short on details and so we all thought it best to have someone who might help us at this front table better able to respond." He sat back down.

The man at the head of the committee had smiled during Damon's talk as the inventor had addressed him as "Mr. Chairman." Now, still slightly grinning, he stated the reason for the meeting.

"As you three may not know, but I'm hoping the individuals on either side of me understand, this current government stands on very shaky political ground. Our support within the general populace of Canada is tenuous at best. Under somewhat secret conditions, the Prime Minister's office of Communications held a series of interviews with about two thousand people across the country about what is going right and what is or feels wrong to them.

"Now, one of the overwhelming things brought up are the government's energy policies. Specifically, dissatisfaction with energy costs and, at least from three Provinces, availability of sufficient energy—specifically electricity—for what they see as the sort of normal life city residents demand."

He looked at the trio and his mouth turned into a grim line.

"With two dissenting votes up here most of us believe the current government has done many wrong, or at least unwise things when it comes to energy. Those two will not be singled out but if they wish to have their say I shall not stop that. To continue, and given that a huge level of federal funding to Canada comes from the mining and partial processing of uranium ore—ore that goes to nearly any nation willing to pay current prices—where it becomes fuel for rectors to make energy, reactors that power ships and submarines capable of delivering weapons with nuclear warheads, and even those same warheads, that we can no long look smugly at each other and say we can't, *won't*, use or allow that same ore and materials to provide a higher standard of living for our citizens.

"You Swifts have proven over more than a decade that you have a safe, reliable and probably more economical way to provide the energy we absolutely need. The one thing we are up against," and he pointed in both directions at the others, "is that we need to have a national mandate and vote to allow full-fledged nuclear reactors be built and operated. Sadly, the best scenario we can find puts that vote out at least two years with possibly another three to five years of hearings where some people will be in favor and will most likely be moderately quiet about it, while a very vocal group will scream, rant and rail against the very thought.

"It will probably mean at least one or two changes in the ruling party during that time, So, it is up to me to tell you a couple things.

"First, we want to officially request that the Swift Organization begin work on a plan to implement between two and five reactor power stations. Second, while you will be compensated for your time, we cannot guarantee you will ever be allowed to build a nuclear reactor in Canada."

He let out a heavy sigh and rubbed his eyes with his right fingers.

"Third, I, personally, and this panel want to know if there is any hope of you coming up with something that does not use our uranium to blast itself apart in a nuclear reaction that is then used to make what we need. Is there any hope or is this nation doomed from our own shortsightedness?"

Tom raised a hand and the Chairman pointed to him.

"Sir... and Ministers. I may have just the answer for you."

CHAPTER 13 /

"BAD, BAD SCOTTISH MAN... NO COOKIE!"

"WELL, THAT was just about totally unexpected!" Jackson told Tom and Damon as they got back into the *Sky Queen* two hours later. The rest of the meeting time had been called off because the Ministers now had far too much information to try to digest.

Without going into such details as the use of antimatter, Tom had told them all about his revolutionary new power generation system that he absolutely assured them did not use or produce any form of nuclear fission.

Of course, for some of them he had to take a side tack and tell than fission was exactly what their idea of a reactor utilized. That it also meant the use of fissionable uranium isotopes and released a lot of radioactivity.

But, he reminded them that nuclear energy—as they knew it—was safe when reactors were made by people who never cut corners. Like the Swifts!

When the best possible materials were used and each and every safety standard was not just adhered to, but surpassed. Like the Swifts!

And, that his new system would not have the possibility of radioactivity being leaked, because there was none. It would use a fuel obtainable from seawater. And, that brought out a question from one of the two Ministers who did not want to be looking into anything other than coal or natural gas generators.

"Do you intend to destroy our coastline with your unmanageable huge and disgustingly ugly power plants?"

Jackson had tapped Tom's foot to keep the young man from speaking. Instead, the lawyer stood up to his impressive six-foot-five-inch height.

"Madam. While I am unsure why the use of invective adjectives in your misinformed description of any facility the Swifts might design and build for the benefit of Canadian citizens... I believe that a slight correction in your perception is in order. Allow me."

He did not give her the opportunity to say anything before continuing.

"First, just because seawater is required for the process of being turned into the very safe fuel for this generator, does not mean two very important things. One, seawater is transportable so while they might be, well, sucking up some small quantities of it at a point along the coastline, that does *not* mean it will be done at a facility that is either large or unsightly. In fact..." and he consulted several pages he'd brought along, "you and your political party recently okayed that a very large facility be built above Vancouver and on Bowen Island, the home of an ecological reserve. That plant, one to simply grind up coal being delivered to a new pier, and is being allowed to usurp nearly ten percent of that reserve land.

"It can be seen from as far south as the Richmond area which is south of Vancouver's airport and all the way into the western portions of Stanley Park and most of North Vancouver. The people over there consider it to be an eyesore."

He looked at her to see if she had anything to say; she was not looking up at him.

"So," he continued, "as to point one, a small facility requiring no greater footprint than an existing building north of Vancouver in a town named Squamish on its main docking pier will be erected with a pipe into the water and through an inlet approximately fifty feet offshore. Once a day a small cargo jet will touch down, vertically and very safely, next to that building that is only a pump and filter location, and take onboard about one thousand gallons of that water, or approximately four tons."

He told them all it would be delivered to the actual generator site or a small nearby site for processing and that the salt would have been taken out of the water and returned to the inlet.

"Anything left over from the conversion process will either be oxygen, that thing we need to breathe to be alive, or a little dissolved nitrogen all just harmlessly released into the air... and nothing else."

The second thing he told her was that the facility could double its output when the time came to support a possible second set of generators.

"So, these will not just be springing up randomly. Now, I need to ask you as respectfully as I am able, why you chose to use insulting and factually incorrect wording to describe the Swift's facility."

The woman shoved her seat back and left the chamber very quickly.

The Chairman had shrugged and asked the recording reporter to note that the woman was officially giving up her seat on the panel and would be so noted in the Parliamentary Notes of the Day.

Now, as the giant jet was preparing to take off from Ottawa's MacDonald-Cartier International, the three men were reflecting on that single negative incident in what they had assumed, coming up, would be a couple days filled with having to defend themselves and their products or services.

"I have to say that when you started pulling out the ten-dollar words such as 'invectives' I nearly choked on my own laughter. Well done, Jackson!" Damon stated giving the man a five clap applause.

"As soon as we get back, I need to truly get on the ball with the design and get the finalized permissions from Scotland and their Parliament for the real test version. Then, I need to get going on building something to prove the antimatter reaction will work.

That made Jackson stare at the younger man. "You mean you don't already have that nailed down? You don't have something to go build in Canada as soon as they officially give the word?" He sounded flabbergasted.

Tom smiled and nodded. "I have just about everything ready. All I need to do is build something small and work my way up."

Minister Jacquie Livingston could not come to Dounreay to meet with Tom, but she had her offices issue him the necessary paperwork, permissions and even identification cards so that he, Bud and Hank could get onto the base. They would need to be accompanied by a Scottish Army officer, but that would be taken care of when he notified the base of his intended day and time of arrival.

Tom's schedule would allow the trip the next week, and so he involved Trent in making the arrangements. Once, the secretary had to involve the inventor on the phone when he was asked to provide a sample of his voice.

It was a strange request, but one easily taken care of in less than a minute.

A half hour later Trend buzzed him to say the schedule was on the computer, with all the necessary paperwork that could be printed out, coming in a few moments.

"The ID cards require I send them official photos of the three of you plus any other pilots you intend to bring."

"I'll check, but I have the feeling Chow might like to come along. He's been itching for a chance to head back there. I think he fell in love with the one helping of haggis he ate the first evening and wants the opportunity to have more and get an official recipe."

"'Course I want ta come along, Tom!" the chef responded when Tom stepped down the hall to the kitchen. "Uhh, can I ask a favor?

Ya see, my wife, Wanda, keeps on about me takin' her along on some adventure. I think she gets a might lonely an' wants ta share in the fun. Could she come?"

Tom said he'd have to have Trent check, and get a brand new photo of her, but she might need to stick inside the *Sky Queen* with Chow and whatever other pilot they might take along. The chef said he'd have her come in later in the day and head for Communications where they could take a high-resolution photo of her.

"Please tell her to not have her hair or makeup any different from how she'll look when we arrive. I remember once having to tell Sandy she had to stay in the jet in Botswana when she fancied herself up for being there and their security guards didn't recognize her from the high school photo ID."

In spite of her husband's instructions, Wanda Winkler turned up late that afternoon with a lot of eye makeup and bright lipstick that she never wore.

"You can't tell me I can't look good for some picture they want of me," she told Chow.

"Darlin'," he told her looking very serious, "if you don't intend ta look exactly like that, they might make us turn around and take you home. Dead serious they are about knowin' who is achully there versus who kinda looks like what they're expectin'."

As much as she loved the man in her life, Wanda needed to wait for Tom to come over to tell her Chow was correct. It was only after he told of Sandy's experience in Africa, and how she had spent nearly three days cooped up in the *Sky Queen*—and how miserable she felt during and after the trip—that Wanda relented. She headed into the restroom and took off all but her normal makeup.

When the ID cards came four days later, she called Tom.

"I want to apologize for the whole makeup mix-up. That was me not listening. Sometimes Chow shoots straight with me on things like that and sometimes I sort of feel he doesn't want me too pretty so he doesn't have to watch out for me. Silly old coot! I tell him and I tell him he's the only man I have eyes for these days!"

Takeoff was just two days away and everyone was excited for the time to come. For Wanda, it would be her first time out of North America.

Slim was excited to be going because he had friends in Aberdeen he would spend some time on the phone with.

Tom and Hank wanted one final site viewing and intended to pound in a few stakes and get a better idea of the layout of the land. Bud, as always, looked forward to the sheer fun of flight.

With the exception of hitting one updraft just to the south of Greenland that caused the giant jet to suddenly rise by nearly five hundred feet, it was a smooth flight

Tom chose, in spite of earlier admonitions, to over fly the ocean side of the Dounreay base. He wanted to get a closer overall look before seeing things only at ground level.

As he stepped from the side of the jet he watched one of the guards stalking toward him. Of interesting note, the man did not appear to have any weapon with him.

I guess what with the base being almost gone, Tom told himself, *not a lot of need for guns.*

"You're nae allowed ta be here!' the man declared with a scowl. "New, get inta that big thing and get out of here!"

Tom, slowly so to not startle the man, pulled his ID card from his shirt pocket. He had the rest of his papers in his back pocket. With a level of visible doubt in the man's eyes, the Scotsman reached out and took the card. His face suddenly changed.

"Oh. All right. Sorry for the confusion. Can I see the rest of your information?"

Tom handed it over and the man spent more than three minutes examining it. Finally, he reached into a leg pocket and pulled out the same sort of card reader other guards had used with the Minister's card. In one end it went and a green light and simple chime came on. He handed it back to Tom.

"Come with me."

"Uhh, I have a few others onboard who are also in possession of proper ID provided you Minister Livingston of the SNP. May I have them come out now?"

The Army man appeared to be slightly put out by the news, but shrugged.

Hank, Bud and even Chow came out. Slim, Tom knew, would not but he was just a tiny bit surprised Wanda had not followed her husband outside... even though she would not be allowed on the base.

IDs checked, the guard asked if there was anyone else to come with them. Tom told him this was it, so the man turned and trudged back toward the gatehouse.

Once inside the fence, the other guard asked if they required one of the base's remaining vehicles.

"I actually need to go back to the jet and pull out our surveying equipment and supplies, so a truck or van would be wonderful."

A call was made to somewhere on base and a seven-seat van with cargo area behind the last row arrived a minute later. It was driven by a young woman with twin Army silver bars indicating she was a Lieutenant in their officer corps.

Introduction were made with her stating her name was Elizabeth Gordon.

Hank asked about the relationship with the Gordon Highlanders and if she was any relation to Dougal Gordon they had met before..

"Nae. Neither. Gordon is a common enough name 'round here, but my mother's side of the family were McIntyres and my father was a Gordon from Wales. So," she said with a hint of mischief in her eyes, "no rampant blood lust or running around with my kilt raised ta scare the English!"

They all took an immediate liking to the young woman. She had her doubts at first, but took to the Americans within moments.

They climbed into the van and she drove them out to the *Sky Queen*. There, she lent a hand at unloading the supplies from just inside the left hatch and got them into the van.

On the way back inside she asked if Tom could tell her anything about what he was going to be doing on the base.

"Not now, mind you. I know this is just a short visit. I was a-wonderin' if there would be something ta keep folks around here. You see, I've taken up with a young man in the town one but next to the east and would hate ta leave the Army ta be with him, and he has an ailing mother he can't leave. So..." and she said nothing more.

Tom took a little pity on her so he told her his plans, once fully approved, would call for some small level of security and hoped the Army might be induce to providing that.

"If not, and we will need to have a Security team here for at least a year, give me your contact information and I'll let you know what we find out."

They all got out and unpacked their equipment once reaching the nearest corner of the property they believed they might be building upon.

Two uniformed men in coveralls were leaning against a tractor about fifty feet to the right side, both men deeply involved in getting as much from the cigarettes they looked to be enjoying as possible. To Hank and Bud they seemed supremely disinterested in the Americans and their escort.

"That hec-o-thing o' theirs sure looks big; a lot bigger'n even a

Texas acre!" Chow commented on seeing the metal posts in the corners and the colorful nylon rope stretched around the site.

"Do you mean a *hectare*?" the Lieutenant asked the westerner. "Oh, and I love your accent."

Chow blushed. "Kinda find I'm partial to how your voice sounds. But, heck, or that heck-tare thing, I got my wife back at the *Queen* so I ought to not be chattin' ta a pretty, young thing like you."

Now, Elizabeth blushed. She was not used to having many men, but especially Americans and a kindly-sounding older American at that compliment her.

They smiled at each other and then turned away.

Tom, trying not to chuckle, spoke up. "That hectare doesn't sound like a very large plot of land, but it looks like about three times what we can ever use. Say, Lieutenant?" He turned to face her. "Is all that fencing coming down at some point, or it is remaining around this base?'

She didn't know but said she suspected, given the types of "things" that the grounds did or had contained, it would likely stay. "Why?"

"Well, I'm wondering if we will need to provide some fencing for surrounding our installation as an added precaution and to even keep any remaining base personnel away. Hmmm?" He turned back to the plot.

Hank was soon standing next to him with the theodolite over his shoulder. Trained at one point as a surveyor, his main duty on this trip was to survey the land and find the exact points for both of the intended buildings.

Suggesting that the chef keep their escort company while he and Hank hammered in a few stakes, Tom ducked under the rope, bringing the pack of wood stakes with colored plastic streamers with him.

As the two men walked away, the Army woman was asking Chow what made something a "Texas acre."

Using the GPS function of the surveyor's device, Hank took readings at each of the corners and then found the exact center point. In went the first of Tom's stakes, this one featuring the only red streamer in the bundle.

Within half an hour, more than half the plot had been marked at twenty foot intervals, checked and verified.

With the local weather being a bit on the chilly side, the Lieutenant offered to drive Chow back to the jet so he could bring out some hot coffee and some sandwiches for snacks.

Tom told them to have a good drive and that he and Hank were going to busy while they waited for them to come back in the van.

*　*　*　*　*

Everyone heard the sounds of a badly muffled truck approaching from the south. All heads turned in time to watch a battered British overland 4-wheel-drive racing toward the fence. It did not slow down. Instead, it hit the outer fence, broke through that and hit the inner fence. That, too, went down under the weight of the truck.

"I thought there were charges between those!" Tom shouted as they all turned to run back to the van.

"Disarmed a week ago!" she yelled. On seeing they were about to be cut off by the interloper, she screamed an order to "Halt!" Even though only Hank had any military experience, they came to an immediate standstill.

The truck didn't come to a complete stop before a single man jumped from it.

The crazed man pulled out what looked like an old military .45 caliber pistol, yanked it up with the muzzle pointing at Tom and pulled the trigger.

The weapon seemed to have jammed so the man, screaming something they barely had time or inclination to try to understand, shook the gun, violently. As it pointed in another direction it went off.

Lieutenant Gordon let out a shriek and dropped to the ground. "That bassa shot my foot!" she yelled as she clutched at her right boot.

As the man raised the gun a second time, everyone heard the unmistakable sounds of a large tractor-like piece of heavy equipment start up nearby. As all eyes swung to the sounds, a big tractor with the initials JCB on the side jerked forward heading right for the crazed man.

In seconds the wide steel blade on the front end hit him at about face level knocking him down. A gash on his lower face began pouring blood.

Two seconds later one of the unarmed Scottish men from the tractor jumped on the man, yanked him into a face down position and got a pair of very substantial handcuffs on him. He then started striking the man about the head screaming about having shot the female officer.

As this was happening, the JCB roared to life, and lurched

134

toward the struggling man. As it did it spun 180-degrees so its rear blade, a narrow trenching digger, could be lowered down over the man's back. The man who'd tackled their would be killer rolled to the side.

Tom and a few others, even though their lives had been saved, had to look away as they believed the man was about to be crushed.

CHAPTER 14 /
INITIAL TEST STATUS, IFFY

THE RETURN from Scotland was uneventful and everyone headed for home except for Tom and Gary. They walked quickly from the Barn to Security and into Harlan's office. There, Gary made a verbal report of the attempt on their lives, and how the Scottish military forces had dealt with the man responsible.

"Generally, I would not suggest that dragging a man by his belt would be anything other than a little humorous," the big man stated, "but their soldiers had already beaten him into semi-consciousness. Plus, they weren't much interested in attending to his wounds. Just hooked the JCB tractor's narrow blade to his pants and up he went."

Tom suppressed the memory of the man's own blood dripping onto the ground as the heavy machinery swung around with its load and headed to one of the miscellaneous buildings inside the fenced area.

At least the good news had been the steel toe protector in the Lieutenant's boots had prevented the attacker's bullet from doing more than crushing that inward. She had to be cut from the boot but she and her toes survived.

The head of Security sat in silence until Gary was finished before turning to Tom.

"Other than the obvious, like are you all okay and did the man give any impression of why he was trying to kill all of you, did you get any verbal clues or see anything my people might have missed during the excitement and their performing their jobs?"

Sitting in one of the chairs across Harlan's desk, Tom concentrated on recalling the events. A moment later he looked up.

"The man screamed something in some sort of Gaelic language. At least I think it was that. It sounded a lot like 'ma hurt the mo fast.' He said it several times as he was raising the gun."

Harlan had a little experience with multiple languages and believed he might understand what Tom had just related.

"If he actually stated, '*mhurt thu mo phàiste*,' then it sounds like he was accusing you of murdering his child!"

*　　*　　*　　*　　*

Harlan walked into the office just after Chow had left with the lunch dishes. "One of these days I'll get here just as he does and he'll tell me he has, for some unknown reason, a third helping and for me to sit and relax," the Security man said as he took a seat in the conference area.

Tom smiled. "You could always call ahead or come over a bit earlier. Always welcome, you know."

Ames nodded, but his face did not show any enjoyment.

"What's up?" Tom asked.

"Just what I was about to enquire," said Damon.

"What is up is that Barbara Felderson, our Security Chief out at the Citadel, has finished her investigation into the power reactor that went bad up in Canada. It isn't dire, but it isn't good. Come on over." He patted the chair next to his.

When all three men were seated he continued. "It would appear that a disgruntled former employee out in New Mexico sabotaged that rod more than a decade ago. No others have been found, so it might have been a one time anger thing."

"How?" Damon asked. "With all our checks and balances, how could one person do that and not have it discovered?"

"Same reason city governments find themselves prosecuting former finance people for misusing city funds, or building inspectors allow shoddy work to happen that leads to injuries or deaths. They are allowed to okay their own work! Nobody else has oversight so they take some money, cover it in paperwork, sign things off and until a disaster or audit, nobody else knows."

He told them the woman, Lawrencia Warhurst, had been on the final check team of three at the facility.

"She had been passed over for promotion to lead the team because she had a habit of sleeping in a bit too often. When she told the management out there she would quit unless they gave her the position, they told her she needed to take a week off to cool down.

"She did that, but when she came back it was just for a single shift. That is when we are pretty certain she did the sabotage. As you both should know, it wasn't dastardly damage, just that she inserted three of the pellets that normally go into the dampening rods right in the middle of that fuel rod."

"Right," Tom stated. "Dr. Slade told us it might have just burned off and the reactor returned to full operation in another five or six months."

"Whatever you say, Tom. The woman left the Citadel at the end of that shift and disappeared. She told people she was heading for

Kansas and a supposed family emergency but called in a week later to say she was quitting and restarting her life."

Tom asked, "Did she?"

Harlan shook his head. "Don't know, Tom. She effectively disappeared right after that. An old neighbor was interviewed who told the FBI the Warhurst woman came back for a couple hours, left with three suitcases and headed out of town. Since the only highway there goes just north and south, we have to believe she picked one and kept going."

Damon pursed his lips in thought. "Next steps?" he finally asked.

"I have Phil and Gary doing detailed Internet scans for any activity we can attribute to her. I had to wait for a search warrant to get her credit card numbers, any associated phones and a few other things, and from here it will take anywhere from hours to days. The FBI is also working from those same things and promise me that we'll hear from them even as they swoop in—if that is possible—to take her into custody."

Tom looked a little unsure as he asked, "And, we are certain she is the one who did the sabotage?"

With a nod, the Security man told them both, "We are absolutely certain. Her fingerprints are on one of those dampening slugs. Now, before you ask about how that is possible, she was not very smart about this. I think she didn't want any computer record of her actions using the Waldoes in that room so she did it manually. Probably picked up a bad dose of radiation."

"Anyone have an idea of what level?"

"If she isn't already deceased, she is likely to be either a very sick woman with little time left. We're even following up on hospital and mortician records for radiation poisoning deaths or even amputations of the arm she used. I will let you both know the moment I hear anything." With that, he stood and left the office.

"I probably ought to call Dr. Slade out at the Citadel and see if he is certain this was a one-time and single rod thing," Damon stated reaching for his phone. As he made the call, Tom slipped out of the office and headed down the hall to the large lab.

Ten minutes later Damon TeleVoc'd his son.

"Tom, The good news is that Dr. Slade tells me that one rod was and is the only one they have ever detected with any sabotage. He also said their security logs show that woman only came into the fill room for five minutes, barely long enough to fiddle with the one. So, I think we are okay."

Tom thanked him before turning back to his energy generator design. As he looked at it, he thought back, briefly, to the Warhurst woman and what a very short period of time it had required to ruin the operation of one reactor. He honestly had to admit he did not know her other than a vague impression they had been introduced once... at some point... and only a quick handshake sort of event. He could not recall her face or even any physical characteristic.

He shrugged now only considering how horrible she must have hated her boss and the Swifts to contemplate, much less accomplish, the sort of sabotage she'd committed. In the end it had been mostly a useless gesture, but a personally harmful one for her.

I have to make this new power generator system foolproof and tamper proof. Perhaps the whole antimatter approach is the best since it will be created on site with no human intervention!

His reverie was interrupted by a phone page from Trent.

"The Minister woman from Scotland in on line three, Tom. She asked if you could take an important and positive call?"

"You bet! Thank you." He pressed the line button. "Tom here, Madam Minister. I have been told by our secretary this is a positive call. Was he correct?"

"Oh, Tom. Your man was so absolutely correct. I have the most wonderful news for you. Full agreement has been given for your test project to proceed in the place we have discussed already. Just there and not in the more rural area you once suggested. If you ken my meaning?"

To Tom she had never sounded so Scottish than with that last question.

"Yes. That is wonderful news, and I do ken your meaning, ma'am. I want to thank you and everyone who took part in that agreement for this. I strongly believe we will all benefit."

* * * * *

When he was told of the news, Damon was excited for both the prospects of a new, clean power source, and for Tom who had been working so hard to achieve it.

"Do you have a complete design ready to put to the test?"

Tom had to admit he did not. "Not yet, but I do have a ninety-five percent good concept for the generators. They definitely will use the antimatter we generate on site to start the other reaction and that will self-sustain for many hours... in theory. Then, and before that sort of peters out we make a little more antimatter and inject that along with a bit more of the fuel to act as our positive matter, and the fusion keeps going."

"Of course you will use the heat generated to superheat a liquid and run that through a generator? I only ask because I honestly cannot see this functioning any other way. Unless..."

"Unless?" Tom asked.

"Yes. Unless you have magically come up with a way to turn that energy release into electricity with no interim step or steps."

The younger inventor had to tell his father he had no thought in mind for accomplishing that. "But, that isn't to say I won't be on the lookout!"

On returning to the lab he sat down and wrote up a couple notes regarding things that had come to mind during his recent discussion. One of them had to do with seeing if the mysterious beads and the cube he had created using the Space Friends' manufacturing box a few months earlier, could be used somewhere.

He was sitting there, very deep in thought, when Hank walked in and sat down. It took Tom a half-minute to look up to see who had entered.

"Hey, Hank. What brings you over to the lab?"

"Well, if you look on your calendar you might see a meeting we have scheduled, starting fifteen minutes ago. When I called over, Trent told me you had just left the big office, so I figured you'd be over soon. You did not come to me, so I am bringing the mountain to you."

The inventor blushed realizing he'd blown it.

"I got caught up in what this new antimatter-fired generator is going to need inside. Sorry. So," he said hitting the **RETURN** key to save out his notes before turning to the engineer, "please remind this old, absentminded inventor what the meeting is about."

Hank smiled at his younger boss and friend. "We were going to discuss the outer shell design with an eye toward whether the test and final units are just different sizes, or if they might be significantly different."

They began by pouring over the various designs Tom had managed to get from pencil sketches and into the CAD program as well as examining the model. The engineer then asked to review the drawings Bashalli had created of the outer look.

"One of the things I notice right off when comparing the inner workings with the outside is that it looks pretty tight inside, and especially space given to the collider equipment to make the antimatter. At least, when I think of the equipment we currently own. Are we going to use that for the test unit?"

Tom shook his head.

"I have been thinking we might make the antimatter here, or take it over mounted to the deck of *Goliath* like we did out in space, load it into a few magnetic containment units, and then... well, almost spoon feed it into the reactor while we check to see how long the actual reaction can be maintained without a little bump."

Hank scratched his left temple and nodded. "Okay. Do you have a reasonable idea of how long that might be?"

"In theory, and that's all we can have right now, it depends on at least two factors. Firstly, to what temperature can we get the fusion reaction initially? Then, what is the nature of the actual fuel we ultimately use?"

When Hank asked if the inventor had a solid idea of what that might be, Tom had a look of bemusement.

"I have been thinking along the lines of an isotope of hydrogen. I've toyed with the idea of tritium because it can be processed from lithium, but the world is using its lithium at a rather alarming rate. So, it will need to be deuterium."

"Right. Made pretty cheaply from seawater. That would be a good match for the Scotland site with its proximity to the ocean."

The two agreed it was looking as if the old Dounreay site would be a successful place to try out the antimatter power generator prototype. Of course, that still left the fueling and cooling needs for any future full-size locations.

It took seven weeks before Tom was prepared, for the most part, to run a test under very strict conditions. So strict he didn't want to do the test on the planet. Instead, he had his specialty team run off two minute charges of antimatter and store them in the same magnetic "flasks" he used in the *Galaxy Traveller*. These were self-powered when necessary and could also be connected to one of his smallest power pods for long-term operation.

The antimatter and matter reaction would take place inside a heavily-constructed Durastress ball of some four feet diameter with an empty interior of only two feet, that was coated inside and out with a quarter-inch of tomasite to hold in any pressure plus stray radiation. None was expected from this type of reaction, but Tom and Damon did not wish to take any chances.

Running into the left side of the reaction ball was a three-inch tube that would carry a cooled liquid form of sodium into the reaction where the fusion process would almost instantly heat it to nearly 620 degrees Fahrenheit (or 600 degrees Kelvin). Out it would shoot, mostly under its own pressure buildup, from the opposite side where it would loop into a spinning generator to make as much electricity as possible before it exited that four-foot cube and ran back around and into the reaction ball. During its time in the tube and when that was exposed to space, it would cool down to about 125 degrees which would be nearly 325 degrees K, allowing it to remain in liquid form.

Then, the cycle would repeat.

Tom's computations told him the nearly fifty gallons of the liquid sodium would race around the entire path about once every nine seconds. He hoped the generator would make its 440-volt output and at upwards of 5,000 watts and that this would continue for more than an hour or until he stopped feeding in the hydrogen isotope.

One of the many things he needed to check was the consumption rate of that isotope; the ship would carry about 10 liters of it. Unless he could keep the reaction going at a controllable rate—and his feeling was that internal pressure would assist in that—his supply of that isotope might run out before the end of the initial antimatter reaction.

Which would be fine. He was definitely more interested in the data than the electricity at this point.

Because the necessary cyclotron resided out on Fearing Island, Tom, Bud, Hank and Mr. Swift packed up and headed there in the *Sky Queen* on a Thursday morning. Starting the afternoon before, the nuclear team—the men and woman who had been Fermilabs' team before Enterprises bought the soon-to-be-scrapped equipment —had started making the necessary antimatter. The first tiny speck of it, or charge-1, was already installed into the first containment vessel with charge number two anticipated to be ready to head into space about an hour after the Enterprises team landed.

Damon had come down to hold several meetings while Tom and his team headed for an orbit around the Moon for their testing. When the time came for takeoff, he stepped outside the Administration building and stood watching the gigantic *Goliath* heading skyward.

On her circular deck just as she rose from the ground he'd spotted one of the largest nuclear power pods made out at the Citadel, Tom's slightly smaller test generator system, and a few things held under what he knew to be woven Durastress tarps. What those might be, he had no idea but had no time to inquire. In seconds, the ship was a dwindling speck in the sky, so he returned to the meeting room and sat back down.

In *Goliath*, Tom was setting a course that would steer them clear of all known objects in orbit. The relatively few tiny bits of assorted space junk would be smashed and destroyed if they hit any part of the ship, and would be deflected by the tarps that covered two heavy-gauge containers holding the individual antimatter containment flasks.

In less that two hours the ship had reached the orbital point, some one thousand miles above the lunar surface and everyone got up to check their part of the upcoming test and their equipment.

"Let's get suited up and get everything uncovered and ready to go," Tom requested. "Sorry for any manual labor out there, but I needed to have this test run more than I wanted to spend another week creating a self-loading system. So, and I plan to do this myself, the first and second charges of antimatter will be hauled over to the reactor, attached via a very strong bayonet-style mount, and then we all come back inside before Hank uses the Attractatron to lift the package off the deck and to move it about a half-mile away."

"Any danger to us if it... ummm, goes up?" Bud asked.

"Not unless there is a surprise concentration of nearly solid matter out there, flyboy. The distance is only to get clearance in case the sodium cooling system ruptures. Even then, it should only travel a few hundred feet before it solidifies and Hank can also use the Attractatron to grab and hold it off."

Nine minutes later Tom and the rest of the crew opened the large airlock at the base of the control tower column and stepped onto the deck. With no artificial gravity that could cover the expanse, and Tom not of the belief in the science fiction magnetic shoe approach, they used the maneuvering backpacks each wore to move around.

While Bud and Hank uncovered the first of the containment flask storage boxes, Tom made a visual check of the reactor.

Everything seemed to be one hundred percent perfect.

He floated over and was in time to take a handoff from Bud of the first flask of antimatter. With the flyer's assistance, he turned around and floated back to the reactor. While the others watched he set one end into a recess on the side of the reactor and pressed it in. Then, he gave it a quarter turn clockwise. His hands felt the clicks indicating it was now locked into place and ready.

Tom backed off and told everyone they could head back inside.

"Okay," Hank radioed back. "I'll head up to the Attractatron controls while the rest of you get things ready. Please give me a one-minute fore-notice so I can get things energized and aimed."

The men needed seven minutes to position everything and to have the experimental package floating away to its test and safety point.

Tom agreed to do a final systems check. In a couple minutes he made the call to his engineer and the process of starting the new antimatter-fired reactor began. And, as quickly as it started it came to a halt!

"Rats!" he exclaimed wondering what might have gone wrong.

"What can we do, Tom?" Bud asked, a look of worry crossing his face. "I hope we don't need to jettison that test thing."

With a visual sweep of his readouts, the inventor shook his head. "First, I have no idea why that didn't work. Then, I also do not see anything registering that would say we have to get rid of that and head out of here."

After giving everyone a two-hour break, Tom set about looking at all the recorded information from the initial test. At best, the results had been on the "iffy" side. The reaction had most definitely started as the minute bit of antimatter was magnetically shoved into contact with a larger piece of matter and the deuterium fuel was sprayed onto the miniature conflagration.

It had nearly sustained the consumption of the fuel, but the temperatures inside the reaction chamber cooled so suddenly that once the initial reaction concluded—about five hundred seventy milliseconds after it commenced—things just petered out. And, a scant two seconds later there was nothing happening inside the sealed chamber.

He knew there would be a similar result from a second experiment and so Tom decided to pack things back up and head home to try to figure out what went wrong.

CHAPTER 15 /
BASHALLI'S DAY OF INSPIRATION

BY THE next day Tom received word from Harlan that the man in Scotland had been identified as a mercenary for hire. His name was Duncan McNaire, had an extensive list of previous charges, many for menacing people he evidently did not know, and had spent about a third of his fifty-two years of life in one prison or another. In several cases those had been in foreign nations.

"McNaire survived in spite of his treatment and is in a prison hospital in Glasgow, the Barlinne Prison. His wounds were described by one of the physicians as 'egregious' but he is expected to survive and face life in an even more secure and harder time facility."

Tom was both relieved the man had not perished, and at the same time was coming to grips with the incredible anger he felt at a man who would have shot everyone in his group had his gun not jammed. That could have started with Tom!

When he asked if Harlan knew of the man's reason, Ames shrugged.

"A check is being made of his finances. If he has had a sudden increase recently, my guess is he was paid for the attack. He has never shown much reluctance to harm others for money, one of the many reasons he is likely to never breathe air outside a prison for the remainder of his life."

Their talk turned to the inventor's hope that the others were taking advantage of counseling that Enterprises offered all employees in times of stress or trauma. Doc Simpson had cornered Tom an hour after he arrived back at the company with the demand that he, Tom, sit and talk things over for at least half an hour.

"It won't take a lot out of your day, but if you can think back to when Sandy was kidnapped back when she was, what... eighteen or nineteen? She did not seek out help and it showed. That's when you and Bud and Bashalli took her to Seattle and entertained the depression out of her."

Tom lightly grinned. "Are you asking me to go to Seattle with you, Doc?"

The physician, who had known Tom since the boy was about fifteen, snorted. "Hardly! But, I am very serious about you needing to unburden yourself of things that are starting to gather inside." He decided to go for broke as he sensed Tom's reluctance. "It is either on a voluntary basis, here and now, or I can go tattle to your dad. As an executive here at Enterprises, you have a signed agreement to attend to such things as this via the best professional mechanisms."

Tom sat back and sighed. He did have a few things going through his mind that he could not shake. He nodded and sat forward again.

Over more than an additional hour he unburdened himself to the man who had saved his life more times than could be counted, or remembered, and who was also a friend.

The tears came more than once as Tom told him of his one and only thought at the moment the gun had raised and clicked, but had not fired.

"All I could do was think of how I was letting Bash and the kids down... once again!"

Doc gave him a moment before asking, "How were you letting them down? To anyone's understanding, you did not court this deadly advance. You did not foolishly stand there, chest bared and daring the man to shoot. Did you?"

"No. Of course not."

"No. Of course you didn't do that. You have a good and level head on those shoulders I have patched up a couple times. You have a wife who actually understands what it is that makes up Thomas Swift. She might feel occasional fear over these things, but I believe you do a pretty good job of minimizing her emotional exposure to the worst."

Doc offered to arrange for some family therapy in case Tom's wife or his older two children had any fears over his recent experience.

By the time he left the physician's office, Tom felt much better about things and realized that he was not there only because of luck. He was there to continue doing what he did because of everything that had and had not happened in that place and at that time.

He called Bashalli to tell her he was coming home early. He felt they had a few things to talk about.

As an inventor, Tom understood the usefulness of keeping track of all past experiments and even miscellaneous notes. On more than just a few occasions, either a thought of his own, or something casually mentioned by someone else, had him searching databases and even old files kept in the permanent archive building at Enterprises for something to remind him of a previous... something.

148

This day it was a mention by his wife the previous evening as they discussed the lack of success with the first antimatter test in space that sent him into search mode.

Bashalli was not a scientific thinker by characteristic or by training. She was an artist and often saw things more in terms of shapes, colors and patterns than in logical ways. But, when Tom spoke of the enormous heat necessary to sustain the reaction—and even if she mostly missed the deuterium part—her mind returned to an occasion before Tom had even proposed to her.

At that time, she had been nearly bowled over to find out that Tom and his father both knew the actual President of The United States and were on speaking terms with the man. To top it off, he had even complimented her on her beauty, something she remembered as if it has just been a day or two before.

When she mentioned that incident and the invention Tom had devised, asking if that was the sort of heat he meant, it caused Tom to sit and stare at her for so long she thought she'd said something wrong.

When he assured her that her idea was an incredible one and that he needed to rush back to Enterprises, she begged him to make some notes and to do his searching the next day.

Whether she had exhibited her fear or not on hearing about the Scottish "incident," it had affected her strongly and she wanted him to remain close to her that night.

Tom acquiesced on seeing the look in her eyes.

So, today he was at work and had just checked into the Archive Building with his iris scan, palm print and lengthy alpha-numeric code sequence. The computerized security system responded with, "*Recognized: Tom Swift. Authorization: full access with no restrictions.*"

When his wife's very own voice inquired what he needed to gain access to—Tom never tired of hearing the official voice of Enterprises and its products that had been recorded by her a few years earlier—he told the computer:

"Access to all files and notes on Cyclonic Eradicator project."

"*Location desired?*"

"Physical archives."

A door in a nearby wall opened exposing the elevator to take him down to the files room.

Once there, "Bashalli" asked him what files he specifically needed.

When he told "her" she responded with the specific aisle, cabinet and even the drawer number where they could be found. After accessing that location Tom set the three folders in a tray next to the elevator asking the files be copied and sent to his computer.

Back at his desk an hour after first leaving the office, Tom used the access code he'd been given to open the set of digital files. Then, he spent the rest of the day pouring through everything, being reminded of several aspects that had slipped his mind over the intervening years... more than a decade of them.

Almost at the time he needed to head for home, he located the notes and specifics of the thermal energy ray he'd built to pour incredible power into the water of a swirling hurricane or even tropical storm that split the molecules of hydrogen and oxygen apart, excited them so much the hydrogen exploded furiously consuming the oxygen and effectively blowing apart the storm.

He made a fast call to his father's desk where the older man listened and agreed it was a very important thing to experiment with.

"If that is the answer to starting or sustaining the reaction you need, then we might need to investigate what happened all those years ago and come to the conclusion that you actually created a fusion reaction back then!"

Tom arrived home in a better mood than he'd been in for several weeks. So much so that he held Bashalli in his arms, kissed her with a passion he had not had for those same weeks, and danced her across the room. All this to the amusement of his three children, but especially Bart who laughed and laughed at what he believed were their silly antics.

When she disentangled herself from his embrace, she casually asked what might have him in such a good mood. She secretly believed she knew, but wanted him to have his moment.

"*Your* idea," he said emphasizing it was all thanks to her mention of the Eradicator project, "was an absolute winner, Bash. I found all the notes in the archives, just as you thought I would. And, the best part of it is I am certain I can apply some of that technology in this new generator project. Even dad thinks this could be the secret winning element!"

By noon the following day he had come up with a way to include his energy beam technology into his little test antimatter reactor as a sort of preheater plug of the sort diesel engines had relied on for more than one hundred years. In this case it would preheat the chamber as well and impart a blast of heat into the deuterium fuel as the first of it was injected into the small maelstrom that was the antimatter and matter explosion.

The actual work took nine days, but on the tenth day he and his small crew took off from Enterprises in the *Sky Queen* with every part of the new equipment to be installed into the reactor that was waiting for them under guard and inside a heavily protected hangar at the island base.

Together with Hank, the two men installed and swapped over from the old equipment to the new and tested every circuit both in the reactor as well as on the *Goliath* that would, again, take them out to orbit the Moon for their next test.

"We'll take the night off and head up tomorrow morning. If all goes well, we will be back on the ground about thirty hours after we depart. Get a good sleep, please."

Twenty-nine hours after leaving the ground on Fearing, Tom and his team returned all with huge smiles on their faces. The firing up of the reactor had taken an extra two seconds while the first of the deuterium fuel had been nearly exploded just before the antimatter had been introduced. As matter and antimatter hit each other, the heat factor had risen to nearly sun-hot temperatures, but as Tom noted with glee, as more deuterium was introduced, the reaction continued.

It was only at hour nine the reaction began to cool enough Tom believed he needed to send in the second shot of antimatter.

"Did that do it?" Bud asked watching Tom's face more than he was watching the instruments.

Tom nodded and began to laugh.

"Bud... and everyone," he called out to the other in the upper level of the living area, "we have success. Now, without having a continuous supply of antimatter up here, or the fuel for that matter, we will stop the reaction in about nine more hours, check everything, pack up and go home. I suggest a rest period for all of you while I monitor things. See you all in five hours."

After landing and asking that the reactor be packed up for a return to Enterprises—it would be picked up the following day—the men headed back to Shopton and a good night's sleep.

Now that he had the secret to a successful small-scale reactor using non-nuclear ingredients and technology, Tom needed to create a test system to take to Scotland. This included the systems to generate the antimatter, a scaled up version of his preheat system, and everything necessary to run in a self-contained and self-fueling single case device.

"Do you have a target size," Damon asked as they had coffee a week after the successful lunar test.

Tom slowly allowed a little breath to escape through his nose before answering. "I believe, if I want this to all be inside one building, that it will need to be as wide as the current cyclotron—about forty feet across at the base, with everything above that down to reduced scale. So, I'm thinking this first one will be about thirty-eight or so feet tall. Circular rather than a cube, of course, and if possible installed about one hundred feet from the ocean."

"I see. Are you proposing to use salt water for cooling?"

Tom was nodding but then stopped. "Okay," he stated a bit guiltily, "and there will be a desalination system set up between the water and the generator."

Swift Enterprises already built a mid-size desalination system for use in small communities close to a body of salt water. Its output would be more than the test generator could ever use, but as Tom had discovered, the similar desalination plant at the base in Scotland had been shut down rather than repaired a month earlier when the seals inside had begun to deteriorate. Since that time, all water had to be trucked in.

Because of newer technology and materials, the Swift DeSal-1 unit was expected to run for a dozen years before anything needed to be checked or replaced, so it would do for the installation's needs, including some small level of personnel the Scottish Parliament had agreed to leave on the site to monitor the generator after the Swifts had run their initial weeks of tests.

It would need a few people there at all times to monitor both the reactor as well as the power being generated and sent into the nearby trunkline for distribution to the local area.

As each day passed, Tom watched all the necessary things come together to construct the test facility. His schedule called for them to complete pouring the base for everything in just another eight weeks. This would give the pad a full ten days to set and be ready for them to land and build.

Knowing the generator's weight allowed him to decide that steel rods for strength were not going to be necessary. Instead, he would send over a bundle of about one hundred pounds of Durastress strands that would be mixed in to give the concrete an additional forty percent strength factor, without adding any weight.

All that would allow the base and the structure to be built a little closer to the edge of the available land and not put any stresses or be subject to ground shift due to weight.

When he traveled over to look at the site just a few days before the concrete was to be poured, a team was setting out the forms for the forthcoming work. In all, the perimeter of the pad would extend five feet wider than the structure and feature a one-foot wall to keep any leaking water contained. The free space was nearly ten percent greater in capacity than the amount of water inside at any given moment.

"I must say that is looking like we are in for an impressive sort of installation, Tom," came the Minister's voice from behind him. Turning to face her, he smiled.

"Sneaking up on a poor American, Madam Minister?"

"Tom? If you will do me the favor of just calling me Jacquie when we are out here, please?"

"Of course. And, I hope what you see in your mind turns out to be impressive to you, but not so much that it attracts attention. The last thing we want is for this to have the press flying all around at all times of the day or night. In fact, the building will appear to be more a water storage tank than anything exotic."

She returned his smile before turning serious. "I need to ask you how you feel about the, uhh, attack on you and your people?" She added that she was embarrassed about the incident and wanted to do whatever was necessary to make amends.

"For myself, I have had a good talk with a very wise man followed by another talk with my exceptional wife, and I feel better." He glanced around for a moment. "Since this is the approximate area where things happened, I admit to a moment of apprehension when I stepped out here today. I am over that."

"And, the people who were with you that day? Are they all alright?"

He said they were as far as he knew.

"How is Lieutenant Elizabeth Gordon? I've heard her foot was not badly damaged."

Jacquie smiled. "She is so good that I have suggested she take over the security detail here to protect both government property as well as your installation."

Together, they walked around the perimeter of the circular forthcoming pad discussing the next steps. When he told her the installation was going to take only three days from delivery of everything—and they were bringing a desalination plant—she could scarcely believe how fast that would be.

Or, the fact the personnel remaining at the decommissioned base would be allowed to take advantage of the water.

During this they had been looking at the area around them. Where once more than a dozen buildings stood, there were only three remaining. Most of the rubble piles that had been buildings were now gone. One still standing was the Administration building they had their first meeting in, one was the housing barracks, and the final one was the only remaining reactor on the grounds. It was now scheduled to be shut down just one week after Tom's anticipated energizing of the new test system and the spent and remaining fuel rods removed by a robot and stored in a concrete and lead-lined bunker sitting over closer to the airfield where they would remain basically forever.

The next time he saw her was three weeks later when he came over to inspect and to start the antimatter reactor. Before she could allow him to proceed, she had one question.

"Can you assure me, officially, that this is not a nuclear reactor? I ask that officially and as a representative of the Scottish government and in the name of the people of Scotland."

Tom nodded. "I can assure you, your government and the people of Scotland this is not a nuclear reactor, Madam Minister. I will also tell you this technology has been tested by my company recently with one hundred percent success."

Minister Livingston nodded and smiled. "Then, by acclamation of the Parliament of Scotland and the Prime Minister of our body of government, and in the name of Greater Britain of which we are no longer a part of but maintain favored nation status, I give you permission to start your new generation generator."

Tom bowed. "Thank you, Madam Minister." He turned to face the entrance to the circular building and smiled. One of his structural engineers had spotted the similarities between this structure and a water storage tank located atop one of the many small hills around Shopton, and had suggested adding the same sort of hatch you might see on such a structure along with a ladder heading down one side—and totally locked away behind an unbreakable Durastress cage to keep anyone from climbing onto it.

With no windows and only the partially disguised door looking like a steel entrance hatch on a ship, it was easy to see this as only a tank and nothing more.

Tom turned and motioned to the Minister asking if she wanted to come inside for the startup.

"It won't be very impressive," he assured her, "mostly because the actual controls are inside the desalination building over behind you."

"You go ahead and do what you need. I'll stand out here looking all innocent and like this is something a Minister of Parliament always comes to. You know... dedicating a water tank?"

He did not close the door as he reached over to pull down an old-fashioned electricity breaker. Now, everything outside would control everything inside.

Re-closing and locking the hatch, Tom and Minister Livingston headed for the nearby building. Inside she watched in fascination as his fingers moved over various panels and pressed buttons here and there all the while watching a set of readouts.

In the next room water could be heard starting to move though the pipes.

"How long will it take before you generate power?"

Without going into any details of the process, he responded that the "warm-up" would take four hours. What he did not say was this was the time when the first of the antimatter was being created.

"If you wish, we can go to my aircraft, the *Sky Queen*, and be comfortable while all that happens," he offered.

Hank, who had been standing outside, offered to monitor everything and to keep the inventor, and Minister, updated with any information.

By the time they returned—with Chow serving a light lunch to them—the process had started.

The test antimatter generator had begun to whine as the generator turbine was spinning and electricity was heading from the generator and into the nearby power lines.

CHAPTER 16 /
(NOT TOO) HEAVY EQUIPMENT

WITH THE much smaller test version of the antimatter generator now up and running in Scotland, and proving to be both a success from a physical ongoing as well as power generating sense—just having passed week six of continuous operation—Tom turned his efforts to planning for the British Columbia placement.

Soon to be a twin tower approach, each one likely to be more than four times as tall as the Dounreay generator, the site had been chosen from among fifteen parcels of government-owned land that had little, if any, commercial value. Each had been selected for its distance from populated areas along with accessibility for both construction crews and for getting all building supplies in with minimum fuss.

Of the two finalist sites—at least so in Tom's opinion—one was close to a former surface mine area that could be leveled and easily allow for the landing of any of the Swift's cargo jets. It did not have sufficient area for a runway, but the vertical take-off and landing nature of the aircraft meant it would be just fine.

Either a series of trucks or several heavy lift helicopters would do the job of final site transport for people and supplies.

The other site was about thirty miles away and did not have any place ready to use for landing or staging materials, but it did have a larger river closer in case it might be necessary to assist the natural airflow with a water jacket for cooling. Tom was considering this need based on the second cooling jacket he'd added to the Dounreay site shortly after it had begun operation.

Tom, Bud, Hank, Red Jones and Slim Davis flew out to B.C. in the small cargo jet Tom and Bud had tested months earlier. With the ability to land vertically it gave them both the size and abilities they required.

As the five men took the one-mile hike into site one, Tom made a series of notes on his tablet computer regarding the state of the current road, the temperature—which for July was pleasantly cool—the pathway, and other aspects of the surroundings.

"Beautiful spot," Red commented.

"Kind of like some of the hills in northeastern Washington where I grew up," Slim added. "Nothing too steep and a lot of greenery around. And, unlike Washington State, which is close to Canada, this *is* Canada!" He grinned.

Tom agreed. "If we do need some source of water my guess is there will be enough to be had if we drill down a few hundred feet. Might even consider building a pond or semi-enclosed tank for storage of what we need."

Tom and Hank spent the first half hour performing LASER measurements of the cleared ground to ensure there would be little or no need to remove any existing plants.

After kicking at the ground and with Bud pulling out a collapsible shovel and digging down about a foot so they could take a soil sample back, the team walked back down the hill to the waiting aircraft.

With great dismay they all could see that one of the tires on the left side had been slashed open!

They immediately crouched and looked around them. Nothing and nobody could be seen. Hank and Bud told the others they were going to check out the aircraft while Tom got on his satellite phone to call back to Enterprises.

Nothing other than the tire—and the nearby machete that had been used and abandoned—were found. Hank carefully wrapped the large knife in a length of plastic packing and set it in a storage locker inside while Tom made the decision to take off without trying to change out the tire.

"Whoever did that obviously isn't too bright," Bud said. "Heck. If they saw us come in, they would have seen we did that vertically. The tires are just so much padding under there. Plus, they only got the one of that side."

Red asked, "Are they total amateurs, or was that just a little message? My vote is for them being new at this and fools."

Tom agreed, and with Red siting in the right seat, he got them into the air a few minutes later. They turned toward Vancouver where they set down at the airport and took advantage of the facility's commuter aircraft lift to get that set of wheels off the ground enough to change to the spare they were carrying.

An hour later they were heading to site number two.

"Why don't I stay here with my hand close to an eGun just to make certain nobody comes to fiddle with the jet this time?" Hank offered.

While the others headed the four hundred yards to the possible site, Hank sat in the cockpit watching the monitors giving him all-around view of the area.

When Tom and company came back in less than an hour, he reported no activity had been seen.

"Good. Before we leave we need to head back to Vancouver so I can let the Mounties know about the damage and even to see if they wanted to lift some fingerprints off that machete."

On the way, Tom made a call and spoke to the Commandant's adjutant, a man who practically begged to be allowed to come to the airport with his fingerprint and latent evidence team.

"If we can get just one good print, and match that to any of the many morons who do these things, we'll get them in jail before they can blink!"

Tom wondered if the man were not just a little too eager and was overstating the ability of his people, but agreed.

"We should set back down in eighteen minutes. The last time they directed us to one of the four parking areas to the west of the main terminal. You ought to find us around there. If we are moved, I'll call this number and hopefully you'll get the info."

As they winged back over the U.S. border a while later, Slim asked what Tom thought of the sites.

"I like the first one better than the second, but no matter what we choose, and as long as the Canadian government lets us build, I believe we will be able to bring in most of our heavy equipment, just not too heavy. The big stuff might have problems negotiating the hill."

"What has the Scotland site shown you about the natural approach to cooling, skipper?" Bud asked as they were walking around the pathways of the main building area at Enterprises one afternoon the following week. Nothing had come from the machete; no fingerprints had been left, and it was an old one with no way to trace who had bought it or when.

"Basically, one we knew going in and one we found out. Before the unit had run a full day we found we needed to add a one-inch thick water jacket just outside the hardened Durastress retention case, along with a fairly thin radiator band at the top of the containment plate to take out some of the excess heat that was building up. It keeps that generator at a nice temperature. Luckily, we had sufficient clear space for that inside."

"Yeah. Hank told me about that. What's the other one?"

Tom grinned, ruefully. "Well, after two days of operation we noticed something on the video monitor. Each time a new speck of antimatter gets added, and the Eradicator's heat beam sends thing back up to running temp, the casing for the reactor, which is, I need to say, not perfectly circular for a variety of reasons... anyway, it sort of bulges."

Bud's eyes went wide. "Bulges?"

The inventor's head tilted to the right. "Yeah. By only a few millimeters, but it definitely bulges out for about thirty seconds. Before you ask, it's nothing I believe that is going to do any harm to the generator and certainly won't cause it to blow out, but it is annoying and puzzling to see."

"Oh. What can you do? Or, do you just not do anything?"

Tom thought a moment. "I believe we ought to attend to that in the small generator as a proof of concept, but especially in the full-sized ones. There, the bulge could be a quarter inch or so. That, I do not want to just let go in case it is a project killer."

He was interrupted by a TeleVoc call from Phil Radnor.

"Tom? Harlan is on the phone with the Mounties but asked me to call you to see if you can come over in a few. I'm fairly sure it has to do with that tire sabotage the other day."

Tom promised to be at the office in less than ten minutes.

"Tell him I am on my way."

When Tom stepped into the Security chief's office, Harlan was still on the phone. He pointed to a chair across the desk for Tom to take, and then another one for Phil who had stepped into the room.

"Right," he said to whomever was on the other end of the line. "I understand that, but I would hope you could admit this does not have the stuff of making for our unquestioned trust in the Mounties." He paused, then, "Please explain how 'losing the files all of a sudden' makes any sense? Did someone there strap roller skates on those files and let them escape? Your Commandant assured me, personally I will add, that your records were among the most complete rundown on these ecoterrorists to be found. Now, you say they cannot be found. So?"

He looked at Tom and Phil with a tired roll of his eyes.

"Yeah. You do that and have her call me. If I do not hear from you or her within the next hour then we supply all our own protection and the Mounties will have to sit on the sidelines with a whole heap of egg on your faces." Another pause for a listen and another eye roll." It is a well-known saying. Egg on your face? You've honestly never heard that? Tell Commandant Dimmock about that missing link in your education. Goodbye."

160

He hung up and dropped his face forward, his head landing in his arms and remaining there for more than twenty seconds before he looked up.

"I was so hoping the two of you might have crept out while I had a brief meltdown. But," and he sat up straight, "since you are here, it would appear that not only has the RCMP 'lost' the machete used to cut the jet's tire, but their files with the fingerprints of about fifty ecological terrorists they have arrested over the years are gone. Paper files, missing, and computer files seemingly erased!"

Tom raised a hand. "Teacher? Can I make a suggestion?"

Harlan feigned looking around the room before coming back to the inventor. "Okay. What is that?"

"Call them back and tell them we will resurrect their files if they give us permissions and access. I don't want to get accused of hacking, but unless the actual server those files were sitting on has been destroyed, and they have steadfastly refused to do any backing up of anything, I am about as certain I can find them as anything I've ever done."

Harlan knew Tom was not making an idle boast. Three times in the past his skills had saved vital files that had been considered to be lost. Each time it took him fewer than nine minutes once he had the names of what to look for.

Without another question, Harlan picked up his receiver and pressed the buttons to do a recall of the previous number.

"Now, just stop saying anything and listen, Sergeant Preston. And, yes I do know the reference but I also know it is your name. So, we have the means to get your files, computer type, not paper based, back to you so you can do your job. I honestly do not give a... darn about protocols or permissions, I just want you to get us into your computer and let us save your bacon. That is another saying you may not be familiar—okay. Fair enough. Just not your Canadian back bacon, okay?" He listened and smiled. "Sure."

As the man on the other end placed him on hold, Harlan covered his mouthpiece and told the other two, "Preston agrees they blew this one and while they try to find out how... or for my money *who* did those files in, he says he thinks we ought to be allowed to... Yes, I'm here and listening... Good. Connect us, please."

"He found Cheryl Dimmock. Oh, hey, Cheryl. It's Harlan in case your Preston didn't mention it. Now, before you say much of anything, he told us about the missing paper and trashed computer files. Tom Swift can and will get those computer files back and in about the same time it will take for you to walk a permission slip over to someone at a higher level... Oh, nobody higher? Then, can we please get you back up and running so we can all get the bad guys?... Cheryl? I owe you the best darned dinner in British Columbia. Let me put Tom on the line."

Two minutes later the inventor asked to use one of the computers in a quiet office.

Eleven minutes later he came back to say he had found the files. They had not been trashed but had been placed into an invisible directory and that had a cryptic name.

Harlan got a phone call just before quitting time to say that three of the eco-saboteurs had just been arrested with a bunch of photos of Tom and most of his team that had come to British Columbia, along with a hand-written note telling them to:

Do as much possible damage, even if that means taking a few people out, and do it quickly! These Yanks are out to kill the lot of us and we cannot be stopped!

"Mr. Swift," began the Minister for Mineral Exploration, "The Canadian government readily acknowledges the contributions your company has made to our nation in the past. What with all the ore you discovered while surveying for our version of your speedy railroad, is of course to what I refer, we are a stronger nation. But, even with that we cannot give you a pass on heavy restrictions for this... ummm, what was it again?" He consulted some notes on the table before him. "Oh, right. For this exceptional heavy cable transmission system you propose."

He stood there looking at the inventor, and Tom could almost see a glimmer of intelligence in his eyes. The problem was, there was also a slight nervousness in those eyes the owner might be on a totally wrong track.

"Mr. Minister, and all you other august members of the Canadian Parliament. It would seem there is a small level of misunderstanding and that may be due to insufficient information from Swift Enterprises." He looked around the room all the while thinking, *Except we laid it all out in that two-hundred page report!* "So, let me go back over a few of the items that will, I believe, allay your fears regarding our intentions."

He told them of the power generating systems and how the test generator in Scotland was a rousing success. He reminded them of their own troubles in getting electricity to many of the areas within their largest Provinces, Yukon and Nunavut, and how he intended to run lines into five distribution points from which the Canadian

162

power companies might sent it along to those in great need. Tom knew that the tribal leaders in Nunavut would not allow any power generating facility within their borders. So, he was building in the northern portions of British Columbia.

"Each and every line out of the generating facilities—facilities that will be as out of the way of anything as possible—will be laid underground inside our very secure and unbreachable tomasite and Durastress piping. That pipe will be laid concurrent to the cabling being constructed at a rate of about two miles per day."

He could see the Minister rising again and sought to cut him off.

"And, I assure you all that no heavy equipment will be involved. Your own internal companies running anything from four-inch— uhh, about eight centimeter—water or natural gas pipes typically plow a swath of from three meters out to fifteen meters devastating that area for many years. Our equipment, on the other hand, runs on low-pressure pneumatic tires and merely presses the natural grasses and such down, but does not destroy anything. The actual hole dug to accommodate the cable will be fewer that eleven centimeters wide and about two meters deep."

"But, what about all that heavy equipment you will need to use?" The man's voice was almost pleading for Tom to agree with him.

Tom shook his head. "We use no heavy equipment, sir. The total weight of one of our machines might be higher than an average family sedan, but the wide and squishy tires spread that out so any square centimeter receives less than half that weight of an auto weighing in at some three thousand pounds, or—"

"There is no need to try to do the conversion, Mr. Swift," the woman Minister to the questioner's right told him. "We regularly do such math in our heads because we can't all agree on whether to remain with the metrics or go back so we more closely work with the United States."

"Thank you, Ma'am," Tom responded with a small nod and a smile. Turning back to the main body, he continued. "There will be some areas where we traverse very rocky soil or even mountainous parts of the country where we will need to use our earth blasters, which simply use great heat to melt and vaporize the rocks leaving behind a clean trench. Those would be filled back in as we pass over them setting the pipe and cabling inside."

The committee meeting broke up ten minutes later with Tom agreeing to resubmit his working documents, some of which had been mislaid (although those Ministers told him they were never received.)

Tom and Bud were flying home thirty minutes later with Bud

163

taking the controls. He understood his friend needed some time to think a few things over.

In his mind Tom had been going over what else he intended to use by way of equipment. Foremost would be his one-time revolutionary flying vehicle he had called a Workcopter before changing that to Workchopper. Designed for skywriting he quickly repurposed one to lay out his repelatron skyway in a small third world nation. The twin rotors on either side of the boxy fuselage had been—he had to admit—actually too small for the craft.

Because of this they needed to spin at about twice what normal helicopter blades turned putting a lot of stress on the hubs. Those hubs had nearly given out during that first major adventure and had been replaced about every three hundred operating hours since.

Still, the aircraft worked for some interesting projects.

Now, he intended to rebuild one of the remaining two of them using similarly-angled twin rotors as he used in his Whirling Ducks. The blades could be considerably longer and intermeshed directly over the center of the body. By using these better-designed rotors, the craft could now lift about three times the load as before, the new QuieTurbines that powered them could turn them at a more normal rate, and with advances in materials they would last thousands of hours between maintenance.

Using a pair of Tom's smaller power pods the new version could remain airborne for more than ten hours at a time, only pausing about twelve hours at night so the pods could regenerate their electricity capacity. Tom had a better plan in mind.

When he was asked about them by Bud as they flew back to the U.S. and Shopton, Tom smiled.

"We need to be able to resupply the trenching and laying equipment so those can operate nearly around the clock. What I'm going back to calling a WorkCopter will be able to fly at about two-fifty to supply depots we set up, pick up enough of the piping and cabling for about three miles of installation and bring it all back fast enough to keep things running."

"Individual sections of cable?" the flyer asked.

"Well, one cable mega-spool run for every four of the piping. We're going to build in waterproof quick plugs on both ends so it should take less than three minutes to change from one spool to the next."

"I see, only I really don't. How do you get one end into the pipes and still be able to connect pipe after pipe? I mean, it sounds counter to what I think I believe." His eyes told the inventor he was seriously worried Tom's scheme might have a flaw.

"Okay," the inventor said huffing out a breath. "I forgot to tell you that at the very lead end of each cable run will be a small robotic vehicle that will pull it through a run of already laid pipes. It'll have five drive wheels and the power to pull the cable all the way through to the next interconnect point, which will be where pipe work pauses waiting for the next spool to arrive and the ends mated."

"Got it!" He paused then asked another question that popped into his mind. "So, if you have the one WorkCopter getting rebuilt, and it can run about ten hours or so, *and* if you plan to work around the clock... uhhh, how does that work with the power pods?"

Tom chuckled a little. "That's the easy part, Bud. We'll have three sets of them with quick swap connectors. As soon as it sets down to pick up any load after about hour seven of runtime, a crew pulls the tired ones, shoves in a new set and runs the self-checks. It will take less time to swap power than it requires to put a new load under the cabin and get in cinched down."

The flyer grinned. He knew his friend generally thought of everything, but always felt obligated to mention such things. At least three times in the past decade such queries had let Tom to rethink some things, and that had led to improvements.

CHAPTER 17 /
SITE CLEARING (AND A LITTLE BIT MORE, STARTING WITH A CAPITAL T)

ONCE ALL permissions came through from the Canadian government, Tom set the gears in motion to get their site clearing equipment up to the selected location in northern British Columbia.

For the most part, all that needed being done was to level out the specific placements for the two towers, use one of his earth blasters to dig down about twenty holes around the perimeter of each to a depth of two hundred feet and then to fill those holes with Durastress rebar-reinforced concrete piers everything would be held on and secured to the bedrock.

Unfortunately, Tom's first choice of land had proved to be a no-go as it was directly under the flight path for Vancouver's International Airport, so this second—still more that adequate—property had been secured.

Well, that plus widening and repairing the one-lane, heavily rutted dirt road that vaguely followed a nearby stream from a Provincial highway five miles away.

When he and Bud arrived, half of the advance crew had completed the surveying of the road and taken core samples to determine suitability for the roadway they required. Only one place had shown any tendency to slide, that being a sandy patch over a basalt skid of rock just thirty-four feet down.

"We're of a couple minds on this, skipper," the foreman reported.

"I'm listening, Emelia. What are the best options?"

She smiled brightly at her boss. "Either we float a ninety-foot section over the top with enough arch to help support weight, or we dig the section out to rocks, possibly sink some vertical support beams before filling back in with the stuff we took out. That would have added binders so it should not shift."

Tom knew the woman was one of the top individuals in her field and had been "in the real world" for eleven years before joining Enterprises three years earlier. He trusted her judgement, so he asked what her choice would be.

"From the standpoint of keeping the environmentalist off our backsides, the right thing to do is the dig out and fill back in method. It will take a bit longer and be a bit more expensive, but we can replant with native flora so a year from now you see nothing other than the wider road just like everywhere else along this stretch."

"That sells me," he responded. With a motion to Bud the two climbed back into the small ATV they'd brought along in the *Sky Queen*, which was parked several miles away on the old strip mined area off the nearby Highway 97. Three minutes later they arrived where the two towers would be eventually erected.

Another team had begun pounding in a series of stakes and colored plastic streamers indicating where things would go, and what sort of work was needed.

Something did not appear to be right, so they got off the ATV and started approaching the small team. One man noticed them and called out to "Stop!"

Bud shouted over, "What's going on?" as he and Tom came to a quick halt.

The second site foreman began a weaving route to walk back toward them. At a distance of twenty feet he came straight to them. "We've got a huge problem. Trouble with a capital T! Somebody mined this area! One of my men, Chuck Morris, is standing on top of one. He was in the Army so once the ground dropped two inches under his foot and we all heard the *click*, he froze. He can't move for fear it will blow his legs off."

"But, you came back out. There is a safe path?"

"Well, yeah, but I can't figure out what to do for Chuck."

Tom considered the options before turning to Bud. "Go back to the *Queen*, rig a harness underneath and get a Durastress blanket attached to it. We're going to yank him off that mine!"

As the flyer raced off, he said to his foreman, "Bill? Go back out there at tell the other men to come out here. Tell Chuck we have a pretty good plan, but he might end up with a few strained back muscles. Stress to him he will not move until we are all ready and we're trying like heck to protect him. Okay?"

"Don't have a real choice, do I?" With that, he swiveled around and worked his way back out to the others.

Before Bud got the *Sky Queen* back in the air, the team—minus, of course, Chuck—reunited with the inventor on safe ground.

"Chuck said do tell you that once one of some types of mines goes up, that explosive concussion can set off all the mines within hundreds of feet." Bill sadly shook his head; he was imagining the loss of one of his best men who was also a good friend.

Tom's TeleVoc announced an incoming call from Bud.

"Skipper? Deke is rummaging through some of our supplies but tells me he thinks he saw the sort of heavy blanket you want. We're just in the air and will be over you in two. Want me to fly out over Chuck's position?"

"No. Far too much force coming down from your lifters. Stand off over about where you and I parked and drop the blanket to us. Then, head up to about three hundred feet and slowly sideslip over once I tell you it's okay. No earlier."

"Got it!"

The blanket bundle was dropped off and the giant jet headed straight up.

Bill volunteered to carry the blanket out to Chuck and to help get it secured around the man's lower body and to use some zip ties to hold it as far down over the man's boots as possible.

When the trapped man asked for the truth about his chances, Bill smiled and said, "The skipper is pretty darned sure that once you feel even the slightest tug up, bring your legs up and tuck them under you. That way the blanket should protect you. Oh, and there's a beer with your name on it once we get back to town tonight!"

They shook hands and Bill moved back along the now well-trodden path to the rest of the men.

Three minutes later, and with Chuck now soaked in his own sweat, the harness was lowered from the maximum height the available line allowed—four hundred twenty-five feet.

Fortunately for all, no mines were pressed upon to the point of ignition, and Chuck was not blown over... one of Tom's secret fears.

With Deke Bodack looking down using the SuperSight on the jet, they waited for Chuck to give them a thumbs up sign. As it came, Bud announced via the outside speaker they were on a three-second countdown.

He carefully took up the slack and when the construction man felt a little of his weight being taken off his feet, he tucked his legs up and his head down and was yanked so quickly he nearly lost consciousness due to blood being forced into his lower body.

His fuzzy brain barely registered the explosion below that not only set off the mine he'd been standing on for over forty minutes, another seven of them also blew.

The pilot arrested their upward motion and moved to the side so that when he lowered Chuck, it was to the arms of his comrades. It was only with the best of fortunes the man sustained no injuries other than a strained neck. So, Bud came down on a relatively flat piece of land, Chuck was taken onboard, and the *Sky Queen* flew to the southwest and Vancouver where an exceptional hospital awaited their arrival.

By the time they all got back, Tom had formulated a plan of action. He directed Bud to bring the jet in over the suspected area at about twenty feet. When the flyer complied, eight additional mines blew themselves apart, plus a lot of dirt, into the air. Another pass saw just a single mine go up and a final pass had no more explosions.

"That doesn't mean it's safe out there," Tom told everyone as he suggested they all head into the *Queen* for the time being while he arranged for a mine detection device to be delivered.

Nobody complained.

The detector—mounted on what appeared to be an armored garden tractor—came the next morning, as did Harlan and Phil to do a full security check. With them was an explosives technician from the FBI dressed in civilian clothes.

In the two suitcases he brought was a full lab to determining what they were up against. Tom thought to tell the man the *Lab* part of Flying Lab was well earned and all tests could be performed inside, but he did not preferring to allow the man to do his job.

"Simple C4," he announced within minutes of having a sample returned from one former mine site. "Home made and fairly sophisticated for the type. Two part switch so press down and it arms, allow the spring to shove back up and detonation. Luckily, these seem to have about a half-second delay in firing off, and are bodied in simple PETE plastic. Enough force to knock someone down and possibly break a leg or ankle, by no real shrapnel to do further damage."

Tom looked a bit askance at the man. "Soda pop bottle plastic?"

The man nodded and shrugged. "I'm going to go out and do a search for more of them but as these are meant to be triggered individually, I am surprised that you say a lot of them blew at the same time. Very unstable meaning very poor handling and moisture resistance."

A four-hour search found no more mines in any of the proposed building or storage areas.

Harlan was only mildly satisfied, and he told Tom it was time for calling in the Mounties.

*　　*　　*　　*　　*

170

The following day Commandant Cheryl Dimmock and fifty of her officers and lower ranks appeared on the hill. Approaching Tom and Harlan she saluted them reporting the Mounties were officially on duty.

"If I might ask Mr. Ames to brief my senior team members I need to speak to Tom," she suggested.

With a shrug the Security man headed for a group of five officers. As soon as his back was turned, Cheryl stepped forward and hugged Tom.

"Not protocol, but once I heard about the ecoterrorism here I had a sudden dread you might get hurt, and I know Anne would storm up here and absolutely kill me. I'm happy to see you are just fine."

The two headed for the *Sky Queen* and some coffee and conversation.

"Your Mr. Ames is hearing this so you should as well. We know we have some home grown eco-idiots up here and they have made so many proclamations about your intent, most contradicting the previous or future ones, that a lot of people are asking us to put a permanent end to them." She raised an eyebrow that told the inventor she meant others wanted them "removed from existence."

"Well, I don't want to be called the cause of any of their deaths, but I'd really like to not have to walk on eggshells and continually look behind me. So, Cheryl, anything your folks can do will not be challenged by us."

As she told him of their beliefs and intent, he got a small grin on his face. It was only once she showed him a photograph on her cellphone that a full-fledged smile broke out.

Three nights later and because he had made a promise to take her to a fancy dinner once he returned to Shopton, Tom sat on the side of the bed putting his socks on while telling Bashalli about the new issue with the antimatter reaction causing the casing to be placed under enough pressure for a few seconds that he feared nothing he built would be capable of standing up to it over a period of time.

She sat on the padded chest at the foot of the bed carefully unwrapping her pantyhose and starting to bunch one leg up so she might slip her foot inside. As she slid it upward and Tom noticed how it stretched out from a very compact state to follow the contours of her leg, he stopped talking.

She turned her head and looked to see him staring at her legs. "Still like the way they look?" she asked with a wink.

"Hun? I mean, yes, I do. It's just that I'm really amazed by those hose. How they are all scrunched up and wrapped around that cardboard rectangle, but once you start putting them on they just keep stretching until they are a perfect fit. Uh, can you take them off, slowly, so I can watch how they react?"

"Do you mean see how *you* react?" she teased him.

Tom shook his head. "Actually, I need to watch how the woven fabric in those returns to its shrunken size. Umm, how many time can you put those on and take them off before they sort of, I guess, stretch out and stay large?"

Bashalli shook her head. "They always go back to the way they came in the package. The only reason I buy an occasional replacement is they get snagged on things, like my beautiful rings, and that tears one or more of the tiny strands and that..." and she let go on the leg she'd been slowly uncovering and her hands made a sort of explosion motion, "is about it for that pair."

He thought about what he was seeing a moment before reaching for the bedside phone. "Got to make a fast call then we're out of here for the Yacht Club."

Dialing a number from memory he soon was speaking to Hank Sterling.

"Sorry for the dinnertime bother, Hank, but you and I've been racking our brains for some way to mitigate the expansion in the new generator, and I think Bash just showed me something great."

He turned in time to see her grin and blush.

He asked his Engineer to picture a pair of pantyhose. "You know how they are all small and puckered before they get put on? Then, they stretch out while worn before going back to their small state at the end of the evening? Finally, the do not stretch beyond a preset size."

He heard a sharp intake of breath from the other end of the line.

"See where I'm going with this?"

"I absolutely do! And, since we are dealing only with heat and pressure expansion and no radiation, we've been trying to come up with a new solid material band to handle that. But, well all I can say is wow! I'll come over to the office first thing and we can look into this. Okay?"

Tom said that was just fine. Now he had a truly good idea how to handle that expansion, he was going to relax and have a nice evening. He and Bashalli did, and ended up exhausted from more than two hours of dancing after their dinner.

The first words from Hank as he walked into the office were, "Durastress fibers and something synthetic like nylon. DuraLon? NylaStress?"

"The first one, I think. Do we know if weaving them together will make for something that is tight enough at first plus gives us the ability to grow and shrink?"

The two men did about eighteen minutes of calculations before siting back and sighing.

"Well, mine show we can get the stretch and retraction necessary, but I'm not sure about the initial holding pressure. Seems to want to stretch and relax a little under normal conditions," Hank admitted.

Tom nodded. His calculations had showed about the same thing.

The two thought about it for another quarter hour before Tom told Hank to head back to his workshop. They both had more thinking and work to do.

Three minutes later he was out of his chair heading from the office. "I'll be over at Uniforms," he told Trent. "Back within the hour."

The drive over gave him a moment to organize his thoughts on how he was going to ask the manager what her thoughts were on making a giant pantyhose leg.

The Major—a nickname Marjorie Morning-Eagle had garnered over the years—greeted her boss with a rare smile.

"What can an old squaw do for you, kid?" she asked, referring to her Native American heritage. It was meant as a wink-and-a-nudge and indication she had a good sense of humor and was proud of her roots.

He described his needs for a flexible yet exceptionally sturdy restraining band to go around a forthcoming power-generating tower. Actually, he required two of them. The more he told her the more she edged over toward a chair, moving her hand around almost blindly until she found the seat back, finally taking the seat and staring, slack-jawed at him

Finally she asked a question. "You want us to make you a pair of girdles for some hot towers?"

When he only nodded, it got through to her he was about as absolutely serious as can be.

"How wide?" He had told her that earlier on, but all the other information coming in had crowded that out.

"Likely to be about eighty feet in diameter, at least where we

173

need the *girdle*, as you call it, and about that same in height. It will need to fit in between at least two sets of guy wires that will keep each tower stabilized no matter what wind conditions might happen. Those will attach at specific ring points just above and below where this band needs to be."

She let out a voluble sigh. "Come on, Tom. Let's go to my office and get this down on paper so I can visualize it better."

To start with he helped her call up the outer view of both the small Scottish installation as well as the beautiful renderings Bashalli had made of the Canadian—and hopefully many more future—set of towers.

They performed the math to give her the outer length of material she would work with and multiplied that by the vertical height of the bands. The band for the Scottish site only needed to be about eleven feet tall.

Giving Tom a much more relaxed look, the Major sat back. "Overall," she told him, "that ain't half as bad as I imagined. Nothing to compare in size with the Mars colony domes, and so simple compared to the underwater growing domes that a second year seamstress could make it. Just one thing. What the heck is that made from?"

He said the word, "DuraLon," and she snorted.

"Another one of the famous Tom Swift made up wonder materials I'd imagine."

Tom grinned at her and admitted he and Hank had come up with the notion the day before but were still working out the exact details. "He is pretty sure your loom in the back can turn it out once we get the exact fiber mix into production."

"So, who will do the fiber work? We can make that Durastress thread and even weave it, but it will take a specialty house to do a mix of something that is, well, stiff along with something that soft and stretchy like nylon. But, you probably want me to make a suggestion; right?"

"I was hoping..."

With a whoosh of air escaping her mouth, the woman pushed herself up from her chair. "Okay. I need you to understand a couple things about the fiber industry. First, if they think you want them to do something really special, they jack up their prices and claim it is something to do with 'working with exotic materials.' Then, once they do their own internal testing and see this might be something really nifty, they'll steal the idea and start selling it before they even deliver a foot of finished thread to you."

He could see her sadly shaking her head. "It's one of the reasons I jumped at the chance to get out of that business and come work for you and your dad. It's even worse in the finished goods industry. Sometimes I wonder how anyone getting into clothing design thinks they can ever make money on what they come up with. The knockoff shops can reproduce something from just a blurry photo through an unblocked window!"

Tom was scratching the back of his head in wonder as he sought to come up with a possible solution.

"How does the military not have secret information and fibers leak out?"

She shrugged. "Possibly because they generally own the plants and the machinery. Now," and she looked at her young boss, "I am not suggesting we go out and purchase all that equipment; I don't believe we'll ever have enough need to justify that. I do think I have a contact in a place Id rather keep secret, at least for now, who possibly has a portable thread maker we might borrow... for a fairly hefty price but a lot less than buying anything."

"How much?" It was a blunt question she had no actual answer for.

"A bit plus a bit more. No tax, though!"

He told her to look into it and get back with some costs.

"One thing I ought to mention, Tom, is that this equipment could have a bit of a dodgy history and is not a high capacity unit. I have to tell you it could take as much as a month to make enough fibers to make both of those power girdles of yours."

Tom smiled and told her that was faster than he'd hoped for.

"Just not two months, please!"

CHAPTER 18 /
THE NEXT-TO-LAST PUZZLE PIECE

GOOD TO her word, the Major had the facts, costs and a delivery date for the equipment they needed to keep the DuraLon a company secret. Her contact agreed to provide the machinery just as long as it was a money up front deal and that Enterprises could come pick it up and bring it back within ten weeks.

Damon had already been told about the nature of what she was planning to obtain, had only asked if it was coming from a nation the United States had active "Do Not Trade With" orders on, or if it she had the notion it could have been stolen by the new owners.

Her answers has been: "It will be coming up from Central America, and it has a storied history going back to a questionable fire in a neighboring country a dozen years before." She would not, or could not, tell him anything other than she had seen it in operation, seemed to be of very high quality when new and also appeared to have been maintained it top working order.

"Normally, my often impetuous young son, I might suggest that we steer clear of questionably legal things like this, but I have done some research and the Major is correct; that industry is built on thievery, imitation and cheapening the process. A certain U.S. Senator whom shall remain unnamed for the time being assures me the Navy had to ship back an order of several thousand chemical warfare protection suits to a manufacturer that used a cheap thread to sew things together and they leaked like sieves.

"In the end, the FBI had to raid the place and arrest the owners, which was not an easy thing to do as they were in China. That, by the way, is not for discussion even with Bud! Peter— I mean the *unnamed* Senator, told me you could know but only because he trusts the two of us."

It was arranged for the *Sky Queen*, ample in cargo space for the job, to be readied and flown on a humanitarian mission down to Costa Rica with a load of food and medical supplies to bolster that nation's ability to care for its own following a bad storm season and rather massive forest fire.

Four pilots and six others volunteered for the flight that would take them down—quite visibly with lots of pre-announcements—one day with an unannounced and IFF off flight up one country in the middle of the night, on-loading of the machinery at a private airfield, and return before dawn to Costa Rica where they would take back off for the U.S. amid some fanfare for their valiant work.

Somehow, even the Senate got into the act with a declaration of the wonderful work the Swifts were performing in that area. By the time the *Queen* arrived back at Enterprises—and offloaded its cargo directly into the Uniforms building—the only thing the general public knew was that some faceless people is some foreign country many had never heard of, were going to be okay.

Even Dan Perkins at the *Shopton Bulletin*, often given in the past to making up sensational things about the generally mundane, only gave a quick call to George Dilling in Communications to ask if he might get a copy of the small press release.

Two days later the first of the combination thread came out of one end of the machine and was quickly spooled for future use.

By the end of the first full day, the Major announced she had enough thread to weave a test strip of about two feet in height and a circumference of twelve feet.

Before responding, Tom checked the circumference of his test generator in Scotland.

"If you can hold off until you can make a band that goes around something with a circumference of one hundred and six feet, even at that height, I can use it in a real world test. Everything after that can be held until we need it for the Canadian installation."

The Major agreed and told him it would require another three full days running the equipment for eighteen hours in each twenty-four, but would have things set on the loom to make that band is less than a full day after that.

It was closer to the end of the time before the first of the full-sized DuraLon girdles would be ready and Tom sat in his underground office and lab wondering if he had missed any details, or was ready to build things in Canada. Just some little thing that might ensure success, or increase the output of the generators.

With a groan he realized he never really tested the small box made using the Space Friends' manufacturing device even though it had been brought back along with the bead condensers that had received fairly thorough testing.

"Just how do you propose to give it a test?" his father asked that morning. "To my knowledge, you did test those blue bead things, and they ultimately did not give a high enough output to make them candidates for your antimatter power generators. Right?"

"Yeah," the younger man replied, sounding a little dejected. "I think I tried to impart into them a higher degree of what they are meant for... only I have no idea what that is. Bud saw one and likened it to a bead condenser from an old movie."

"Sure. *This Island Earth*. I have to admit," Damon told his now slightly shocked son, "that was my first thought as well."

Tom closed his mouth. Then, opening it again, he asked, "Did everyone *except* me know about that movie?"

His father let out a hearty laugh. "Oh, Tom. When you were younger your mother and I watched tons of movies in the evenings. Loved the 50s science fictions ones especially. We tried, and I mean *tried*, to get your nose out of books and come watch, but you seemed to only put any faith behind printed words and not something from Hollywood. Please tell me you encourage the kids to watch movies, especially ones that can expand their thought horizons. If not, perhaps your mother and I ought to steal them in the evenings and sit them down in the living room with some of the classics."

"No. We do want them to watch good television, but try to limit what Bart and Mary watch. Time-wise that is. Bart watched the movie and loved it!"

They returned to the subject of using the alien technology.

Damon suggested a few things Tom might try, at least two of which he already had in mind. After excusing himself, the younger man headed for the lab down the hall. It was there Bud located him an hour later.

"Oh, you really are in the building," the flyer exclaimed.

"Present!" Tom sang out as he tightened a connection between a trio of wires and the underside of a small box. He was inside the safety chamber to the side of the lab but soon stepped out and closed the door.

"What's going on?"

Tom pointed to the chamber. "I realized I had only tested those bead things from the Space Friends and not the box they appear to fit into. At least, not much. So..." and he again pointed to the equipment in the chamber.

"Okay," was all Bud said as he pulled over a stool and sat on it, watching his best friend.

"That's it? Just, 'Okay'?"

"Sure. Unless you want me to ask what is it you are going to be doing as a test." He looked expectantly.

"Well, when I pried the top off that box, I found three places inside where those blue beads fit as if they were designed to be there. I tried using a multi-tester to trace what is going *where,* and all I could figure was whatever you feed into the left bottom terminals goes through each of those beads. Not at the same time. More of a case of in one, out and into the next, and so forth."

The look on Tom's face said there was something more, and possibly more interesting. Bud waited.

"Here's the odd bit, and I have to tell you I have no idea how it happens or why it works, but if I put in, say, ten volts it races through some circuitry I can't get to without breaking the box, into the three beads, and then... it runs through the beads *a second time* before heading for the exit terminals!"

The flyer nodded. "And, of course, we both know that sort of thing is impossible. I mean, the next cycle of power coming in would then either double what is racing around inside, or it sort of packs the thing full and eventually goes *kaboom* or at least can't take any more. Right?"

Tom had to say he only had a theory and was about to test it.

"I think the box somehow knows how to filter out the power that has had its second lap around and lets it out just as the next cycle of power comes in. If that is true, the box only has a double charge running through it at any time." His eyebrows rose as he tried to find words to describe how that might be possible.

Certainly, not with Earthbound physics.

Both men had been inside the lab when something blew up, and even with the tilt out wall panel to keep pressure from building up in case of an explosion, things had exploded with them as witnesses. Twice, the tomasite window had ruptured because the pressure built in microseconds and the wall didn't have time to move.

Even tomasite was prone to sudden pressure shock failure. That is why Tom and visitors now donned protective facemasks and heavy leather aprons... just in case.

The inventor gave a countdown so Bud could brace, or take a breath, or whatever he did; Tom never knew because his attention was always on what was inside the chamber. All he knew was he instinctively took a breath and held it the first two to three second.

As with earlier experiments, the power began fairly low and built up. When things reached the point where he was feeding in two hundred volts, the box was outputting nine times that level.

And, then it evaporated in a puff of purple smoke!

*   *   *   *   *

Hank and three engineers headed for Dounreay and the installation of the girdle for the test generator. It was deemed to be very safe and so the system was not shut down for the eighty-seven minute job. Most of that was in running a stiff "snake" of metal around the outside of the generator and inside the outer concrete shell of the building.

Because most of the heat tended to collect toward the top of the cylindrical reaction chamber, the band of coolant Tom had installed a few days after startup was not affected, nor was it in anybody's way.

One end of the new fiber band was attached to the snake and pulled around everything. It was going to be short enough and therefore tight enough once installed, that the technicians had to use a trio of old-fashioned come-alongs. These were hand-cranked tighteners first used in the cattle industry to stretch barbed wire from post to post.

As each was cranked another full swing of the lever arm, all three simultaneously, the band started to stretch. It was not a fast or a particularly easy task, but they finally had the two ends next to each other.

At that point, Hank did some hand-sewing to connect the ends using a special curved needle and some extra twenty feet of the DuraLon threads.

A triple knot he'd been shown by the Major finished things. The band would not pull apart at that connection point. It was as strong as the fabric itself.

As Tom received the great news he was making the final logistical arrangements for building the twin power generators in British Columbia. Already up there and working away were two WorkCopters in the air along with small ground teams digging the narrow trenches for the cables that would begin being dug in the following week.

And, because the Canadian government was suddenly being cooperative with just about everything Tom needed to do, the work was moving along at the rate of seventeen miles per day of preparation. Once the first pipes and cable started to go in, that part of the process could run as fast as fifteen miles per day.

With their primary and initial target being a high capacity trunk line just three hundred miles away, this part of the build would be finished with weeks to spare.

*   *   *   *   *

Tom flew out to British Columbia for a day to watch and help the crew surmount a rocky bit of previously unseen hillside. It had so much vegetation covering it that it looked like it would just be a seventy degree vertical dig.

It was not going to be that easy.

Tom was standing in a brief valley below the rise looking up at the eleven hundred feet they would need to find a non-destructive way in which to embed their power line.

The WorkCopter stood two hundred feet behind him and the portable digging machine another forty feet past that.

The dig manager, Stanley, coughed politely in case the inventor was deep in thought.

"Hate to be a bother, but we are just completely stumped on that. We've sent a climber up to try to see if there is dirt along our path, but he came back with a report of solid rock covered in four inches of mossy weeds. We're kinda stuck right now. I'm really sorry about this, Tom."

Turning to face the man, Tom shook his head. "Nothing for you to be sorry about, Stan. It's Mother Nature and her way of coming up with constant surprises. I do have one idea how your crew can continue until I find a solution to this."

He suggested they use the dye marker function of the WorkCopter to lay a line straight up to the top and to transfer their machine and efforts to that point and resume the dig.

"I hope by the time you are another day or two down the line, I can come up with something."

Within a half hour the excavation team had reached the new starting point at the top of the hill, and they had moved the digger to create the first fifty feet of the trench... by tying it down and sending it back toward the precipice. As it started to tip, it was reversed and came back leaving the most ready-to-use trench as possible.

Tom called his father who, in turn, called the chief Minister they were now dealing with. She told him that the area was declared to be a wilderness, with emphasis on the wild.

"I cannot believe that even if you need to install your enclosure pipe with brackets holding it to the outside of that cliff, that Nature can't cover your tracks within a few months. Consider this to be approval to run that pipe outside those rocks. The only thing we would ask, if possible, is that the pipe be painted with some sort of permanent coating that is a shade of green like the native plants."

Once that was passed on to Tom, the younger Swift asked that an appropriate amount of interconnectable pipe be extruded with a green coloring.

"We'll have that run by tomorrow morning, skipper," Arv Hanson who was filling in for the day back at Enterprises promised when the request came to him. "Look for it day after tomorrow in the morning!"

"Many thanks, and be sure to include enough brackets to attach it every ten feet or so." He detailed the sort of rock the bolts would have to pierce and was promised a portable impact driver to do the job.

Because of the working conditions on the cliff face, it took three men two days to get everything mounted, but when Tom stood back about a hundred feet along with Bud, neither said they could immediately spot it except for the fact they knew it was there.

While this was happening, Tom flew back to inspect the new site. All forms for the base had been built and the Durastress vertical support and stabilization beams had been sunk in deep holes filled with expanding concrete.

They would not move or be able to be pulled back out.

As he hiked up from the landing area, Tom spotted the first of the Swift Heavy Lift helicopters coming in from the company in Victoria their special concrete mix was being batched. Hanging underneath was a three hundred gallon bucket he knew was filled to about the ninety percent mark making the load about seventy-five percent of the helo's capacity.

The bucket featured five cables hanging thirty feet down. Those were grabbed by a team of five men and helped to center the bucket's delivery spout in the correct spot.

Tom held back until the bucket was emptied, the cables released, and the helicopter was heading back for another load.

He walked to the edge in time to see another team, these were the finishers, just climbing up into the wet concrete with their wide, flat boots that allowed them to stand on top while they pushed and smoothed every rock and air bubble down and into the proper locations.

"How many total loads will those take?" he asked the lead man on the finishing team.

"Seven more for this pad and eight for the other one. Give us two full days and we'll have these smooth and pretty. Eight days after that we reach max strength and the other construction can start!"

*   *   *   *   *

"I had a thought," Bud stated as he entered the lab three days later. He and Tom arrived back at Enterprises the night of the first concrete pour and both had been busy with various normal duties.

Tom looked up from his notes. "Just the one thought, flyboy? Should we call Sandy and let her know? Pop open some champagne?"

"I'm breaking up with internal laughter, Tom. No, this is a serious one." He pulled over his favorite stool and sat. "The new generators need a real name. I think I've come up with one that isn't actually a pun and describes them fairly well. What do you think of Swift Antimatter PowerGrid Generators?"

With a little bit of wonder why his brother-in-law was being serious about the name this time, Tom sat pondering it.

"Well," he began slowly, "that does say what they are and do... and, well, I can't think of a good reason for them to not be that. At least for now, we'll call them Antimatter PowerGrid Generators, and I'm assuming one or both of those words has a capital letter in the middle."

"I was thinking of the G in PowerGrid."

It was agreed that would be an unofficial name for the time being subject to the people in Marketing and Sales and Legal—and Damon —having their say.

Bud changed the subject to the full-size generator girdle bands. He'd heard of them, felt that he understood the basics behind them, but could not get beyond the image of Sandy struggling to wear even pantyhose because of the pressure they exerted on her hips and behind.

She hated it and had hated what she termed "leg stranglers" since her first pair purchased in secret when she was fifteen. At the time she and a few of her friends thought they would be the height of sophistication to be wearing them.

Not only had her mother found the secret pair barely covered in the teen's underwear drawer, her mother insisted on purchasing another two pair to celebrate the girl's sixteenth birthday. Within two weeks, all three pair had mysteriously been ruined.

Bud asked about the sturdiness of the bands the Uniforms team were making.

"The DuraLon threads they have been making over there, and we have talked about those before, have proved to be both slightly stretchy—exactly what we want—and incredibly tough—another win for us all. I had Hank rig up a stress test for a one-inch strip. You know, like we do for metal fatigue studies at the Construction Company?"

"Sure. I can even recall seeing the old video of the first test your dad did over there when he started building the first *Pigeon*."

"Right. So because this bends the only test to do was to try to rip it apart end-to-end."

The flyer wanted to ask how it had fared, but he knew Tom was only pausing to build a little suspense before announcing the results. He smiled encouragingly at his friend.

"And, the winner is..." and the inventor made a drumroll on the edge of his desk, "stronger than even SpiderSilk by a factor of nearly two times!"

Jetz! Bud thought, knowing that the man-made product was about the strongest fiber the Swifts had ever tested.

CHAPTER 19 /
ECO-TERRORISM REARS ITS HEAD, AGAIN

THE BOTTOM rings of the two generators took shape and were given a week to properly cure so they would support the rest without any weaknesses. Durastress and steel bolts held the rings to the base plates.

At the same time, both the sets of power pods and the twin cyclotrons were nearing completion.

Bud had asked him why they could not share one cyclotron, and Tom's answer had been simple.

"If we start running these both at the same time, how do we keep that up unless they are on opposing fueling schedules? Doing it like this means both get a dose of antimatter about the same time and both have the full cycle to build more of it."

"Do you think one could, well, go down at some time and the other pick up the slack until the Swift Cyclotron Repair Team—'Always at the ready to serve you'—get out to fix things?"

Tom had to grin at how quickly Bud could come up with ridiculous comments like that one.

"Yes, and no. Yes, it could conceivably take over, but we'd have to change the cycles so they were exactly opposite, if we decided to run each generator at a slightly lower rate. Then, there is the fact we do not have the ability to transfer between towers. But, I honestly do not believe we'll find we have to do that. Those cyclotrons are pretty sturdy and have a lot of checks and balances to notify us if anything is out of whack before it becomes a problem."

Bud gave an emphatic nod. "Good! Now, for the truly important question: when are we having the lunch we swore and promised the ladies would happen no later than today?"

The inventor glanced at the clock on the wall above the door. It showed **11:23**

"I would have to say that you call Sandy and I'll call Bash and tell them we'll pick up the blond in ten minutes and the brunette in twenty. Sound okay?"

Bud nodded but had to ask, "Where are we taking them. Sandy will want to know. Mostly because I think she doesn't believe it when I tell her we are going for a *nice* meal."

"Then, ask your picky wife if Herd of Chickens sounds good to her, and I know Bash will like that idea. She keeps asking me when we are going back. If not Herd, then ask my picky sister if Morrie's Deli downtown meets with her approval. Bash also likes their pastrami on light rye."

Of the two, Sandy chose the closer one, the deli. She had a meeting right after lunch and Herd of Chickens was a twenty-minute drive, each way.

Just to surprise Tom, Bashalli had the chicken soup with matzoh balls and the chopped liver with onions and rye bread crackers. Sandy made a face when her sister-in-law ordered the liver dish, but she rallied and ordered one of the place's giant boiled ham on a wheat bun sandwiches with extra mustard and a little sourkraut.

On the way back to work, and after dropping both ladies off at their work places, Bud asked Tom if he thought one or both of their wives might be... *expecting.*

"I've never known Bash to be a liver eater," the inventor admitted, "but she's never said she hated it. You?"

"I think Sandy had decided her days as a bathing suit model are coming to an end. She's put on about three pounds to the seven I've gained since we got Sammy. Still looks nice in a bikini, and sorry if I put that image in your mind, skipper. But, the fact is she might have slightly softer curves, but she is still a beautiful specimen. Remind me to hug your dad and kiss your mom for what they gave to her."

Tom was just standing up when he spotted Harlan walking across the cafeteria floor two mornings later. The Security chief seemed to be headed toward the inventor, so he stood and waited.

"Hello, Tom. Thanks for not turning and running. I seem to have that effect in places like this. Guess there are a few people who are nervous about the cop in the room." He and Tom grinned as they sat down.

"So, the reason I was coming this way was not specifically to speak to you, but I figured I might just as well. I'll lay a guess that you well remember the name of Lawrencia Warhurst?"

With a grim look, Tom said he did.

"Fine. And we all believed she had hightailed it back to her Midwest home and then moved quickly from the area, never to be seen again. Such is not, as I have just found out, the case. She did make it out of town, and that was amusingly Lawrence, Kansas, and up to Lincoln, Nebraska. That is where her trail ended."

"She just disappeared?"

"No. She died. With no ID on her or in her belongings, she went to the morgue as a Jane Doe where she was autopsied and determined to have passed from an advanced cancers of the spleen, liver and intestines. Then, unclaimed, the body was eventually buried in a city grave."

Tom was trying to follow, but needed to ask about how Harlan had found this out.

"Wonders of technology, Tom. All her information was entered into a national database of unsolved deaths. All genetic and forensic data. Now, as you know, our companies ask for DNA mouth swabs from all employees. What you may not know is that periodically our computers do a data search of the national ones looking for things like hidden criminal records."

Tom smiled as he believed he knew the next part. "So, her medical records popped up?"

Harlan made a sort of hole with his left hand and shot his right one up through it. "Like a weasel being flushed out by a terrier. Bad analogy, I know, but up her information did pop. This morning I was able to do a human-assisted cross check and verify the body was hers."

Now, Tom sat a little confused. "So, are you saying that her fairly brief exposure to the radiation in the rod she fiddled with gave her those cancers?"

His Security man shook his head. "Nope. Turns out this was a situation where she likely knew she was already on her way out. We found her doctor in her home town who verified she had been diagnosed the year before while on vacation. She had been late stage 2 then but refused to do anything about it." He sighed. "I guess a lot of people just hope something like this will spontaneously go away. For her it did not. The radiation she picked up might have even helped prolong her life by a little. It may have acted like a small dose of radiation therapy. Not enough."

He looked at Tom and could guess what the inventor was contemplating. "Don't give a split seconds thought to whether she picked her cancers up at the Citadel. These were genetic. Her mother and father both died from those same cancers."

There were more things the inventor wanted to ask, but Harlan excused himself to attend a meeting of his department.

After the weekend Tom announced he was to lead the construction team that would be starting to build the two antimatter power generators. With the base plate and the support rings for the bottom of each tower in place, it was time to get going on the things.

First to go in would be the basic lower twenty feet of the outer walls. Those would surround the antimatter generating equipment and be the strongest part of the structure being more than two-feet-thick and heavily reinforced with Durastress beams both vertical as well as cross braces. This was both a safety measure along with being a structural necessity as the rest of each tower above that level would weigh in at about forty-one tons.

Given the footprint of the towers, that would be about like a skyscraper's per square foot weight.

Into that would go the trio of power pods surrounded by the cyclotron equipment. But that would not even be packed up for about two more weeks.

"Before I let you go out there," Harlan was telling Tom—a conversation being witnessed by Damon Swift who, the Security man knew, needed to hear what he had to say— "I want you both to understand something. I am outfitting my entire team of eleven with eRifles complete with double energy packs."

Damon began to open his mouth before realizing he had nothing to say to contradict this statement. Even though he truly hated weapons, the effectiveness of Tom's eGun and the newer eRifle he, himself, had okayed, was a proven method of dealing with those who would do others an injury.

"There's more," Harlan admitted. "I am also having twenty more of the eRifles made and will provide them to the Mounties of the protection detail. I'd rather have them shooting shock charges than bullets, and believe me, they will be outfitted with sidearms and even more deadly service rifles."

Tom was nodding. Like his father he did not like what standard weapons could do, but understood that sometimes you had to do something to protect yourself and the ones you loved. His eGun had already saved him several times, along with Bashalli, Bud and Sandy when they had once been kidnapped by a small group known for killing their captives even when ransoms had been paid.

"Okay," he said. He looked to his father whose eyes were slightly downcast, but the man was nodding.

"I agree with Tom. I only hope the Mounties understand our rifles must be the first line of attack or defense with their own to be used only in the most serious of attacks. You can make that point with their Commandant?"

He received a smile and an assured nod. "Cheryl Dimmock and I are in total agreement about this," he told the two other men.

Damon was now thinking how he could believe the man in front of him had already taken care of everything before bringing the information, now a fact, to him. He could not fault Harlan for this.

*   *   *   *   *

The final construction and test team headed to Canada on Monday morning six weeks after the initial concrete had been poured. Tom had been out for site visits about once in every three days.

With most of the major aspects finished, they would be placing "the hat" on each silo—lifting, setting down and welding on the domed top part for each—as well as running a thorough set of simulations of all components and subsystems.

This work included filling the water jacket and circulation pumps for each, and digging a well to provide additional water when needed. Without a lot of testing of the area, they had lucked out when it was discovered there was a layer of subterranean water just two hundred thirty-seven feet down.

It was going to take the remainder of the week so Tom insisted they bring along everything necessary. This included a team of eleven Security men and women who, in turn, insisted on bringing along an arsenal of e-type weapons. Each of them carried an eGun in a quick-release holster on their belt as well as eRifles slung over their shoulders. Those e-weapons were a special issue for the Swift's Security department. Each one had fast-swap energy cartridges that took less than three seconds to change.

Now, the hand-held eGuns could fire shots at about one-second intervals and keep it up for more than three total minutes.

The eRifles with their higher power output could do the same but in two-second shots over about six total minutes.

Harlan had insisted each of the other team members carry at least a standard eGun with them at all times.

"We are looking at a possible threat by an eco-enemy determined to not listen to anything but their own prejudices and hates. Most of them are not well educated, and many have criminal records going back to their teens. While our Mountie friends are going to be on patrol around the vicinity, I do not expect they will be able to provide all-around and all day/all night protection. So, we will be going through a morning of response and firing drills before you go."

That had been on Friday. By closing time even the normally doubtful and cautious Security manager felt Tom and his team could handle most situations.

He silently prayed his people and the RCMP could take care of anything else.

For the first two days and one-and-a-half nights things went smoothly. Even the Mounties seemed to relax a bit.

It was just past 1:00 am on Wednesday when the night was split open by the sound of guns firing from the dark perimeter of the encampment. With most people opting to spend nights in a series of two-man tents closer to their worksite, a lot of them were out in the open.

Tom was awakened by both the sound of a shot and the side of his tent poking quickly in toward where he was on a foldable cot. By design, the Durastress and Tyvek materials moved to absorb the impact but did not tear open.

More shots started coming at shorter intervals as he and Bud—and from the sounds of it everyone else in camp—were getting dressed and outside.

As he unzipped the tent from a prone position to offer less of a target, he heard the first **ZEERACKKK!** coming from one of the eRifles. It was a lower tone that the handheld guns. That was followed by more and from different directions around him.

ZEERACKKK!

ZEERACKKK! ZEERACKKK!

Tom and Bud checked their eRifles and made certain the night vision scopes were activated before crawling to a nearby tree. Each man took a different area and scanned around them.

"I can sort of see a few of them, Tom. Not out in the open enough to try for a hit."

"I may have one..." Tom trailed off as he raised his eRifle. A second later it fired and he leaned back with a sigh. "Think I got one of them."

Shouts of curses came from the darkness outside their clearing.

An equal number of orders were being quietly communicated via TeleVoc pins and walkie-talkies. The shouters seemed disorganized and haphazard where the Swift team and Mounties were definitely more organized.

"I hope all those shots of theirs are going wild and our side are hitting with each an every one they take.

"Since our guns have no recoil, Bud, and theirs certainly do, combined with the dark and my not seeing any signs of infrared scopes on their guns," he held up his eRifle and pointed to the scope, "I have to think our side is being a lot more accurate than theirs."

A warm body suddenly slid up against the inventor. "It's Cheryl Dimmock," she stage whispered to the startled man before he or Bud could react. "Just taking a little break." Shots from the enemy's guns came faster than the e-weapon shots, but soon it seemed as if there were fewer and fewer gunshots heard.

"Got to go!" she declared jumping to her feet and running away to what Tom believed was the north. Several gunshots rang out.

Then, and it made Tom's blood run icy cold, a cry came from about thirty feet away.

"Geez! I'm hit!"

It was Cheryl Dimmock's voice!

Either because she was incapacitated or so to not draw attention to her position, the woman made no other sounds. Tom felt hot tears welling up in his eyes as he pushed himself up from the relative protection of the tree and did a running crouch toward where her voice had come.

He fell over her because she was closer than he'd believed.

They both made noise with hers being one of pain and his from slamming into the ground with an "Ooofff!"

Several shots sounded and at least two bullets impacted within just feet of them. But, as each of the terrorists fired, it only helped the Swift team and Mounties zero in on them. Muzzle flashes and sounds gave them away and for each bullet fired there seemed to be a pair of ZEERACKKK! sounds.

The enemy was not so fortunate as the ZEERACKKK! of the e-weapons echoed and seemed to come from all around.

Risking it, Tom grabbed Cheryl's collar and, with a fast whispered apology for the discomfort he knew she was about to experience, dragged her back toward the tents. Seconds later he felt Bud grab more of the woman's clothing and helped get her back to relative safety faster.

The battle continued to rage around them, with many shouts of either commands or outright cursing and threats, but the two men had only a single thought, and that was to save the RCMP woman.

It was so dark inside the tent that Tom had to feel around to find out where she had been hit. The pain had made her pass out about half way through the dragging process.

Starting at her feet he found the hole and a more than minor dampness two-thirds up her left leg on the outer side. *At least that's away from a major leg artery,* he told himself. He started to be thankful he had not needed to feel any farther when it occurred to him she could have other injuries. So, after telling Bud to grab a tee-shirt and make compress to hold over the leg wound, Tom took a breath and continued up trying to be as clinical as possible. But, he found himself sweating from the experience.

He found nothing on her front up to the neck, and a fast run over her face and head with a hand brought up nothing more than some dirt where she'd fallen, so he directed his assistant to hold tight.

"Got to turn her over, Bud." Together they eased her onto the side and then on her face. The cot made it a softer experience for their patient.

The backside exam came up with nothing other than the fact she had picked up dirt and some pine needles.

Back she went onto her back.

Each tent had a first aid kit, which Tom pulled from its straps. Opening it he found what he needed. A SwiftSplint and Tourniquet. He also brought out the kit's scissors and split her pants leg up to a point several inches above the wound before slipping the tubular device up. Bud kept pressure on his makeshift compress until Tom told him to pull out.

With a squeeze to push the splint in so it applied pressure to the bullet hole, he touched a small switch on top and it immediately stiffened holding exactly the pressure he'd given it.

Sitting back on his heels, Tom listened.

He only could hear Gary Bradley's voice yelling about "sweeping the area," and another man's voice—certainly to be one of Cheryl's people—calling for a headcount of his and the Swift's team.

There were no more shots and no more e-weapon energy blasts.

"I'm going to check things," Bud declared. While he unzipped the tent and left, Tom turned back to Cheryl. He could see, in the very dim light, her eyes were open, and she appeared to be in pain.

"Did I make it?" she asked through clenched teeth.

Tom nodded. "You did. Took a bullet in the leg but we have the bleeding stopped. Just lie there and I'll get a light on and find the pain shots."

She placed a hand on his forearm and squeezed.

"You make me proud to know you, Tom. Did you really do a stupid thing and come out into the field of fire to get me?" She sounded both happy while trying to sound scolding at the same time.

194

"Yeah. Momsie would have skinned me alive if she ever found out I'd left you out there. Besides, by that time there were more of our energy shots than their bullets."

As he located and gave her a pain shot just above the tourniquet, she told him she needed to find out if there had been any losses. "Both sides," she requested.

When he came back three minutes later she was drowsy but asked for the information.

"No Swift personnel hit. Two Mounties hit, including you, with yours the worst of the injuries. Three of the eco-terrorists hit by their own people's gunfire. One dead and two to be taken to a hospital. Now," he directed gently pressing her shoulders back into the cot, "off to sleepy land for you, little Mountie!"

Cheryl Dimmock grinned at him and nodded as she drifted into sleep.

When Tom called his mother to tell her of Cheryl's injury, he heard a gasp from the other end of the line, a click, and then got a dial tone.

"Oh, yeah," he told Bud pocketing his cell phone. "Momsie is on her way out to Vancouver even as I speak. Guess we need to arrange for a car from the airport for her."

CHAPTER 20 /
SHROUDED IN PERPETUAL FOG... AND THAT'S GOOD!

BECAUSE IT had been an all out battle of two disparate ideologies, the eco-terrorists had, indeed, come in their full numbers. Even their elusive leader was there and was, ironically, one of the two men shot who survived their own friendly fire.

Once Red Jones, on duty in the *Super Queen*, had managed to get the jet into the air and slide it over to a point where it could temporarily land, the first person to be taken onboard was Cheryl Dimmock. Two of her Mounties helped Tom gently lift and carry her up to the small sick bay room before he told them they were likely needed elsewhere. As they and others attended to getting the two wounded eco-terrorists on and locked up, plus all the other prisoners who were crowded into a forward storage room on the lower deck, Tom checked her tourniquet band.

As designed, it had loosened up for a few seconds to allow some blood to get through, and some of that had leaked into the makeshift compress.

His first duty was to cut away the remainder of her pants so he and medical personnel could access her wounds. This he did without embarrassment, much to his surprise.

He ripped open a sterile compress and, with deft hands, turned the constricting device off, slid it down her leg enough to take off the packed and blood-dampened tee-shirt and replace it with the real compress before repositioning and tightening the band and stopping any more blood loss.

With a thought of what Doc Simpson would tell him to do right now, Tom pulled out one of the self-administering hydration cuffs he and Doc invented nine years earlier. It would, once placed around her arm, close down and seal automatically to the correct pressure, locate a proper and accessible blood vessel, insert a needle into it and begin dispensing sterile water at a rate that could be selected. He put the cuff around the drowsy woman's right arm, pressed the button to get the first liter of liquid into her in over just thirty minutes, and sat back.

He was physically and mentally exhausted and momentarily thought about taking a fast nap, but he knew he had to attend to the wounded woman.

In an effort to consider both her comfort and to cover her nearly naked lower half, Tom pulled out a blanket from a storage drawer, removed it from its sealed pack and gave it a shake. A self-heating layer inside, once agitated, would warm it to about 105° in seconds. Not hot but enough to keep her warm for several hours. He pulled it over Cheryl and considered this was about all he could do for her at the moment.

Five minutes later he felt the aircraft lift off, turn to the left, and head, likely as not, for Vancouver.

When he called forward he was told they were transporting everyone, Mounties, Swift people and prisoners.

"Nobody left at the site?" the inventor asked.

"Evidently no need. According to at least one of the bad guys, he believes their entire organization was called in for the attack. It could be they are no longer an organization with any members!"

Three of the gunshot victims made it to the Vancouver Airport and where taken away in a pair of ambulances; one was for the Commandant and the other two were the eco-terrorists crowded into the second vehicle.

All made it to hospitals in the area and all would recover.

The other injured Mountie had only taken a graze wound to his upper right arm, and was driven to the hospital by a fellow officer.

After spending the rest of the night sitting on the tarmac, along with half the day, and with everyone in the *Sky Queen* getting at least seven hours of sleep, the Swift construction and Security teams unanimously agreed they wanted to get back and finished their work.

All but a single Mountie, a very young man with a younger wife he had made the decision to call with a report of the attack, felt he needed to be with her as she was in a screaming panic over the thought he might have been injured.

So, at a few minutes past 1:00 that afternoon, the jet rose into the air and turned toward their construction site, where they intended to get right back to work.

Tom, Red, Slim and Bud, along with half of the Security detail— recalled on orders by Harlan—headed for Shopton.

Using a WorkCopter, along with one team at the supply depot they'd set up on the island above Victoria, and another on the ground as cable and protective pipes were laid—with the original machine they had used for digging following along moving the dirt back to cover everything—the entire first stretches of electrical lines —two hundred ninety miles one direction to the Northeast and eighty-nine the other toward the Northwest—were finished within and tested thirty days.

Pipes that came off the auto-loader of the air lift vehicle—and were manually interconnected with a quarter-twist, self-sealing in seconds awaiting the high-power cabling running through at the same time the WorkCopter moved another fifty feet ahead—had taken an additional three days, but it was well within Tom's schedule.

"I have to tell you that Canadian contractors never—and I shall repeat that because I find it to be an incredible statement—they *never* get something even as straight forward as twenty kilometers of transmission line installed in less than a year." This had come in a conversation with the Minister for Energy at a debriefing meeting before the first kilowatt of power had been sent out from the power generator station.

She informed the inventor that her department had received a new charter and would no longer pursue a national non-nuclear-only policy, "...in the areas where we can have some say in the matter." She had rolled her eyes at her own statement.

"However, if this new generator station turns out to be the perfect solution, we will definitely be heading that direction. That goes double for both British Columbia as well as Quebec. Both province governments have declared themselves to be nuclear free with Quebec making a declaration that prohibition will be for eternity!"

Tom secretly wondered if, as governments do, he might have to bid to provide the systems only Enterprises would ever be able to build.

Harlan called Tom and Damon to tell them the Scottish man, McNaire, who had tried to kill Tom was now ensconced in the highest security prison in Scotland.

"It turns out he was hired by that same Yemeni Sheik who tried to get Tom to sell him some earth blasters. Held a fierce grudge, but their government is taking care of that... and him. Check off one more bad guy from out lists!"

The rolling hills around the first pair of Antimatter power generators were just about continuously a light green and moderately damp nine months out of the year; it was only slightly less green and a bit drier the other months of August through October. With the lease of the land had come eleven homes formerly occupied by workers at a nearby, yet totally empty, uranium mine. Each one sat along the single road coming up from the major Provincial Highway 97.

The site operators and a couple Mounties who were stationed at the generators occupied all of them, and all had been extensively repaired and modernized.

Looking like very futuristic grain silos—as reported by one television reporter who had overflown the area during the weeks of mid-construction who told his viewers "This must be some sort of joke. Those are not, and I know what I'm talking about, any sort of power generators!"—the gray-greenish blue of the outside panels stood starkly contrasted to the hillsides and the browner grassy area just between the two towers and the first of the houses.

And yet, along with their twenty-four sets of eight-per-group hold down cables that stretched from the mid-ring area down to the ground and out about forty feet, they somehow seemed to fit in with the landscape.

The great number of cable ends interweaved and crossed about twenty feet up from the ground. Because of this and to take advantage of each generator's weight, Tom decided to pour additional concrete between the two circles to create a single, large oval pad for mounting them on.

"Much better strength for holding things absolutely stable," he'd explained.

The environmental conditions were even better for Tom's plans during the first test run at low settings when the towers seemed to generate a sort of mist all around that flowed out nearly a half mile and up to about the one thousand feet mark above the installation within the first twenty-four hours.

That first night, the soft glow of the generators had tinged the fog a light blue allowing the red aircraft warning rings of light to make it all evenly glow.

The high levels of mist came with the release of the heat from the exchangers at the top of each tower. By that time it was nearly the same temperature as the surrounding air, but the added moisture overpowered the ability of the air to absorb it, so it hung as a man-made fog.

"That," Damon commented as he and Tom stood a half-mile away just looking at the new additions to the scenery, "is incredible. I find it to be sort of serene to the eyes. Great job, Tom. I hope of goes without saying, but I am so proud of you!"

Much to everyone's satisfaction, the Canadian government had declared the area extending two miles all around and up to five thousand feet altitude to be a no fly and no travel zone with the exception of the few trucks that used the nearby highway. This ruling had come into effect the day before a Quebec television station's "investigative reporter" and her cameraman had rented a small private airplane with pilot, so when they landed back at the airport in Vancouver the three men were taken into custody for a day and the television station was fined heavily.

"How did your power test go, Tom?" his mother asked as he, Bashalli, Amanda and the three children sat at the Swift home a week later.

Her son's smile ought to have told her everything, but she wanted him to be able to explain it all and take the credit she believed he was absolutely due.

"We brought the cyclotrons on line at noon so they would be outputting the tiny amounts of antimatter we need for the test. Luckily, the Canadians relented on those once the U.S. convinced them they are not nuclear reactors. I guess even the Canadians have to admit whenever their laws do not cover something specifically, such as this, so they need to allow it."

"And, not try to pass something retroactively?" she guessed.

"Exactly! Anyway, by nine that night we had sufficient materials all held in the magnetic vacuum flasks that we could start the initial firing up process."

Everyone stopped eating as he described the controlled intermixing of the positive matter and the negative, or antimatter, inside each of the giant generators.

Atoms collided with negative atoms releasing large levels of non-radioactive energy and heat that started the actual fuel ignition and tremendous heat, which flashed the circulating coolant around the main core area into superheated steam and that drew the heat out and away. As the super hot liquid was allowed to run through a trio of generator turbines in each tower, they began sending electricity out of the tower and into the substation set a half-mile behind the towers.

"It was very consistent power and we fed that into the grid once it had all been leveled out and stepped up to Canadian standards. It may have begun as a trickle, but electricity did go out into their power grid"

*   *   *   *   *

And, that wasn't the only success.

The following week in the state of Oregon, once home of the Trojan Nuclear Power Plant along the Columbia River, the local power provider approached Swift Enterprises with a request to enter into negotiations to replace that decommissioned facility with a new pair of Tom's generators—now being officially renamed to sound less ominous as the Swift PowerGrid System—to be built on that older site.

It was hoped they could supply the needs for electricity not being serviced by either hydroelectric or wind power over the coming decades.

In Arizona, the owners of the Palo Verde Generating Station called to say their site was within two years of their useable life; their reactors one and two were due for decommissioning at that time with number three just a year later.

The more than three-point-three megawatts of power generation needed to be replaced. Sooner would be better, Damon was told. And, their budget was barely enough to perform tier one maintenance on the first single reactor. Replacement was their only hope.

"Good thing we can make the Antimatter PowerGrid generators for just a little over that. Will they stretch their budget to buy ours?' Tom asked once he had been informed.

Damon nodded. "Like nearly all government projects, they want the sun the moon and the stars for the price double-wide trailer home. But, yes. Peter Quintana, through whom the inquiry got to us, said to expect their final budget will be enough to cover a two-silo system plus annual maintenance for the first five years. Plus, they are in negotiations with Texas to lease a small plot of land by the ocean for the seawater extraction."

To top things off, Tom received a visitor the following week. Still hobbling on crutches, Cheryl Dimmock was ushered into the shared office by Trent.

Tom nearly tripped over his own feet jumping up and rushing over to hug the woman.

After greetings and a few more hugs, she made a sound he interpreted to mean she needed to sit.

"Try one of our comfy seats behind you," he told her as he assisted her in turning around.

Once she was in the chair, and her crutches had been moved to one side, she smiled at Tom.

"During my life and a couple careers, I have run into one woman whom I hold in higher esteem than just about any other human on this Earth. That is your mom. But, now I have someone who has saved my life and did so without much evidence he was trying to duck and cover. My Mounties all reported your heroism in getting to me and dragging me off the field. Thank you, Tom." She reached over and placed a hand on his left knee.

"I also was not so far out of things that I didn't feel you checking me for other entry or exit wounds." She blushed mightily causing Tom to do the same. Seeing his discomfort she laughed. "Don't let it get to you, Tom. You did the right thing. And," now she looked at him with a sparkle in her eyes, "you were *very gentle!*"

This caused an even greater blush to flow up his neck and face.

"You are a great man, Tom Swift. Your wife, Bashalli—who I met this morning when she and your mom came to the airport to pick me up—is not only beautiful, she is also so very proud of you. Well, make that two women I drove in with plus me!"

Tom stammered a little as he told her, "I-I sort of was only trying to think about the gunshot, Cheryl. But, I will tell you it wasn't an altogether unpleasant experience. I hope you are going to be okay."

She told him she was absolutely on the road to recovery.

And, that evening, staying with Tom and Bashalli, she told Bashalli how very honored she felt to know the Swifts.

"They are two for two in the 'save Moose's life' events. I love them both." That forced her to tell everyone the tale of her former nickname.

Tom blushed throughout the entire narrative.

Eleven days after the PowerGrid was "lit" all tests showed the reaction to be easily self-sustaining and for periods in excess of even Tom's best computations before more antimatter had to be added.

On this trip he and Bud invited their wives to come see what a wonderful sight the generators were.

Bashalli stepped from the van that had brought everyone up the hill, keeping her eyes closed and holding tightly onto Tom's right arm.

"Go ahead and look," he prompted her. Now she reached out to steady herself by grabbing onto Sandy's arm on the other side.

"Oh, my god! It... it is just what I imagined!" She turned to look up into Tom's face. "It's just what I painted. How did that happen?" She was totally amazed at what she had never imagined would make it from paper into reality.

Tom laughed and gave her a hug. "Well, the simple truth is that once everybody saw your sketches and then the final, color paintings you did, we all thought that was precisely what these needed to look like. They are big, and would be imposing and perhaps a little stark, if they was been realized as gray things sticking up out of this hill. Your imagination, and sense of color, has made these the beautiful things they are."

As the final crew finished the very last of the outside cleanup, and the test team continued with every test Tom had designed, Bashalli stood looking at the two towers, tears of joy streaking down her cheeks.

The next time Tom visited the Canadian site, a month after the first tests of their ability to generate electricity had gone down the transmission line, he noticed something they had not encountered with the installation in Scotland. Fog, thick and blocking out about fifty percent of the sun—expected but not at the current density—hung all around the antimatter generators even in the heat of daytime (when it thinned out slightly but did not dissipate). A small level of night fog had been expected, but most believed that would disperse each time the sun rose.

With a mental shrug, Tom put that thought aside.

To the skin it felt slightly cool even though the temperature of the air was a steady fifty-seven degrees.

"Kind of like a wind chill factor," Bud said as the two men stood looking from the left side of the installation at their surroundings.

"You know, Bud? That is exactly what it feels like."

"Think it'll last?"

"I don't really know, but that meteorologist from Vancouver told dad this is an area of increased humidity. It just wasn't all that noticeable most days because it never gets all that warm. I think this will work to our advantage."

When the flyer asked how that *would* work, Tom chuckled.

"Wet air naturally will carry away more heat. I'll have to run some numbers but would make a guess this fog, if it sticks around all year around, will decrease our having to pump much water up from the well to do the same thing. After all, we atomize it and let that run around the heat exchangers on top." He stopped speaking for a moment.

"All in all, I'd say this fog is going to be an advantage to us, Bud."

He was right. Over the following week as the Antimatter

PowerGrid generators ramped up to full output, the fog stayed in the area. It did not get appreciatively thicker, but the ambient temperature around the generators dropped by three degrees. A flight in the Skeeter told Tom the fog hung all around the hills out to about five miles and rose to above one thousand feet.

His calculations told them all this was going to keep the generators running about nine percent cooler overall, and it would reduce their reliance on the nearby well water by greater than fifty percent. That also meant those pumps needed to be run only once per day for a couple hours to fill the large tank he'd had installed so that water could always be available for the towers and the people running them.

As a bonus, and after carefully studying video taken by an infrared camera from one hundred feet away, once the fog had passed through the upper area of each generator, it came back out, warmer for certain, but still in the form of heavily water-laden air simply mixing in with the rest of the fog and quickly cooling back down.

There was a detectable and slow swirl to the air above the domes that had its own kind of beauty.

In just two more days the first of the full strength electrical power was to be released. It would be travelling out on the pair of high-tension power lines with enough power to take care of the needs of greater than thirty thousand homes.

And, that would be just the start.

* * * * *

Tom and Bashalli came home to a warm welcome from his father and mother, and her father, mother and brother, and a special welcome home dinner at the senior Swifts. It was a pleasant meal and everyone in the returning party told their stories.

But, Tom's real reward came that evening from Bashalli. As they snuggled together in bed she cleared her throat, letting him know she had something to tell him.

Or, an important question.

It was both.

"So, now that you have your antimatter generators up and running, and believe me when I tell you I have loved having you here on this planet and not rushing around the oceans or dealing with nasty dinosaur aliens or flying through the sun or whatever, but I wonder if you are going to stay down here forever." She sounded both hopeful and a little sad because she knew Tom and knew he didn't *plan* to run off under an ocean or around the solar system, but she was a realist. It just seemed to happen.

"I'll tell you this right now, Bash," he said giving her a little hug—gladly and warmly returned—that I have no intention to rushing off to someplace other than right here in Shopton and to be home every night." *Whenever possible*, he added in his mind.

What the inventor could not know was that a chance discovery by a team from Fearing Island about three months later would have him back in space heading for a seriously strange adventure.

For now, he reached over and turned off the lights before turning back to concentrate on his wife.

<•>—< End of Story >—<•>

This has been book 31 in the *New TOM SWIFT Invention Series*.
Read them all, and then read them again:

...with more to come in the further 2020s!

Manufactured by Amazon.ca
Bolton, ON